Praise for

The Spice Box

"Bridget is a delightful heroine . . . accurate historical details of the mystery provide wonderful atmosphere . . . the series should quickly become a favorite for culinary mystery fans and historical mystery fans alike." —*The Mystery Reader*

"Food mixes well with history in *The Spice Box*, an appetizingly lively mystery . . . The series is off to a roiling start."
—*Fort Lauderdale Sun-Sentinel*

"Hard to put down, like a bowl of pudding." —*Booklist*

"Temple further brightens her dark landscape with a mélange of recipes, cooking hints, and tidbits of Manhattan history." —*Kirkus Reviews*

"This is one book that should not be read on an empty stomach . . . a delectable culinary historical mystery."
—*Midwest Book Review*

"Charming . . . A delightful mix of upstairs and downstairs characters, a vivid picture of the city's seamy underside, absorbing details of Sephardic Judaism, and a fittingly melodramatic climax make this a memorable debut."
—*Publishers Weekly*

continued . . .

THE
Spice Box

THE
Spice Box

LOU JANE TEMPLE

BERKLEY PRIME CRIME, NEW YORK

THE BERKLEY PUBLISHING GROUP
Published by the Penguin Group
Penguin Group (USA) Inc.
375 Hudson Street, New York, New York 10014, USA
Penguin Group (Canada), 90 Eglinton Avenue East, Suite 700, Toronto, Ontario M4P 2Y3, Canada
(a division of Pearson Penguin Canada Inc.)
Penguin Books Ltd., 80 Strand, London WC2R 0RL, England
Penguin Group Ireland, 25 St. Stephen's Green, Dublin 2, Ireland (a division of Penguin Books Ltd.)
Penguin Group (Australia), 250 Camberwell Road, Camberwell, Victoria 3124, Australia
(a division of Pearson Australia Group Pty. Ltd.)
Penguin Books India Pvt. Ltd., 11 Community Centre, Panchsheel Park, New Delhi—110 017, India
Penguin Group (NZ), Cnr. Airborne and Rosedale Roads, Albany, Auckland 1310, New Zealand
(a division of Pearson New Zealand Ltd.)
Penguin Books (South Africa) (Pty.) Ltd., 24 Sturdee Avenue, Rosebank, Johannesburg 2196,
South Africa

Penguin Books Ltd., Registered Offices: 80 Strand, London WC2R 0RL, England

This is a work of fiction. Names, characters, places, and incidents either are the product of the author's imagination or are used fictitiously, and any resemblance to actual persons, living or dead, business establishments, events, or locales is entirely coincidental. The publisher does not have any control over and does not assume any responsibility for author or third-party websites or their content.

THE SPICE BOX

A Berkley Prime Crime Book / published by arrangement with the author

PRINTING HISTORY
Berkley Prime Crime hardcover edition / May 2005
Berkley Prime Crime mass-market edition / April 2006

Copyright © 2005 by Lou Jane Temple.
Cover design by Amy King.
Interior text design by Tiffany Estreicher.

ISBN: 0-425-20665-3

BERKLEY® PRIME CRIME
Berkley Prime Crime Books are published by The Berkley Publishing Group,
a division of Penguin Group (USA) Inc.,
375 Hudson Street, New York, New York 10014.
The name BERKLEY PRIME CRIME and the BERKLEY PRIME CRIME design
are trademarks belonging to Penguin Group (USA) Inc.

PRINTED IN THE UNITED STATES OF AMERICA

10 9 8 7 6 5 4 3 2 1

To my grandson, Jackson Thomas Walker,
with whom I share
our birth date.

ACKNOWLEDGEMENTS

The research for this book was fascinating and I thank those who have chronicled in book form the history of the City of New York and the Irish immigration. Thanks also for the Library of Congress website, which was invaluable for Civil War information. The New York Historical Society and the New York Public Library answered the most obscure questions over the phone with patience and humor. Thanks to the friends who gave me a quiet place to write: A. Cort Sinnes for naming his guest room the Temple Suite, Lenny and Jerry Berkowitz, Andrew Hoffman, and especially Ed Rollins, for it was at his home this idea hatched.

CHAPTER ONE

BRIDGET Heaney shivered. She'd been standing on this corner of Fifth Avenue and Thirty-Fourth Street for at least twenty minutes. The wind was whipping down Fifth Avenue, and she had a cape as thin as a cat's whisker.

In the nine years and six months she'd lived in New York City, she'd been this far uptown only once before, one of the many trips looking for her sister.

Some of the girls she went through the orphanage with, the ones who were still alive, talked about all of them going up to that new Central Park and having a picnic. It would almost be like they weren't in New York anymore, they said, like being out in the country. But they had never got around to it. Mostly, their lives played out below Fourteenth Street.

Bridget shifted her gaze from the house on the opposite corner to the rest of the street. It sure smelled nicer up here.

The houses were so big and she knew that only one family lived in each of them. The German woman she had been cooking for until yesterday told her all about it. And of course, her friend, Mary Martha, talked about it, too, when she came down to the boardinghouse on Sundays, her day off, to visit with Bridget. Mary Martha was the reason her life had gone topsy-turvy in the last twenty-four hours.

Bridget inspected the gutter. There was no garbage or the contents of someone's chamber pot in the gutters to cause you to hitch up your skirt and jump across. She glanced up and down the street. And there didn't seem to be a fishmonger or a butcher to empty all his remains in there, either. No pigs fighting with each other to eat up the scraps.

They'd pretty much done away with the pigs running wild in New York City now, making folks keep them way uptown. She remembered how the pigs had frightened her when she was little, when she and her family first came from Ireland.

That had been back in 1855 and Bridget had only been ten. Now it was 1864, the country had been at war with itself for three years, and Bridget was almost twenty.

It really did seem like a lifetime ago when they left Ireland. At ten, she'd been plenty old to have memories of her life there but it was all just a blur. It was as if the trip across the ocean had wiped out "before," and what happened "after" was all there was. The men in the pub and the ladies in the apartments talked constantly about what Ireland had been like, sounding as if they missed the place yet all the while complaining about not having anything to eat when they lived there. But Bridget didn't have those bittersweet longings. New York was her home, for good or bad.

An omnibus pulled up at the corner, going down Fifth

Avenue. The big trolley was hitched to a team of horses, their hooves the size of plates. The bus driver—they were known for their recklessness and derring-do—snapped his long six-horse whip in the air. One of the horses relieved himself while they were taking on passengers, and immediately a young Irish boy jumped off the back of the bus and swept the droppings into a burlap bag attached to a broomstick. He was back on the bus quick as a cat. No wonder the neighborhood doesn't stink, Bridget observed. The buses didn't pick up after themselves downtown; that was for sure.

Bridget noticed there were no outhouses in the back of these mansions either. That certainly would help with the smell. Bridget thought of that hellhole of a place they lived in when they first got to New York. The landlord must have never cleaned out the outhouse behind his ruin of a building on Elizabeth Street. Bridget and her sister would relieve themselves in the alley; they hated the stench of the outhouse so much. It didn't help that every room in that rickety building was packed with mothers, fathers, children, and grandparents; people who didn't even know each other shared rooms to save money. There was just too much crap for one little outhouse.

Bridget could close her eyes and see their own room and remember how others in the building were jealous because there were only three of them tucked in together—Da and Maggie and her. Imagine being jealous of such a pit, with its two tiny ash-covered windows and its dirty gray walls. Of course, looking back on it, it was better than some places that came after.

That was before Da disappeared and all the children without parents got rounded up and sent off to places like the Home of the Friendless. Bridget could visualize the old neighborhood for a moment: so many people, and so noisy— the noise of boats being unloaded down at the harbor, horses and mules being yelled at, children laughing and crying but mostly crying, drunks breaking bottles and fighting, peddlers and corn girls calling out to sell their wares.

Bridget was glad she had landed in the Friendless; she truly was. She learned how to read and to cook there, and those were two skills that she knew no one could ever take from her.

But the thought of their life on the outside with those crowded streets full of filth and danger and that God-awful first room and Da, then she and Maggie being on their own, made her a little sad and homesick, not that she would ever admit to missing something that dreadful.

Bridget turned her attention back to the house across the street. It was huge, a mansion if there ever was one, and made out of those big slabs of stone. Granite, she thought it was. Once down by the docks, she'd seen a man crushed when a big slab of stone like them on the house had slipped off a flat bed cart he was trying to hoist it on, and as he lay there gasping his last breaths, the onlookers had talked among themselves about how heavy granite was.

The house was at least three stories aboveground and had lots of big, tall windows. The front door was on Fifth Avenue, and there was a pretty little yard in the front that got wider around on Thirty-Fourth Street. An iron fence ran clear around the corner and had a big gate for the carriages to enter in the back. Everything was well tended. There were three gardeners working on the yard right now, and it being November. They went from one tree to another, clipping a little something here and there, one of them lugging a ladder along in case a top branch needed fixing. The empty branches on the trees formed round balls, a style that Bridget was sure she had seen before but couldn't remember where. She thought it looked silly.

There was lots of coming and going. Already, three delivery wagons had left stuff since Bridget had been watching the place. Each time, a stern-looking gent came out of the back door, all gussied up in a tailcoat, and checked the groceries or ice or cases of wine off a list the wagon driver handed him. A couple of little black boys seemed to hang on to the back of all the wagons and they jumped down and did the actual unloading to the door of the kitchen or wherever the door led. The stern fellow didn't let anyone go inside and pretty soon two or three girls, Bridget was sure they were Irish, came to the door and lugged away the stuff.

Were the Irish girls always used for the toting, she wondered, or was it just because of the war that there were no men for the job?

Then the stern fella would close up the back door tight until the next delivery wagon pulled up and rang a big, bronze bell that hung off the side of the house.

Bridget wrapped her cape a little closer. It's that bell I should be ringing right now. She had told herself that she just needed to find out where the help went in and out, that even she knew you didn't sashay up to the front door and announce, "I'm your new cook." But she admitted to herself there was really more than that that kept her rooted to the spot. She was scared to death.

Oh, she also told herself it was smart to watch for a while, get the lay of the land. And she had learned a thing or two, she'd have to admit.

One of the gardeners she'd seen at a pub in the neighborhood she'd been working in, the Kleindeutschland, was known to lose at cards so Bridget figured he would always be short of money. A person short of money could come in handy when you needed something done for a few coins.

The butler—that was what Bridget guessed the stern gent was—favored a plump maid with curly red hair over the two spindly ones with black hair pulled back in buns. They always had to carry the heavy stuff.

Mary Martha hadn't come out to fetch anything yet. Bridget was hoping this meant she was above such duties.

Bridget felt a pang of guilt at the thought of Mary Martha. She's told them all about what a good cook her friend Bridget is. She's bragged about me, how I worked at Delmonico's, how I've been running the kitchen at a proper German boardinghouse, how my potato rolls will float off the plate.

Bridget straightened up, threw her shoulders back slightly. Now she had to go across that street and ring that bell and enter that house and not make a fool of herself or of Mary Martha for recommending her.

Since she learned to make her first pot of soup at the orphanage, she'd dreamed of cooking at one of the great houses of New York City. Now was her chance.

AS Bridget crossed the street, the household she was heading for was in an uproar.

Mr. Fleming, the butler of the house, was serving double duty today as he had recently sent Justin, the steward who usually took care of the deliveries, up to the country house to attempt to retrieve Mrs. Gold. She'd left town in a huff almost a week ago and he could see that Mr. Gold was growing very upset about her absence. The woman really had no sense of duty at all. What with young Master Seth missing and the household being short a cook, Mrs. Gold leaves and takes her secretary, the best coach, the Victoria, and its driver, and now he's been compelled to send Justin after them. The whole mess had given him a terrible headache.

IN the kitchen, Chef Rene was in a bad humor. He could tell that everyone blamed him for letting his assistant get involved with the young master of the house. As if he could walk up to that spoiled brat of a lad and tell him not to put his hands on the help. He'd watched the whole drama unfold. They all had. Children who grew up in houses full of servants didn't even see the maids, the cooks, and all the other ones who made life pleasant for them and their families, until a servant with red hair and a pretty face came along. Undoubtedly Seth thought no one noticed when he'd pull Katherine into the dry goods storage or the silver room. And Katherine, poor, dumb, Irish. She really believed the drivel that came out of that boy's mouth. Believed it until she thought she was pregnant and then she saw how fast he turned her out, or his daddy did it for him. Thank goodness she wasn't going to have a baby after all. Maybe she'd learned something from this, to keep her undies on in the next house she served. In the meantime Rene and his nephew were one cook short and they were sending him another Irish lass. When would they learn?

MARY Martha McBride was almost sick, she was so nervous. She checked the time again, fiddling with the pretty little clock next to Mrs. Gold's bed. It was nine thirty-four. She

inspected the room once more and patted a little bump off
the spread on Mrs. Gold's bed. This morning she had put a
small vase of flowers on the nightstand, in case Justin was
successful in bringing Mrs. Gold home.

She walked around the room and carefully straightened
the drapes. Mr. Fleming said the drapes had to be let down at
night even in the empty rooms, so the house would look balanced from the outside and also to keep the heat in. The
Golds sure did have pretty drapes. Mr. Fleming said that
Gold's Department Store had a whole floor of fabrics and
seamstresses just for draperies. Everyone said the store took
up a whole city block so one floor just for drapes was possible.

Mary Martha looked at the clock again. Nine thirty-
eight. She wished Bridget would get here. The sooner she
started cooking, the sooner the house would get back to
normal.

MR. Gold was anxious for Bridget to arrive, too. He had tried
to read the newspapers, as he always did after breakfast. He
dressed for the store before he came down to breakfast, then
after he ate, he could spend an hour in his library, reading the
papers and going over the day with Mr. Fleming and occasionally Justin as well. Sometimes he went to Mrs. Gold's sitting room and talked to her about their schedules;
sometimes he even took his second cup of coffee with her and
read a paper up there, when she was in a civilized, friendly
mood. That hadn't been lately. When she left town in such a
huff, he had been relieved. But still, his schedule and disposition were ruined and had been for days. His son had gone
off, most likely gambling and whoring like the spoiled rich
boy he had turned into. Seth had disgraced an innocent

young woman and then Mr. Gold had cleaned up after him, as if he were still a toddler.

Mr. Gold paced. Hiring this friend of Mary Martha's would help set the household back to normal. If she would just hurry and present herself.

MARY Martha glanced out the window anxiously and spotted her friend Bridget Heaney marching across the street with her head held high and her brow furrowed as if she was concentrating hard, a worn carpetbag clutched in front of her. Those were the carpetbags they gave them when they left the orphanage. Mary Martha still had hers, too. She flew out of the bedroom, hurrying down the hall and back stairs just as the back door bell rang.

"I'll get it. I'm right here," she sang out. Mr. Fleming's head poked out of the silver room. He'd been polishing for the last few days, getting ready to take the grandest pieces to the country house for Thanksgiving. The Golds kept all their best silver in the city, necessitating lugging it out to the country on special occasions and causing no end of bother for Mr. Fleming. "It's my friend," Mary Martha said in answer to Mr. Fleming's inquiring stare.

"Get her in there. He wants to go to the store," Mr. Fleming said shortly and disappeared back to his task.

Mary Martha opened the door, pulled Bridget in, and closed the door with the same motion. "Where have you been? You've got to go off to the library to meet him right now."

"The tall, bald gent with the penguin suit?" Bridget asked.

"No, Mr. Gold. It's his tradition. No one works here or at the department store, they say, that Mr. Gold doesn't talk to first. Mr. Fleming says Mr. Gold is the only head of a house or a business he's ever known to actually do his own interviewing of the help."

Mary Martha started down the hall with Bridget in tow. "Can't I wash up first?" Bridget stalled.

Mary Martha shook her head. "No. He leaves for the store at ten every day. You're going to make him late." She took Bridget's bag and her threadbare wool cape and put them down by the back steps.

They had walked directly down six stairs to the floor that Bridget knew was the working heart of the house. Most would call it a basement. It was half underground, half aboveground with short windows giving it some natural light. Bridget had observed that real sunlight was reserved for rich people in New York.

Mary Martha pulled her friend down the hall and up the front stairs to the first floor. Bridget strained to look in the rooms they passed but Mary Martha wouldn't let her dillydally. "I'll give you the tour but first you've got to get the job," Mary Martha said anxiously.

Bridget skidded to a halt and pulled at the high collar of her best white blouse as if her air had just been cut off. "Don't tell me I quit my job and I might not get this one." She grabbed the arm of her friend and squeezed tight.

Mary Martha pulled her arm away and tucked a lock of Bridget's red hair back behind her ear. "He's going to love you," she said reassuringly.

Bridget grabbed her friend's arm again. "Why isn't the chef interviewing me?"

Mary Martha freed her arm from Bridget's grasp and then turned her friend toward a massive oak door. "I just told you. It's the house rules. Here we go then," she muttered and tapped firmly on the door in front of them. "Mr. Gold, can you see my friend Bridget Heaney now?" she asked.

Isaac Gold didn't just call for them to come in; he opened the door himself, all smiles. "Bridget, come in. Let's get acquainted. Thank you, Mary Martha. Would you ask Mr. Fleming to send us some tea, please?"

With that, Bridget Heaney followed Mr. Gold in the library and Mary Martha crossed herself, saying a little prayer, then went downstairs to make the tea, even though it wasn't her job. She wouldn't dream of asking Mr. Fleming to do it.

CHAPTER TWO

BRIDGET felt her skin burning. She was pretty sure she was going to faint. She had no idea what to do.

"Please sit down, Bridget, and don't look so worried. This is my usual routine. It doesn't make sense to me to trust my household and my family to people I haven't personally met. I don't trust my business to strangers either, for that matter. It takes so little time to look someone in the eyes, and I can tell you, you can learn a great deal by doing so. Look someone in the eyes and see what is there."

Mr. Gold sat down and gestured for Bridget to do the same. She looked down, startled, and saw her knees were backed up against a beautiful leather chair.

Even though she knew she should say, "No, thank you, Mr. Gold," and remain standing, she just let her knees buckle and down she sank. It wasn't proper, she supposed, for the master of the house to invite his new cook to have a

seat but oh, did it feel good, this chair. She couldn't help enjoying the smell and feel of fine quality leather. Her eyes
closed for just a second and she took a deep breath. When
she opened them again, Mr. Gold was smiling at her, not
making fun of her obvious joy at a nice chair but like he
wanted her to have the pleasure of it.

Bridget ducked her head a bit so she could have a look at
Mr. Gold without bald-faced staring. As much as she hated
people saying certain things about the way the Irish looked,
she had to admit she had done the same with Jewish folks.
Short and round mostly. But the man sitting across the desk
from her was tall and slim with dark hair and dark eyes. He
was handsome and that's all there was to it. Bridget felt her
cheeks firing up again. She knew she was turning red and
felt grateful Mr. Gold couldn't know what she'd been
thinking.

"Mary Martha says you two met in the orphanage, the
one with the strange name," he said to start things up, trying to look both friendly and dignified and doing a good job
of it.

Bridget smiled bitterly and felt a wave of pride at the
same time, just for surviving. Yes, we were the waste children, swept off the streets like the rest of the trash. She finally
felt she could look Mr. Gold in the eyes the way he wanted.
"Yes, sir," she said, "The Home for the Friendless."

"So, both your parents are dead, then?"

How much truth was the right amount? She took a try at
it. "My mother died when we were on the ship on the way
over from Ireland. In 1855." So far all true. She shifted, uncomfortable in the chair, the saying of it bringing back an
image of her mother beside her in that dark place, Bridget
knowing she had passed long before she told anyone, waiting

until she was cold and stiff, knowing what they did with dead folks, tossing them over the side into that never-ending water. Bridget was ashamed to realize she hadn't thought of her mother in weeks. "My father tried to get work and sometimes he would have to leave my sister and me alone, like when he worked on the railroad." The bastard left us for months at a time. Those memories were even worse than thinking about Ma.

There was a little knock on the door and Mary Martha came in carrying a gleaming silver tray with a big silver teapot and two beautiful cups and saucers and a silver sugar and creamer. She smiled at Bridget and gave a little curtsy to her employer. "May I pour?" she asked.

"Yes, please," Mr. Gold said and waited to talk while Mary Martha carefully filled his cup and handed it to him. "Thank you," he said and took a sip.

Then Mary Martha started pouring for her friend, waiting on her as if she was somebody, which was embarrassing to Bridget. Mary Martha didn't seem to mind at all. "Still milk and sugar, Brig?"

Bridget nodded and thought of how many cups of tea she and Mary Martha had shared. At the Friendless, tea and a slice of bread and butter was supper. On Sunday the bread and butter had sugar sprinkled over it for a treat. "Still milk and sugar and thank you," Bridget said and meant it. It was good to have an old friend in your life.

Mary Martha smiled and handed the cup to Bridget, then disappeared quickly out the door. Mr. Gold looked at Bridget, waiting for her to talk, she guessed. She figured he expected her to go on about her family, so she did. "They passed a law that the children on the streets by themselves would have to go to a place. So my sister and me got the

Friendless. We were lucky. Some brothers and sisters got split up."

"And your father?"

"He was killed during this Civil War, sir. Last year, that would be '63." Not exactly the truth but not a lie either.

"I'm sorry for your losses. Bless him for helping his new country through this terrible time," Mr. Gold said softly.

Bridget wanted to laugh. Oh, yes. He was helping all right. He was drunk as a skunk during the riots last year and trying to drag a poor Negro man out of his house to beat him when a Union soldier shot him in the head. Curse the Irish. "Thank you, sir."

"So now it's just you and your sister?"

And me not knowing if she's dead or alive, Bridget thought. "Yes, sir."

"Home for the Friendless, was it a Catholic institution?"

"Oh, no, sir. Run by the Protestant women. They tried to convert us all."

"And did they succeed?"

Bridget chuckled. "Well, Mary Martha is still a good Catholic girl and I'm not much for religion, sir, one way or the other, but not to be talking bad of it. So I guess they didn't make much headway with us."

Mr. Gold nodded sadly. "More harm has been done in the name of religion than anything else throughout history. It's a strange, sad fact."

"Yes, sir, it gets folks all worked up."

He smiled. "Let's talk of something more pleasant. Food. How did you become a cook?"

Bridget wanted to kiss the man's feet, she was so grateful. No lies would be necessary talking about food. "I asked to help in the kitchen at the orphanage. Why, I don't know.

You had to do something and the cooking seemed better than mopping floors. So I cooked for the four years I was in. When you're fifteen, they put you out. One of the women who volunteered there was rich—well, lots of them were, I suppose—but this one knew Mr. Delmonico. They don't let women do anything but take the money in the front and wash the pots and pans but I moved up to peeling onions and shrimp and sometimes shelling oysters. The real chefs never even talked to me, probably didn't know my name, but I watched them, and on my days off I tried to cook a little myself the way they did, not with such good ingredients, of course. Then I started at one of the German boarding-houses, and for the last year, I've been in charge of the kitchen. The Germans like their food." Bridget realized she'd talked way too much but Mr. Gold seemed to be listening.

"How old are you now?"

"I'll be twenty this month." Bridget wondered if Mr. Gold would think that was too old or too young. Telling the truth didn't come easy to her but for some reason she had and now she was stuck with it.

"You've quite a lot of professional experience for your age. I can hardly wait to taste your potato rolls. Mary Martha has bragged about them to me."

Bridget loved that Mr. Gold used the word "professional" when he was talking about her. It made cooking sound important, not just something a dumb girl does when she has to take care of herself, not having a husband. "I'll be glad to make them up whenever."

"Your wages will be twelve dollars a month for the first six months, with room and board, then we'll talk again."

Bridget nodded and almost choked trying to get a word

out. She was floored. "That is a fair wage, sir." And five dollars more a month than she'd ever been paid.

Mr. Gold got up and went over to the fire, poking at the dying embers with a fireplace hook. It was a bit drafty but Bridget guessed he'd let the fire go out as he was going to leave for his store. "I have to tell you some unpleasant news," he said with his back to her, studying the charred pieces of wood.

Her heart sank. What had she said wrong? Had he already changed his mind? Was she let go before she'd done a lick of work?

"It's about the young woman you're replacing. And my son." He slumped back down in his chair, looking older than he had a minute ago. Bridget noticed a little gray hair at his temples. "She, too, was a young Irish immigrant. She was very pretty, and well, she and my son had intimate relations."

Mr. Gold didn't meet Bridget's eyes when he said this and she quickly ducked hers, wanting to make it easier for both of them.

"I wish I could say that my son loved her and was a man of honor. He was not. She came to him when she was afraid that she was going to have a baby and he acted the cad. He came running to me to get him out of the mess he'd made of things. And I didn't have the heart to turn him down. To be honest, he would have made the young woman, Katherine, a very bad husband. And my wife was very upset at the whole situation. She wants my son, his name is Seth, to marry a Jewish girl, of course. So I helped the young woman relocate to Washington, where she is working for a cousin of mine, a distant cousin. We will not run into her again. Luckily, she was not with child after all. I insisted she see a doctor friend of mine. Unluckily, she made a tearful scene. I lost my temper with both her and my son. He stormed out five days ago and hasn't returned home. Even before Seth left, when this whole affair exploded in our faces, my wife fled to our house upstate. That was a week ago." Mr. Gold fell silent, as if telling this sordid story had taken all his strength and his words.

Bridget wanted to dance for joy. This was not a house full of perfect people. How wonderful. She looked up at Mr. Gold and tried to seem serious. "I'm sorry, sir."

Mr. Gold met her gaze and smiled a half smile. "I am, too. And please forgive me for what I say next. But I must ask you to steer my son away if he should attempt the same with you. You are a very pretty girl and Seth obviously has a taste for redheads."

Holy Jesus. He said the word "redhead" like it was the same as a witch or a prostitute. Bridget stood up with as much dignity as she could muster. "I have just worked in a boardinghouse, Mr. Gold, where many single gents live, and while they were not as well off as your son, many of them were lonesome as can be. The good name of the house was very important and I will act here as I did there, with respect for your reputation and my own," she said as solemnly as she could. Don't worry, Bridget thought, I wouldn't sleep with your son or anyone else in this house. I learned long ago you don't have "intimate relations" with the people you work with or work for.

"Don't diddle where you get paid wages, girl," an old cook at the orphanage told Bridget when she was too young to understand what "diddle" meant. It was good advice now that she was old enough to know.

"I knew this would be difficult," Mr. Gold said with concern in his eyes. "I was in no way implying that you would follow in Katherine's footsteps. It is Seth I'm worried about."

Bridget gave a little bow across the desk to her new employer. "You let me deal with him, sir. Thank you for this chance. I won't disappoint you."

Mr. Gold smiled that half smile again. "No, I feel certain you will not." He returned her little bow to indicate the interview was finished.

BRIDGET'S head was spinning. Mary Martha had given her a fast tour of the whole house, pushing and pulling her along, jabbering as fast as she walked. It was grander than anything Bridget had imagined. On the first floor there was a mammoth entry hall with different colored marble making a pattern on the floor like a big star or sunburst right in the middle. A crystal light fixture had lots of dangling prisms hanging down all around and they reflected the natural light so they sparkled. Bridget couldn't imagine how beautiful it must look when the gaslights were turned on and it was dark outside. From there they went into a fancy dining room, then into a keeping room with a big Oriental rug that Mary Martha said had come from Turkey—and there were more like it at Gold's. Next came the library where she'd met Mr. Gold, and another room where the missus met her friends and had tea; Mary Martha called it the parlor. It was smaller than the keeping room, which looked to Bridget like a whole tenement worth of folks could live in there, easy. There were some extra little rooms off the dining room to store the dishes, and one with a lock, for the wine. Then they were back around to the big front hall. The two black-haired girls were in there on their hands and knees polishing the marble floor.

There was a bathroom with a toilet and a sink for the company and another one for the help so they didn't have to go downstairs to take a pee during a dinner party. Bridget thought it all amazing.

They went up to the second floor, where Mr. and Mrs. Gold each had their own "sweet," Mary Martha called them. That consisted of a bedroom and a bathroom and a sitting room, just for them alone, unless they wanted the other to visit. Bridget asked Mary Martha if the Golds didn't get along, them having their own bedrooms and all. She said they got along just fine, that this was a show of how rich they were, that they could afford one of everything for each of them.

They looked into three other bedrooms, the children's, each with its own bathroom, plus another smaller room that turned out to be the nanny's.

"This is the children's wing," Mary Martha explained. "Seth is the only one that lives here at home, or at least he did until the dustup. Mrs. Simon has taken the nanny's room."

Bridget waited for Mary Martha to tell her about the other children, which she knew she would do.

"The daughter is in Spain for a year, living in Madrid. I only just had come on here when she left. Rose is her name. And the other son, Benjamin, is married and works at the stock market, whatever that is, and lives near the department store down on Broadway somewhere," Mary Martha said as she straightened the bottom of a spread on one of the children's beds. The room had roses on the wallpaper so Bridget guessed it belonged to the girl, Rose. "Mrs. Gold, Estella her name is, she likes everything just so."

Bridget couldn't believe Mary Martha hadn't been to the department store. The girl just wasn't curious about things.

Curiosity killed the cat, Mary Martha always said, and Bridget had seen instances where that was really true. She wished sometimes that she wasn't so interested in what some would call other people's business, that she could just keep her head down and her mind on her own worries. But she was curious and that was that.

Now they were going up the stairs to the third floor, where all the help lived. Bridget had her cape and her bag with her. They didn't open the doors, but Mary Martha called out whose room it was as they went by. Bridget couldn't remember all the names. It sounded like a lot of people.

"I sleep in here with Sally. She does the laundry and sometimes helps me on the second floor, with the heavy things, and I sometimes help her with the ironing when she gets behind," Mary Martha said as she opened the door to a plain room with two narrow beds. There was a picture of the Virgin Mary on the wall between the beds and a piece of crochet work on the bottom of one of the beds. Bridget figured the bed with the crochet work was Mary Martha's. She had always been good at handwork such as sewing and crocheting and knitting. Bridget could tell Mary Martha was proud of her place in this household, the upstairs maid she called herself. She shut the door quickly and they went two more doors down the hall. "Here you go, then," she said and opened the door to Bridget's new room.

It had one bed, a chest, a little round rag rug, a slanting roof because it was under the rafters, and a window out onto Thirty-Fourth Street.

Bridget couldn't believe it. She had her own bedroom and a window. At the boardinghouse, she slept in the basement with three other Irish girls that worked there, all four of them in one bed.

"There's a bathroom at the end of the hall with running water and everything. Mr. Gold got the house hooked up to the Croton water as soon as the pipes was laid," Mary Martha explained proudly.

Bridget noticed a bud vase on the little chest by the bed. It had a real flower in it, a daisy. "Did you put that there for me?" She was careful not to look at Mary Martha as she asked because she was sure she'd burst into tears if she did. Little niceties were not a thing Bridget was used to.

Mary Martha smiled. "To welcome you to the house. I really am glad you're here, Brig."

"You're not mad that I got a bedroom by myself?"

Mary Martha shook her head. "Of course not. The cooks all have their own room. That's the house rules. The front part of this floor is the men's. The back part is the women's. There are two bathrooms, one for the gents and one for us. No mixing. The stairs we just came up, don't use them. We use the back stairs. And Mr. Fleming will give you what for if he sees you up front by the men's bedrooms, especially since Katherine."

Bridget sat down on her bed, her head full of questions. Mary Martha didn't give her a chance for even one. "Now you best change clothes. There should be a uniform in that little closet. It'll be a tad big for you but it'll do. I'm sure today or tomorrow Mr. Gold will send someone from the department store over to measure you up. We all have four uniforms, custom made. Mr. Fleming says Mr. Gold knows most folks just have two for their help. Mr. Gold said what happens when something spills and your other outfit is in the laundry in a tub of water? Mr. Gold can afford for us to look the best on the block, Mr. Fleming says. And it reflects on his business if his help dresses nice, I guess."

For the first time, Bridget paid attention to Mary Martha's uniform. It was a pretty dark blue dress with a starched white apron that had intricate pulled work on it at the hem and the top. Her head was covered with something part handkerchief, part headband made of white linen. Just her bangs showed. It was almost like what the nuns wore except much more stylish. Plus it kept Mary Martha's hair from getting all dusty when she cleaned.

"You've got to tell me one thing, no two things," Bridget said, quickly going through all the questions in her head and choosing two.

"Hurry up, then. Chef is expecting you and it's almost time for lunch. You can meet everyone at the table."

"Question number one, what is the chef like?" Bridget asked.

Mary Martha smiled. "You'll handle him fine. He's French but has lived in New York twenty-some years. He's always worked for private families, no restaurants for him. He's good but hits the cognac bottle. The other two are Elsie and a cousin of the chef's who doesn't speak much English yet. I think Chef helps all the ones of the family that wants to come to America."

"What about her?"

"Who?"

"Elsie, the other one in the kitchen," Bridget asked as she started unpacking her things into the little chest.

"Elsie is old. She does the potato peeling and the onion chopping and washes the good serving pieces and keeps track of all the kitchen equipment. And she cooks some for us. Oh, and there's Harvey. Harvey is the dishwasher and does all the errand running. He's just thirteen and a Negro. So, what's your second question, in a hurry now?"

"Mr. Gold told me a tad bit about his son and the girl I'm replacing. What's the real story?"

Mary Martha frowned. "I'm sorry I didn't tell you about steppin' into somethin' a bit messy. But this'll be over in a jiffy and we all have to take advantage of the opportunities that come along."

"I'm happy for the job," said Bridget, "no matter how I got it. But I still need to know."

"We don't have time now. I'll tell you the whole story later tonight. I just wish the young master would come back home. It's a worry to his father and Mrs. Gold, too, if she even knows he flew off in a snit." Mary Martha turned toward the door. "Get your uniform on and come downstairs. Hustle now," she said and was gone.

Bridget sat down on the bed again and looked around. Her hands were trembling and that wasn't like her, to shake like a scaredy cat. It must have been the excitement of her new job and learning a strange house and having to talk to Mr. Gold and all. Bridget had never had a real conversation with a man before, where you told him something and then he told you something. She liked it. He seemed nice enough for a boss. But she still had to meet the chef. It was him that would make her life good or miserable here.

She slipped out of her skirt and blouse and hung them and her cape in the little closet that was cut in under the slope of the house's roof. The uniforms hanging there, the clothes rack was bare but for them, were different from Mary Martha's, not as fancy, which made sense to Bridget since she wouldn't be seen and her job was a messy one sometimes. They were made out of some kind of blue-and-white-striped fabric, like mattress ticking only it was soft. The apron was dark blue with white trim, so it wouldn't show if food got spilled on it. The headpiece was just the opposite, white with blue trim. Bridget slipped the dress on and it was big but not so much she couldn't hitch it up by pulling the apron tight. There was a small mirror on the inside of the closet door. She put on the headscarf and took a look. Not too bad.

Bridget tucked in that one curl that wanted to stray. Then she remembered how the butler gent had seemed to prefer the girl with curly red hair over the black-haired girls and she pulled that curl back out, and one to match it over by her other ear. With those red curls showing, she didn't look like a nun. But not like the hussy type that Mr. Gold seemed to think of redheads either. She hoped she'd put him in his place all right, but not mean. Now she had to tackle Mr. Fleming and the chef.

Bridget took her old carpetbag and shoved it up on the shelf that ran over the metal rod in the closet. Her hand hit something up there that she hadn't noticed. She stood on her tiptoes and took a peek. It was a wooden box. Maybe it was the box to return the uniforms in. She pulled it down and could see right away it was no delivery box. It was carved all over and looked real old. She sat down and looked at it more carefully. The pictures carved on the box were of women with chickens and wheat and loaves of bread in their hands. One was stirring a big pot. One was holding a knife over a goat, looking like she was ready to slit his throat. Bridget had never seen anything like it. Maybe it had something to do with religion or, most likely, Katherine's broken heart. Poor girl, maybe she stole it to take with her, to have something to remind her of this Seth. She must have changed her mind. Bridget stuck the box back on the shelf. "I'll have to return it if it belongs to the house," she muttered, "but not now. Now I have to meet the whole damn staff."

CHAPTER THREE

WALKING into a room full of strangers is never easy, unless it's at a pub, where no one pays you any mind unless you want them to. Walking into this room full of strangers was even worse since they were going to be closer than family to Bridget, her not having a family, except for her sister. Bridget paused at the door, not sure what to do. Having Mary Martha there helped and she gave Bridget a "Be brave" look. They hadn't started eating yet, just taking their chairs and talking all around. Everyone was in an eating room right off the kitchen, except for a Negro boy eating by himself in the kitchen, sitting on a barrel of some kind.

Elsie was putting some platters of food on the table. It didn't look like much to Bridget, some slices of roast beef most certainly left over, cooked cabbage that did smell good with caraway seeds, boiled potatoes, a big bowl of beets, and bread and butter.

Mr. Fleming took over. "Bridget Heaney, I'm Mr. Fleming. I run this house. Now sit down right here next to me."

Everyone sat down then, Bridget included, and Mr. Fleming started the food around, passing it to Bridget after he served himself. He introduced as he passed. "Sally is our laundress, Kate and Karol do the cleaning," indicating the redhead and the two that Bridget had seen toting and polishing marble. Neither Sally nor the other two had on scarves, she noticed. It must be optional. "Elsie, Gilbert, and Chef Rene are your new colleagues," he said and indicated three other people around the table. Those three did have on head coverings, Elsie like hers and the two men short chef's hats.

Elsie was big and plain, but didn't have a mean look in her eye, just a blank, "I don't know nothing, don't ask me nothing" look. Bridget had expected a wrinkled, old woman from what Mary Martha had said. She didn't look more than forty or so to Bridget. She guessed that qualified for old—although Mr. Gold had to be forty to have three grown kids and he sure didn't look old.

Gilbert was cute in a funny way. He looked to be about the same age as Bridget and Mary Martha, with ears that stuck out too far and a big nose. He blushed when Bridget looked his way.

Chef Rene was a nice-looking man with tired eyes, a big waistline, and a little goatee. He nodded to Bridget solemnly. She couldn't make out any arrogance or resentment. Bridget relaxed a little and took a bite of beets. They were cold and pickled with cloves and ginger. Very good.

"Welcome," the chef said with a little smile. He still had a French accent, even after twenty years in New York. "Mr. Fleming tells me Master Gold will not be dining at home tonight. So I'd like you to make supper for the staff. Just look around and make something with what we have here. No shopping."

So that was it, was it? He wants me to show what I can do with scraps by six tonight? Bridget smiled at him. She'd worked with little or nothing many times before. "Supper it is. These beets are delicious. Who made them?"

A pall fell on the little group. "Katherine," Mary Martha said tersely.

Mr. Fleming picked up the slack and returned to his introductions. "Of course, you already know Mary Martha. Then there's Harvey out in the kitchen, where he cleans and also runs errands for me. Three members of our household are not here right now. Justin, our steward, has taken some things up to the country house for Mrs. Gold. It's on the Hudson River north of the city in Westchester County. He'll be back in the morning. Johnny, our driver, is with Mrs. Gold as is her secretary, Mrs. Simon. They will return when she does."

Bridget smiled again, hoping to seem pleasant. "Does the country house have its own staff?"

"A rather diminished one. There is a couple that lives on the premises. The woman cooks and cleans and the man gardens and repairs things. A local girl comes in to help when the Golds are in residence, and Justin and I go up as needed," Mr. Fleming said with a sniff. Bridget couldn't tell from that if Mr. Fleming loved the country or hated it.

The rest of the meal she tried to stay quiet and listen to everyone else. There was some good-natured banter about the presidential election last week and the war. She could tell Gilbert had a crush on Mary Martha, who didn't seem to give him the time of day.

Mr. Fleming, who said he was from Boston, was an

American surrounded by mostly Irish. He acted very superior but Bridget got the impression he liked the way everyone performed their jobs. She didn't think any staff member
would be there long if he disapproved.

Kate and Karol had to be sisters. They ended each other's
sentences and only smiled once, and then it was at the very
same second.

Bridget ate as fast as she could without wolfing her food.
She was suddenly hungry but no one had asked for seconds
so she wasn't sure if it was allowed. Although what else they
could make out of that tired roast beef if they didn't finish it
up, she didn't know. The back door rang, and Mr. Fleming
went to get it. That was Bridget's cue to get up herself. She
picked up her plate. She didn't want anyone to have to clean
up after her the first day, even if they took turns waiting on
each other, like the girls at the boardinghouse did. "I'm glad
to be here and glad to meet you all," she said and went into
the kitchen to find out what was what.

The kitchen was big enough. It had two big cooking
stoves. Both wood and coal were piled in the corner.
There were several long wooden worktables and a smaller
one with a marble top for pastry making. Lots of whisks
and spoons and other kitchen tools stood in large crocks
on the tables. A big iron potholder hung over one of the
worktables, with incredible copper pots hanging all polished and gleaming. There were sauté pans in every size
and even several cast-iron skillets. Bridget's eyes bright-
ened looking at all of them. She'd seen copper pots and
pans at Delmonico's but this would be the first time she
got to cook with them. She heard they conducted heat
better than anything. A shiver of excitement ran through

her, which embarrassed her. Getting excited about pots and pans. Really.

She looked around for food and spotted icebox doors as big as those at the restaurant. She opened them and found a neat-and-tidy walk-in icebox with a huge boulder of ice covered with burlap sitting in the middle of the floor over a floor drain. On one side of the icebox there were items already cooked or prepared in some way and produce. On the other side there were raw ingredients such as cream and cheese and, down on the bottom shelves, in metal pans containing ice chips, containers neatly marked in French. Bridget was going to have to learn the French words for foodstuffs; she could see that. She opened three containers.

There was a tough-looking piece of mutton. Bridget shook her head. She wasn't going to tackle that on her first night. Another container had bones waiting to be made into stock. In the third container were oxtails. Oxtails were perfect. Chef couldn't accuse her of using something too expensive for the staff plus she knew how to cook oxtails. She just wouldn't make them taste too German. French chefs hated German food, or said they did. Bridget had heard the cooks making fun of sauerkraut at Delmonico's.

She left the oxtails for a minute and went out of the icebox dreaming of making ice cream someday with chips from a big block of ice.

She found the dry storage room next. There were plenty of root vegetables: potatoes, turnips, carrots, rutabagas, squash. The acorn squash might be a possibility. Potatoes and carrots could work. Bridget found the onions, picked up the corners of her apron, then filled it with squash and onions, taking them out to a worktable.

Chef and Gilbert were building up puff pastry dough over on the marble, folding it over and over. Puff pastry. Bridget wanted to throw down her vegetables and run over to watch, to learn, but she didn't. There would be plenty of time to learn about puff pastry when she'd fixed a good supper. It did remind her of her own special talent: bread. She didn't have time to make potato rolls for tonight but she could make some bread. She went over to the pastry table and smiled sweetly. "Chef, where is the yeast and flours? I'll make some bread."

Chef jerked his head at an opening covered with curtains, his hands still busy with dough. Bridget went into a large room and found big round tins of salt, three or four different flours, and sugar, both brown and white. There were canned preserves and pickles on the shelves, dried beans in jars, yeast in a crock. She went back to the main room and found some mixing bowls, took one, and returned to the pantry to grab some yeast and sugar. She decided to make whole wheat bread as it was considered more common and she didn't want to put on airs. Also she didn't want Chef to compare it to French bread, which used white flour. And Bridget didn't want to tackle rye bread right away. The bakeries downtown had wonderful rye bread and she supposed the Golds' household bought from them, like most of the city. The Germans had sent her over for rye bread now and then so she had been trying to teach herself to make it. Rye was hard to work with. She grabbed the tin of whole wheat flour in her other hand and went out to the main room.

As she made her sponge in a big bowl, she thought about how she was going to cook the oxtails. She would have to ask Chef one more question about wine, if there were bits from bottles not drunk that could be used for cooking. Surely a

French chef would have a stash of wine to cook with. Red wine, some carrots and onions, potatoes and turnips for the oxtails, and a squash puree on the side whipped up with butter and cream like potatoes, homemade bread, and something sweet. What would dessert be?

Daydreaming and thinking about cooking was Bridget's favorite thing to do. Over the years, it had kept her mind away from the bad things all around her. Now perhaps it wouldn't have to serve that purpose. This place seemed safe and warm and nice. She could see why Irish girls were domestics. Even Kate and Karol, the human mules, both had a nice warm bed and hot and cold running water, for heaven's sake. Bridget thought of some of the places she had spent the night and gave a little shudder without meaning to.

She worked the flour in the sponge gradually. There was a jar of honey in the pantry and so she dribbled just a bit in, along with a little salt. The salt was coarse and she figured it might be kosher. She'd used it before at Delmonico's—they had all kinds of salt—but this kitchen couldn't be kosher or someone would have told her all the rules. She turned out the dough on the table to knead it as she thought about all the questions she had for Mary Martha. Suddenly out of the corner of her eye she saw Chef and his cousin watching her. She could make bread in her sleep but for a minute she really concentrated on her kneading to show off a little, and before she knew it, the dough had a nice sheen to it. She stopped and looked around for some oil to coat the bowl with before she set the dough to rise in it, trying to ignore the men staring at her.

Chef knew what Bridget was looking for and he appeared with a can with a long spout and poured a splash of oil in her bowl. She rolled it around to coat the inside, then picked up the kneaded dough and slid it back in the bowl. Bridget looked around for towels. They were over by the sink neatly stacked on a shelf. She went over and picked one up. It was made of beautiful heavy linen. Mr. Gold probably sold these in the department store, she guessed. As she covered the top of the bowl with a towel, Chef pointed toward the pantry door. "There's a dough box in there if you want to get it out of the draft."

Bridget nodded but didn't say anything. She knew the chefs at Delmonico's didn't like their staff to talk unless they talked to them first. She would try to get in the habit of no words. She picked up the dough and headed for the pantry. Inside the curtained room, she saw the slanted top of the kind of wooden chest Europeans like to put dough in to rise. There had been one at the boardinghouse. She walked over to the corner and bent down slightly, using her elbow to open the top of the dough chest. She balanced the bowl on the wooden edge to keep the lid open so she could use her hand to push the lid all the way up and place the bowl in the chest.

But that wasn't going to work. The dough box was occupied. There was a body bent over almost in two, arms and legs akimbo. Bridget had seen death many times and this was a body, not a person. But she was pretty sure she knew who it had been. The clothes were expensive, the nose just like the father's.

Bridget had found the missing son, Seth Gold.

CHAPTER FOUR

FINALLY, they were going to eat supper. Two or three hours ago, Bridget guessed it must have been three, Mr. Fleming gave her orders to make supper as she had planned. "No one is hungry but everyone needs to eat or else they'll be worthless tomorrow, and we'll have no rest again for days," he said.

Mr. Fleming had been grand through all of the horror and confusion. He took charge right away and was still in charge now as ten o'clock chimed on the clock in the staff eating room. It was a red-eyed group that took their seats around the table.

WHEN she discovered the body, Bridget hadn't screamed out or dropped the dough in a panic. Instead, she quietly closed the lid of the dough chest and stared down at it. She had to tell someone but how? If she ran out in the main room of the kitchen right now, yelling, "Come look," everyone would. She knew Mr. Fleming was the logical person to go to. He had just finished saying he ran the house. But would her direct boss, the chef, feel she went over his head if she just swept past him right now on her way to fetch the butler? Bridget spent a minute sorting it all out. It wasn't as though there was anything to be done for Seth Gold. As terrible as this was, how she handled it would have much more impact on her than him.

After years of institutional living, Bridget knew how much folks valued their position in the chain of command. She would protect that, she decided, and marched out with her big bowl of bread dough still clutched tightly. The chef noticed that she was still holding what she went in to put away and was just getting ready to say something as she stepped close and whispered in his ear. She quickly put down the dough over on the table she'd been working on and turned back to the shaken man. She felt herself trembling for the second time that day.

"Shall I fetch Mr. Fleming?" she asked and Chef nodded, gesturing for his cousin. Together the two men disappeared into the dry storage, the chef speaking French in a low voice.

For a minute, Bridget was lost, stepping out of the kitchen and looking up and down the hall for a sign of something familiar. Then she heard the murmur of voices and saw Mr. Fleming's legs descending the back stairs. The black-haired girls were following with a big box that must have been heavy because it took both of them to carry it.

"What is it, Bridget?" Mr. Fleming asked sharply. She wasn't in the kitchen where she belonged.

Bridget looked quickly at the girls. She knew it was best

to put off the public telling of the bad news. She was sure those two were wailers. "If I may, Mr. Fleming, a private word. It's very important."

The girls didn't hear her. They were concentrating on their task, so when Mr. Fleming stopped suddenly, they went on by, down the hall. "Well?" he said, eyebrows arched. Bridget could just feel his irritation. Is this one going to be a problem? he was wondering.

"I'm sorry to tell you, sir, I just found the young master, or his body. He was dead in the dough box, sir." Bridget felt it was always best to get bad news out of the way quickly.

"Are you sure?"

"Oh, yes, sir. There's no way he could be anything but dead," Bridget said firmly. Folks never wanted to accept this kind of thing.

Mr. Fleming shook his head. "No, how did you know that it's young Mr. Gold. You've never met him." Then he looked suspiciously at her again. "Have you?"

"No, sir. I was just putting two and two together, sir," Bridget said deferentially. She knew this would be hard to manage. Now the butler thinks I've met this lad on the sly somehow, she realized. "The dead man has a resemblance to Mr. Gold and you all mentioned that the son has been gone from the house for several days."

"How do know he's dead, not just passed out?"

"Besides the fact he wasn't breathing? It's not that big a chest, sir. He doesn't really fit. I think his arms or legs must have been broken to cram him in. His skin is bluish. I didn't see any blood, though. Probably his neck was broke."

Mr. Fleming accepted that reluctantly. "Who have you told?"

"Just the chef. He took his cousin into the room where the body is and told me to fetch you."

With that, Mr. Fleming went into action. The whole household would be hysterical soon. He didn't have a moment to lose. "Take me," he ordered.

When they returned to the kitchen, everything was just as it was when Bridget had left. Harvey and Elsie were in the process of taking everything out of a dish cabinet and cleaning it. They didn't even look up. No one else was around. Bridget led the way into the dry storage room.

The chef and Gilbert were standing looking at the body of Seth Gold as if he were a broken wagon wheel or a busted water pump in the kitchen and somehow if they thought on it hard enough they would be able to mend him whole again. They were silent as Mr. Fleming peered into the chest at the young man. "It's Seth, all right. Rene, can we lift him out?" Mr. Fleming asked. There was no reason not to go straight to the point.

Chef shook his head. "We tried. He's, he's stuck. The stiffening is already in him. But he can't have been here too long. I used this box yesterday," the older man explained, proud of himself he didn't mention there was no smell yet. Gilbert was standing over to the side, white as a ghost.

Chef looked almost normal to Bridget compared to a few minutes ago. His coloring had improved from the moment right after Bridget had whispered in his ear. She'd said, "I'm pretty certain the body of the son is in the dough chest. He's dead, no doubt about it." That's when he'd turned a whitish green.

Mr. Fleming looked around. "We'll just have to take the box apart. I don't want Mr. Gold to see him like this. Gilbert, go get a hammer and saw. Hurry," he ordered. Then he went to the curtained opening and stepped out. "Harvey," he barked.

The boy hurried across the kitchen. "Listen to me," Mr. Fleming said, holding Harvey's gaze intently. "You must go down to the store and get Mr. Gold. Tell him I said it is absolutely imperative that he returns home right away. Tell him that Mr. Fleming said he must have his presence. He won't like me giving him orders but I've never done so before so surely he'll know it's important. Do not take no for an answer, do you understand, Harvey?"

Harvey's eyes widened and he nodded, jumping up and down in place, like a runner at the starting block of a race. Mr. Fleming reached in his pocket and took out a handful of coins and shoved them in the boy's hand. "Get a hack. Don't wait for the trolley," Mr. Fleming said.

This alarmed Harvey more than the tone of Mr. Fleming's voice or his instructions. Mr. Fleming had never given Harvey the money to take a carriage before. He took the omnibus around town. Something bad was going on; that was for sure. He turned and left without another word.

Gilbert came running back in the kitchen with the tools and Mr. Fleming looked at Bridget. "Guard this door. Don't let anyone else come in, do you understand?"

"Do I tell them the truth?" Bridget asked.

"You might as well, they'll know soon enough. Try to be brief," Mr. Fleming said, knowing that wouldn't happen. How does one explain how and why the body of the young master is in the dry goods room? And why it sounds like a carpenter's workshop in there? He looked over at Elsie, who had finally got wind of something amiss. She was acting as if she was still cleaning but really she was just watching them. That was how it would be if he didn't get this under control soon. The whole household would come to a stand-still. He turned away, back to the task at hand. He wished Justin were here to help carry the load on this.

Bridget cleaned up the table where she'd kneaded her dough. She didn't think she should take the bowl and the rolling pin to the sink, though. If she got clear across the kitchen, sure enough someone would pop into the dry goods storage and she'd be in the doghouse with Mr. Fleming. She peeked under the towel at her dough. Soon she could make it into loaves. That would take up some time.

The first crack of splintering wood came from the back room, along with a string of French words Bridget assumed was cursing. It shouldn't take them too long. If they just took off one side of the box, they could slide him out. Elsie was walking toward her. It was time for Bridget to do her job.

"What are they doing in there? And do you know where Mr. Fleming sent Harvey?" Elsie asked uneasily. Even a soul like Elsie who wanted to mind her own business and stay out of trouble could tell something was wrong.

"Elsie, it's bad," Bridget started, just to get Elsie's undivided attention. "I found young Mr. Gold. He's dead and someone stuffed him in the dough box to hide the body." Or to make sure the body was found, Bridget thought.

"Oh, dear," Elsie said. "Do you suppose Katherine killed him for doing her wrong?"

"I wouldn't think so. Surely Chef has used that dough box since Katherine left the house. He, the body, hasn't been in there long, I'd guess."

Elsie's eyes widened. "Did you see him?"

"I'm afraid I did. I was going to put my bread dough in to rise and there he was."

"How, how was he dead?" Elsie asked.

"Don't know really. He wasn't all bloody so probably not with a knife. Could have been shot, though. I couldn't see his whole body. He was folded up, like."

Sounds of sawing came from the other room. Bridget could see Elsie's eyes widen. She looked at the curtains to the dry storage room as if they had grown horns. "Do you mind if I tell the others?"

Bridget was relieved. Better they heard it from someone they knew, no matter how much Elsie mucked it up. And she didn't seem prone to hysterics. "Oh, would you? I think it would be better from you. All but Mary Martha. Could you find her and ask her to come down here so I can tell her? And you best do it fast. I think they'll be wanting to put him someplace soon."

"Will the police come?"

Bridget had been mulling that over for a few minutes. She knew that the police wouldn't like what Mr. Fleming and the others were doing right now, moving the body. But in her mind it didn't make much difference because the body had already been moved once, when it was stuffed in that chest. That was what she decided had happened since she didn't really want to think about the possibility that young Mr. Gold had been alive when he was crammed in that box. He'd been killed first, and then put in the dough box second. So, as to moving him again, rich people could do pretty much what they wanted in New York. The coppers most likely wouldn't say much about the travels of young Mr. Seth. "Chances are. Now go find the girls, please," she said, trying to keep her voice calm.

How Bridget acted today, the way she treated Elsie and the rest, would stick with her long after Seth Gold was in the ground. She could make friends or enemies, and she was determined to at least not make enemies on her first day here, no matter what kind of disaster had come their way as a household.

Elsie might usually be slow, but news of this magnitude must have put speed into her feet. Bridget took out her dough and started punching it down. In no more than three minutes, Mary Martha was running into the kitchen. Bridget knew Elsie had already spilled the beans by the look of her friend. "Oh, dear Lord. Is what Elsie said true?"

"What did she say?"

"That you found Master Seth dead?"

Bridget nodded. "Yes, that's true, all right."

"And that Katherine must have killed him. That he was stuffed in the dough box and they were cutting him out in pieces?" Mary Martha reported, fighting back tears.

Bridget couldn't help but smile. "Don't you cry, Mary Martha McBride. We've seen worse than this. Katherine couldn't have killed him unless she came back from Washington where Mr. Gold sent her. And they're not cutting him out in pieces. He just got stiff in that position so they have to cut the dough box apart to get him out."

"Heaven help us. How?"

Bridget shook her head. "I don't know. I didn't touch him. I was going to put this bread dough in the box to rise, and when I opened the top, there he was. His head was all twisted and his arms looked broke but I couldn't tell how he died. And I couldn't see his whole face, thank goodness."

"Someone needs to tell the missus. It'll take hours to get up there."

"Harvey has gone after Mr. Gold. Between him and Mr. Fleming, they'll sort it out. But, Mary Martha, I think they will want to put him somewhere. What about his bed-room?"

Mary Martha looked at her friend and realized for the first time that she herself would have responsibilities in this situation. "It's clean as a whistle. The bed's all made up. There's a fire laid in the fireplace, although the heat might not be good for him." Suddenly Mary Martha was thinking of all the small coffins she and Bridget had seen laid out in the courtyard at the orphanage. The poor little tikes had no one to mourn them but the other children, so they had always filed past those coffins and sung hymns and carried on for days, whether it was in the heat of summer or not. Mary Martha always secretly said the Roman Catholic Prayer for the Dead for them. She started it now. "Oh, God, the Cre-ator and Redeemer . . ."

"Mary Martha?" Bridget said impatiently.

"Oh, sorry, Brig. Do you want me to go up and make a place? Brig, I don't know a spec about Jewish funerals."

"Me neither," Bridget admitted. "Do the Golds attend church, or whatever they call it, much?"

"I've never noticed him going. And the store is closed on Sunday and open on Saturday, which is what they call Shab-bat, their Sabbath, I do know that. He can't be too religious if he keeps the Christian business hours."

"What about Mrs. Gold?"

"I know she sometimes talks about a group of women from her, ah, congregation she calls it. I think she does char-ity work with them. The boy that's married, Ben, I know his wife is more religious. But I get the idea you can be born Jewish and not go to church at all but still be Jewish," Mary Martha said, puzzling over it. It was not like that in the

Roman Catholic faith. You had to keep up with your church going. It was a sin not to.

Bridget looked over her shoulder at the noise from the back room. She'd been forming her dough into loaves while she and Mary Martha talked.

"Christ in heaven, girl, how can you make bread at a time like this?" Mary Martha demanded.

"It calms me," Bridget said as she went over to see which cookstove was on and hot. She figured they weren't both used unless there was a dinner party, or guests in the house. It was the stove nearest the worktable she was kneading on. She could tell by the smell it was burning wood. She checked the oven and then got two more pieces of firewood to stoke the fire in it. "Besides, I'd already made the dough, and if I didn't keep up with it, it would just go to waste. We can't have that."

Just then the other four women burst into the kitchen, all in various stages of shock. Mary Martha was swept up in the arms of Sally, who was weeping. The black-haired girls were clinging to each other, and Elsie looked very pleased to be the one in the know for a change. Bridget figured there would be time enough to straighten out all the misinformation Elsie had delivered. She let them be. They went to get each other drinks of water on the other side of the kitchen.

Bridget looked around and found a baking sheet for the bread. As she was getting the loaves ready for the oven, Mr. Fleming stepped out of the dry goods room, followed by the chef and Gilbert. He eyed the women, who had moved to the eating table in the other room. He would have to regain control of them in a minute, but right now what he needed was a good, stiff gulp of brandy. He had dispatched Chef to go get his hidden stash. He walked over to Bridget. "How are they?"

She glanced in the other room at the women and then took her bread over to the oven and put it in. "I let Elsie be the one to tell them so I imagine they have things a little confused," she said as she walked. "You'll probably need to go have a talk with them. How are things in there?"

"He's on the floor, his eyes are closed, and I want to cover him. Gilbert's gone to get a sheet from the laundry room. He's still curled up but I think the stiffness disappears in a while. They go limp again. Then we can straighten him out." Chef and Gilbert came back in the kitchen and went directly into the other room. Gilbert was carrying a sheet and Chef had a bottle down at his side. Mr. Fleming followed them.

Bridget thought a nip sounded like a good idea but she knew the men would never say, "Let's give the lass that found the stiff a little brandy." She cleaned up her table again. She didn't really belong in there boo-hooing with the girls and she wasn't welcome with the men.

Bridget heard the next arrivals before she saw them. The ladies in the dining room did too. They shrank together in a little knot of fear and misery. There was sympathy involved, too. Mr. Gold was home and he was going to have to bury his own child. Poor man.

He burst into the kitchen, Harvey on his heels proclaiming he wasn't told anything, which was true. "What's going on?" Mr. Gold demanded. There was no one to hear him but Bridget.

"Mr. Fleming is in the dry goods room, sir. I'll go fetch him," she said but it was too late. He'd made for that door as soon as she identified Mr. Fleming's whereabouts. She hoped they'd already had their nip and put the bottle away. It would be bad enough to see your son dead, without having it look like the staff was toasting with a bottle of your cognac over his body.

The next sound they all heard wouldn't be forgotten anytime soon. It was an anguished cry of heartbreak. You couldn't tell from the sound if it was from man, woman, or animal, but they all knew it came from Mr. Gold. The cry was so full of loss that it utterly emptied out the soul of every one of them who heard it. Although she didn't feel them or notice, tears started running down Bridget's cheeks.

THE chef and Gilbert and Mr. Fleming put Seth up in his room. Mr. Gold said that the body couldn't be left alone and asked someone to stay with him until the ladies from the congregation got there. He'd already sent Harvey downtown again to whatever they called their church—Bridget wasn't sure if the word "congregation" meant the building or the people—with a letter he wrote himself right at the staff eating table. People called it the dining room, just like the one upstairs. The rest of the staff had congregated in there, too.

"I'll be glad to stay with him, sir," Mary Martha said. Bridget thought that was a good choice. Mary Martha wouldn't be weepy about it.

"Thank you," Mr. Gold said, his voice still quivering a tiny bit. "In our faith, everyone who comes in contact with a, a body"—how hard that was for him to say—"must wash their hands, whether they touched the body or not. I know none of you are Jewish but I beg you to follow these rules for me, please. It is a ritual more about respect than about having dirty hands," he said, and went into the kitchen and washed his own hands. They all followed him, washing right there in the kitchen so all the rest would know they did it. This was out of respect for Mr. Gold, not especially for Seth, Mary Martha told Bridget later. After they were all done, Mr. Gold addressed Mary Martha. "That was cowardly of me to ask anyone else to stay with Seth. I'll do what a father should do. Mr. Fleming, could you please come sit with me for a few minutes so I can tell you what must be attended to?"

"But of course, sir," Mr. Fleming said. He threw a look at the chef and Gilbert, and they all three went into the dry goods room. Mr. Gold remained in the kitchen standing by the door with his head down.

Then off they went, Gilbert and Chef and Mr. Fleming trying to carry Seth's covered-up, curled-up body so he wouldn't look too undignified, Mr. Gold in front so he wouldn't have to watch his son getting bundled that way. In a minute Mr. Fleming ran back in for some candles. The Golds had gas lights, so candles were used only on the fancy dinner table, but now Mr. Fleming took a whole box of them up to Seth's room.

Bridget took her bread out of the oven. The loaves looked nice and smelled good but no one noticed. She put them on the baker's rack to cool, and then she split the acorn squash, seeded them, and put them in the oven, feeding the fire with another log. She figured they'd use the squash tomorrow, if not tonight. And she had to keep busy. She wouldn't know what to do otherwise.

She peeled some onions and carrots. The chef and Gilbert had never returned to the kitchen and she imagined they were up in their rooms, trying to drown the memories of the last few hours. Bridget didn't blame them a bit.

She heard the back door bell ring at the same time that Harvey ran in the kitchen. "The ladies from the church are here. I let them in with me," he said importantly. "They went on upstairs."

Sally, Karol and Kate, and Mary Martha looked at one another. They were still around the table, drinking a cup. They weren't sure what to do about strangers coming in the house and just making themselves at home. Mrs. Simon usually took care of social things that were out of the ordinary. Or Mr. Fleming did. Mary Martha made a decision. "I should go. He's on the second floor after all," she said and took a last sip of tea as she stood up.

Just then Mr. Fleming came in the kitchen. He looked relieved to see Harvey. "Boy, go down the street to the hack stand and ask who wants to go up the river to Westchester and back. If no one says yes, tell them there's big tip in it. Talk till you convince someone to go, and bring the driver in here first. I must talk to him and also give him this." He held up a sealed envelope, and then slid it in his pocket.

"Sally, go up to the third floor and get Chef and Gilbert. I want to talk to everyone," Mr. Fleming said and walked into the staff dining room. "Girls, stay here." Then he went back in the kitchen and spoke to Bridget. "Please go ahead and make dinner, Bridget. But come into the dining room first," he said distractedly. "I need Harvey to break up the rest of that chest and take it away," he said, talking more to himself than anyone else.

Before Sally got back downstairs, Harvey returned with a hack driver. Mr. Fleming talked to the man in a quiet voice, and gave him some money along with the letter. They looked up at the clock, both nodded, and the driver left.

Bridget had no idea where Westchester County was, or if it took an hour or a week to get there.

Sally, Chef, and Gilbert reappeared, and, Mr. Fleming turned his attention to the staff. They were back in their dining room. "In just a moment, I'm going to have to go to the police station and let them know Master Seth was apparently murdered. The Metropolitan boys will be here soon. This will be the end of our peace and quiet for a while. The good news is that the rabbi is upstairs with Mr. Gold now, and they inform me that if Mrs. Gold were present, the funeral would be tomorrow. Since she most likely will not arrive from the country house until the morning, the burial will be the next morning, day after tomorrow. Then the mourning period begins, which I will explain to you as they explained it to me."

"What'd he die from?" Sally asked bluntly.

"Two gunshot wounds to the chest. Quite a neat job, really. But then his neck was snapped and his legs and arms were broken. Or that's how I would prefer to imagine it happened. He was shot dead, then he was made to fit in that chest after, by making certain parts fold in ways they aren't meant to."

Bridget changed the subject as fast as she could. "You said the mourning comes after the burial?"

"Yes," Mr. Fleming said, giving Bridget a grateful look. "Before the burial there are a few things you must attend to, however. All the mirrors must be covered. One of the women has gone downtown to tell Seth's brother Benjamin what has happened. He works on Wall Street, as most of you know. They will stop at the department store to tell the managers and get bolts of black fabric for the mirrors. When they return, please take care of that, ladies."

Mary Martha said, "Of course, sir."

Mr. Fleming continued. "The women from the congregation, Shearith Israel is its name by the way, who sit with the dead evidently do this for everyone who passes on. It's a very prestigious group, a holy society, and they are called 'Shomerin,' which means some kind of guard. While they are at work, I suppose you might say, with the body, they may not eat, drink, or perform a commandment in the presence of the dead, and there are some six hundred commandments so I would think they can't do much of anything. It is because the dead cannot do these things again that the Shomerin don't do them either. Chef, I want refreshments for them when they get off duty or change shifts or whatever, but these women keep the dietary laws so you must get the food for them from a kosher bakery."

Chef nodded. His eyes were bleary and so were Gilbert's. They both seemed drunk, but not so drunk they couldn't understand Mr. Fleming's instructions. After all, most of the workingmen of New York City went to their jobs half looped.

"Did Katherine do it?" Elsie asked. It was though Mr. Fleming hadn't uttered a word since he told them how Seth died.

Mr. Fleming's eyes flashed. He had to regain control of this group or the next few days would be unbearable. "Now, how would I know who killed him, you nitwit! Little Miss Katherine did not leave a letter stating that she shot her lover, no. Nor is there anything to indicate she did not go to Washington with Mr. Gold's cousin, as she seemed to be doing when she walked out that door there. And young Mr. Gold was alive after she left. So what in the world gave you that silly idea?"

Elsie took it as a legitimate question. "Well, sir, I thought since Mr. Seth and she—"

Mr. Fleming held up his hands, palms down, and sliced through the air with them. "Enough. The police department of New York City will have to determine who killed Seth Gold. Since they are generally just a peacekeeping organization with very little in the way of detecting skills, I assume we will never know how this tragedy occurred." He looked at them as if he dared anyone to speak. "Now, on to the mourning period. After the burial, a close friend or relative will prepare the first meal for the mourners. Chef, you must make your kitchen available for this, although I understand it is usually just eggs and bread. Shiva, the first mourning period, is observed for seven days. Parents, children, spouses, and siblings of the deceased observe Shiva. That will include our employers and Master Benjamin and I guess his wife. Mistress Rose will not know about this until word can get to her in Spain. Shiva begins on the day of burial and goes until the morning of the seventh day after burial. During that time the mourners cannot bathe, put on fresh clothing, work, or shave and some other things that don't affect you. Then there are things that can't be done for thirty days, like attending parties, shaving, cutting hair, or listening to music. I gather that for religious families, there is a daily church service for a year that relates to mourning, but since the Golds are not religious, this does not apply. That's the basics. I'm sure there is much more, but right now just remember that you don't take tea or a bite to eat to the women sitting with the body, and get ready to cover the mirrors. Bridget is cooking supper and I'm going to the police station. Would you all give the house a good look to make sure the fireplaces have fires laid and everything is spotless? I'm afraid there is no way to prevent our family from being invaded by outside forces for a while," Mr. Fleming said sadly, and then wheeled and left the room, stopping only to talk to Harvey about removing the broken chest. Everyone else followed him out of the dining room and upstairs. The thought of Harvey bringing out the dough box where the broken body had been found seemed to have taken the desire to be around food away from them.

Bridget was glad to have a job to focus on for the next hours. The squash were tender and she peeled them. She found four bottles of opened wine in the pantry next to the vinegar and used two of them to braise her oxtails. The rest of the household buzzed in and out of the kitchen, functioning again after their initial shock.

"The police are here," Elsie told her excitedly. She'd been put on back-door duty and gave Bridget a report every time someone arrived or left.

Bridget didn't expect the coppers to do any real investigating, such as interviewing everyone who lived and worked here. That would be too much trouble for them and from her experience, they only worked when there was something in it for them.

"The material is here. They're covering the mirrors," Elsie reported a little bit later. "Oh, and Master Benjamin and his wife arrived."

Mary Martha rushed in. "Master Benjamin and his wife are staying here. I've got to get a hot water bottle for her," she said breathily and rushed out again. Bridget wondered what the other brother was like, if he was handsome like his sibling and his father.

"The master won't leave the library," Sally reported as she went into the laundry for clean towels.

*   *   *

AND now it was ten o'clock and everyone was gathered back in the staff dining room. The group had come to realize how much work this death was going to mean to each and every one of them. As they sat down, they all seemed to be complaining: about the firewood not lighting, about covering the mirrors, about the women sitting with the body on little stools they had brought with them, and of course, about the police.

Bridget served her first meal to the household. They all ate like there was no tomorrow, but no one complimented her on the food or paid any mind one way or the other. No one seemed to remember it was her first day on the job. Morning was a lifetime ago.

CHAPTER FIVE

As Elsie and Harvey were clearing dishes, Mr. Fleming pulled Bridget aside. "Would you please take a supper tray to Mr. Gold? Not that I think he'll want it, but if you take it up, he won't feel obliged to be nice. That is, you haven't been with us long enough to be considered family and that's the way Mr. Gold treats his household, like family. After that you go on up to bed. I'll pick up the tray later."

"Of course, sir. Mary Martha took a tray up to Master Benjamin and his missus just a minute ago but they were already in bed, poor dears. I'll give it a go," Bridget said as she went over to the uneaten tray Mary Martha had returned right before they sat down to eat.

She tipped the oxtails back into a copper saucepan and put them on the warmest place on the stovetop. The squash would just have to be at room temperature and the half loaf from Mary Martha's tray was fine. It was all she had.

In a few minutes, Bridget was standing in front of the library door, wondering what you do when you have your hands full like this. "Mr. Gold, it's Bridget, sir."

"Come," a voice said. It had no resemblance to the voice that had greeted her this morning.

She was able to open the door without letting go of the tray, barely. She stepped in and took the tray right over to the desk. Mr. Gold was sitting with his desk chair facing the fireplace but not close and cozy, just pointed in that direction. He had been holding his head in his hands but straightened up when Bridget came in.

"I brought you some supper, sir. I know you're probably not hungry but—"

Mr. Gold cut her off. "I need to keep my strength up. I know. Bridget, what a terrible day for you to have joined us." He seemed to appreciate an excuse to think of something else.

"I'm so sorry for your loss, Mr. Gold. I just can't figure out how or why your boy ended up in . . . where he did."

"None of it makes sense now. The police weren't very helpful either. They said it was probably some ruffians, out to rob him. They said life is cheap in New York City," Mr. Gold repeated bitterly.

"Well, he was a well-dressed young man. I guess his coin purse or money was gone, yes?" Bridget asked.

"That's the strange part about it. He had more than one hundred dollars in his pocket. I have no idea why he was walking around with that much money but it couldn't have been a robbery."

"What did the coppers, ah, the police say to that?" Bridget asked.

"They said we had no way of knowing how much money he had with him, that he could have had much more, that maybe he gambled, that maybe the robbers were interrupted or didn't find the pocket with the cash."

Bridget snorted. "Yes, they were so interrupted they were able to break him up and stuff him in a wooden chest in an inner room in his own house." Bridget couldn't believe she'd said that. How rude, and to a man who had been so nice to her. "Lordy, I'm sorry how that came out, Mr. Gold."

"No, that was a very good point, Bridget. Seth wasn't found in an alley somewhere. He wasn't even found on the outside stairs, trying to open the door of his house. He was found inside the house and not only inside the house but in that chest. It must have taken some doing to get his body in there. That takes planning. There is no way that whoever did this wasn't trying to send a message of some kind."

"What do you think the message is?"

Mr. Gold shrugged. He was at a loss. "That they can get in my house if they want. It could be simple: they wanted to make sure I knew Seth was dead and found his body. Or it has something to do with this household or my business perhaps. Seth worked with me, you know."

Bridget thought about Katherine and how Elsie had assumed the death was her doing. "Mr. Gold, did you ever meet any of Katherine's kin? Could she have an angry father or brother?"

"I never heard her speak of her family. But I think that's one of the first things I need to discover. Did someone want

to even the score with Seth for what they considered, what
was, an injustice?"

"So will you ask the police to find out?"

"Nonsense. As soon as Seth is buried, I'm going to look
into this myself. I refuse to just let my son be shot down like
a dog. I will find the person who did this."

Bridget was glad to hear Mr. Gold talk so feisty-like. Not
that she figured on him having any success but it was nice
he wasn't just willing to be a victim. "Anything I can do to
help, you just let me know," she said as she left the library.

Bridget went up to her room but she certainly didn't feel
tired. There was so much to sort out in her mind. Someone,
Mary Martha she guessed, had turned on the gas light for
her so the room seemed inviting even if it was a strange one.
She got out of her clothes and into her nightgown and lay
down on top of the cover to think.

From a selfish point of view, Bridget thought the day had
turned out pretty well. It was a tragedy, yes. But she had
shown herself to be someone who could be counted on in extreme circumstances. No one might realize it yet, but when
Mr. Fleming had a chance to think about the day, he'd see
the new girl had been someone who hadn't stopped working
through all the craziness, who did as he asked with a mini-
mum of questions, and didn't fall apart when she found a
dead body. Also, she hoped someone had noticed, those were
damned good oxtails!

There were still so many questions. She thought about
going down to Mary Martha's room but she was probably
already asleep and Bridget didn't want to wake her. She did
want to know something about the mistress of the house besides the fact that she liked the country better than the city.
And what about this Justin? What did a steward do? There

was a lot still to learn, but all in all, Bridget felt good about her place in the house. A day is like a month when there's trouble and by suppertime no one had paid her any mind, just talking away at a clip and asking her opinion on the murder like she was one of them.

The murder. That was more of a puzzle. She couldn't see an Irish father killing a rich young cad because of his daughter. Asking for money, yes, for the terrible disgrace to the family name. Yes, that would be something Da would have pulled. But killing? And then going to the bother of breaking into a great house like this to leave the body? And doing it so no one could hear? And not taking a hundred bucks, no matter if there had been a hundred more? No Irishman she knew would play that game.

Bridget realized she should try to get some sleep. She went down the hall to the bathroom, a bathroom of all glorious things, washed her face, and took a pee. It was quiet. Everyone else had the sense to sleep while they could. On the way back to her room, she heard a commotion on the second floor. Doors were banging and she heard sobbing. Someone was talking in low tones, talking to Mr. Gold. Bridget could already recognize his voice as he responded. He must have come out in the hall. The crying came from a woman. Bridget guessed Mrs. Gold had traveled home as fast as she could, wanting to believe there was a mistake, and now she knew it was true. One of her own, lying there, broken, all the dreams she must have had for him over.

Bridget stood transfixed at the head of the stairs. She was on the men's side of the house, which was forbidden, but she just couldn't help herself. She could hear the soothing noises the ladies staying with the body were making to try and get Mrs. Gold to calm down. Bridget had forgotten about them.

She was surprised that they were still there. But she guessed "someone must stay with the body" didn't mean only in the daylight hours or just until midnight. Bridget wished she could fix a cup for Mrs. Gold, or a dram of brandy would be better.

She was ready to return to her room, but suddenly the noise downstairs became louder, more intense. She stayed, listening in the dark.

"Enough of this, Isaac," the woman Bridget assumed was Estella Gold yelled, her voice full of so many emotions Bridget could hardly sort them out: loss, grief, anger, spite. "I don't care who killed Seth, or why, for that matter. He's dead and we'll mourn him forever. But I'll tell you the truth, I would have killed him myself rather than seen him marry that little tramp," she spat out. Mr. Gold must have pulled her back into a bedroom because their voices became muffled. Bridget could no longer hear them clearly, but she could tell the Golds were in for a long night. She made a beeline for her bedroom, cold suddenly from the iciness of the last statement. What kind of a woman would talk so mean about the departed, who also happened to be her son?

When she was falling asleep, something that didn't take as long as she thought it would, she remembered the box in the closet. She must ask Mary Martha. Tomorrow.

CHAPTER SIX

THE next day was a blur. Mr. Fleming hired two more Negro boys to help Harvey, and the three boys spent the day taking messages around town to people the Golds wanted to know about the burial. That's what they called it, not a funeral, Bridget noticed. Bridget was sent downtown to pick up a whole list of foodstuffs that she guessed Mrs. Gold had ordered. Chef also gave her a list of things that weren't from their regular delivery grocer and Mr. Fleming gave her money and told her to get receipts, which she knew to do. She had a nice time shopping with money in her pocket for a change. The Germans were very frugal.

That took up her morning. Mr. Fleming told her to go to the corner and hire a hack to stay with her, so she could just get right in the carriage with her packages and toddle on to the next stop like a real lady. When she got home, there was some unloading to be done. Bridget remembered how

Mr. Fleming hadn't let anyone in the house when she'd watched him—was that just yesterday? So she and the driver unloaded, she paid and gave him a nice tip for all the stopping and starting, and then rang the bell, her packages all piled around her.

Suddenly, out of nowhere, a young man was standing beside her. He had on a suit and a proper hat, a bowler, and clutched a notebook and a pen. "What's going on in there? I hear Mr. Gold's son was murdered. Word from the Metropolitans is his arms and legs was chopped off, maybe his head. Can you help me, lass? I'm with the *Recorder*."

"Go away. You've been fed a pack of lies, you have," Bridget said. "Don't you have better to do?"

Mr. Fleming opened the door and stepped outside with authority. "Yes, that's a very good question, Bridget. Don't you have better to do, young man?"

While Mr. Fleming and Bridget loaded themselves up with packages, the reporter tried to get a peek in the house. "I'll give you a buck to see the corpse," he offered. Mr. Fleming kept his body between the reporter and the door. He wasn't about to let this outsider breach the gates of his household.

Bridget had lots of questions for the reporter, like who down at the police station had gypped him out of a pay off with that story about Seth being chopped up. But Mr. Fleming pretended the fellow didn't exist so Bridget did the same. As they were closing the door in his face, he threw a business card in one of the bags. "Send for me if you want to talk. My name is Michael Murphy but everybody just calls me Murphy. Who's Katherine O'Sullivan?"

Soon they were inside and the door locked behind them. Mr. Fleming walked with her to the kitchen and put down the bags he'd been carrying. "When you find that card, destroy it. We have enough trouble," he said, looking much more addled than he had yesterday, when they'd had only the dead to deal with, not the living. He hurried away.

Bridget started unpacking her purchases, and when she came to the reporter's card, she disobeyed Mr. Fleming and put it in the pocket of her uniform. She didn't know why. It sure wasn't for personal gain. She wouldn't have sold information about the Golds for any amount. She felt strongly that someone in service in a household never told tales about the people she was working for. She didn't believe in telling on people under any circumstances. She'd learned that lesson on the streets early on.

She had a vague idea that maybe the reporter could help Mr. Gold, not the other way around.

All of a sudden, the back door opened again and there was another bustle of activity. A booming male voice rang out, "And don't let me see you around here again, young man." Bridget guessed the reporter was still out there.

Sally went hurrying by. "Thank God, Justin's back," she said.

Bridget had assumed the whole group from the country house had returned in the middle of the night. She stuck her head out in the hallway to take a look. Lots of luggage was being carried down here to the staff floor. There was a very thin older woman in a suit, a disheveled Irish-looking gent, and a big, tall, older Negro who seemed to be organizing everyone else. The missus must have come back with the hack driver, and the thin one was Mrs. Simons, the secretary; the Negro was the driver; and the other one was Justin, the steward. They must have stayed until morning to wind up the other house, although it was odd Mrs. Gold didn't bring her secretary with her.

"Johnny, take the horses over to the stable and give them an extra ration of corn. That was a hard ride." The Negro seemed to be telling the other what to do. Had she been mistaken? Was the Irish-looking' fella the driver and the Negro the steward?

Sally, Karol, and Kate swarmed around the Negro, all talking at once. The thin woman went upstairs. Mr. Fleming joined them next, and sent all three of the women back to what they were supposed to be doing. He and the Negro stood there talking in low voices for so long that Bridget stopped watching and went back to her work.

In a few minutes, the Negro came into the kitchen. "Bridget, I'm Justin Morgan. I'm the steward of this household. I hear you had quite a first day. This is a terrible thing, yes it is."

Bridget gave a little bow in the direction of the man. He was such a powerful presence she was a little intimidated, and that didn't happen often to her. She could understand why Sally had been so happy to see him come home. He just radiated a power that gave you confidence.

"Glad to meet you, sir. I feel sorry for Mr. Gold, that's for sure, and Mrs. Gold, too, of course. It's just that I haven't met her yet."

"Something to look forward to," Justin said dryly. He glanced around the kitchen and then stepped into the dry storage room where Seth's body had been found. "I feel responsible for this tragedy. I sleep down here on this floor, along with Harvey. If I had been home, no one would have dared try such a thing." His voice was shaking with indignation.

"First thing, sir, you were doing what Mr. Fleming and Mr. Gold wanted, as I understand it, in being upstate, so there's no fault there. Second, I'm pretty sure Master Seth was killed somewhere else and then brought down here. You most likely couldn't have done a thing to save him. Third, those guns have more than two bullets in them as I recall. You could have got yourself killed along with the young master. And if Harvey sleeps down here, why didn't he wake up? It must have been noisy, what they did with the body in the chest," Bridget said. She hadn't given a thought about where the Negros slept or them not being up on the third floor with the rest of the help.

Justin gave a little smile. "I'll take the third part first. Harvey's a child, and when children go to sleep, they don't hear a thing. If he did, no one will know until he's an old man and he spills the beans to his grandchildren that he heard some murderers one night when he was young."

Now it was Bridget's turn to smile. "I can just see Harvey as an old man, telling that tale."

"As for Master Seth being killed somewhere else, the fact that no one in this household heard a gun go off would indicate you are correct about that. Mr. Fleming assures me it was quiet as usual that night, although I, too, can't imagine the perpetrators were totally silent. And the first item you mentioned, that by going away from New York to attempt to retrieve Mrs. Gold I was merely doing what I was told by my superiors, that is an excuse that's been used by soldiers, servants, and other assorted scoundrels for years as they try to absolve their own guilt. It does not convince my heart. I'll always believe that if I had been here, things would have been different."

It was funny, Bridget thought, how you could not know a person one minute and have such a real and true conversation with them the very next minute. She had a good feeling about this man. He sure did talk like a professor or such, and he seemed street-smart along with the big words. She was surprised—no, shocked would be a better word—that he was a Negro and Mary Martha had not mentioned this.

The Irish and Negroes had a funny relationship in New York. They lived in the same tenements and many of them competed for the same jobs and the same women. Bridget had seen lots of Irish girls fall for Negroes, and the Irish lads didn't care for it, that was for sure.

"Well, only time will tell, sir. Can I ask you a question that shows my ignorance?"

"I doubt that will happen. Mr. Fleming says you are sharp as a tack and have behaved admirably throughout this ordeal."

"I appreciate Mr. Fleming saying that. What I don't know, sir, is what is a steward? We didn't have one, or a butler for that matter, at the German boardinghouse. I'd heard of a butler, though."

Justin nodded. "Mr. Fleming is the one in charge of the house. However, I share his duties somewhat. He works directly with the Golds, serves their guests, and sees that everything on the first and second floor is as it should be. I am in charge of this floor. I am the one who usually takes care of ordering, accepts the deliveries, and looks after the accounts. Mr. Fleming and I have a weekly meeting where we go over the books, and a monthly meeting with Mr. Gold concerning the household. In many ways we partner. I am just not seen."

Bridget figured he was stuck in the downstairs because

he was a Negro. "Can I ask how you got to be a steward? Is there training you go to?"

Justin smiled. "When I was a boy, I worked at Mr. Gold's parents' house, doing a job similar to what Harvey does for us now. Mr. Gold and I grew up together and we have a fondness that sometimes develops through that shared experience."

Bridget laughed. "A fondness through shared experience. Some brothers and sisters have that, some don't."

Justin nodded in agreement. "When Mr. Gold married, he asked me to come to his house and help him out. I've been here ever since, not in this fine house, but in Mr. Gold's service. He is a man unique in that he does not see the color of someone's skin. He sees what a person's character is, what his accomplishments are, and judges according to those criteria, not their race or religion. His parents were fine people as well. They insisted that I learn from the fancy tutors right along with their children."

"I guess that means you can read and write?" Bridget asked.

"That I can."

She couldn't help but brag. "I can, too. Isn't it wonderful to be able to read books?"

Justin took the bags and boxes she had emptied. He turned to go and smiled. "It's the best."

IT was two o'clock when she met the missus.

It was then Mrs. Gold came down to the kitchen. Mrs. Simon and Mr. Fleming accompanied her. Chef had asked Bridget to organize the smoked fish and other things she'd purchased and she was in the walk-in icebox when the three of them appeared.

The first thing that shocked Bridget was Mrs. Gold's torn bodice. It wasn't that it was revealing anything. She was wearing a black dress, and a black camisole was showing through the tear. But she either was unaware, and in that case surely Mary Martha would have told her, or it was part of the official grieving. She added that to her list of questions for Mary Martha, whom she'd barely seen today.

The second thing that surprised Bridget was how young Mrs. Gold looked. She sure didn't look old enough to have borne grown children. Bridget would have guessed her to be in her early thirties, while Mr. Gold looked in his late forties to fifty. But Bridget also knew that a woman with access to all the things they sell at a department store, cosmetics and all kind of face creams and the like, maybe didn't show her age like the women downtown.

It worried Bridget that she would turn out looking like most of the Irish did, old way before her time.

Mrs. Gold was pretty; that was for sure. She looked foreign in the same way Mr. Gold did, dark hair and dark eyes that flashed, and sharp features. In fact, if they weren't married, Bridget would figure them for brother and sister. Mrs. Gold stopped talking mid-sentence when she laid eyes on Bridget. She and Mrs. Simon both stared at the girl, and it wasn't friendly.

Mr. Fleming was smooth as silk. He realized Mrs. Gold's reaction to Bridget could be a problem and tried to head it off. Bridget was beginning to see firsthand what a good butler really did. "This is our new cook, Bridget Heaney. She was a great deal of help yesterday, and on her first day here at the house, too. By the way, Bridget, Mr. Gold asked me to tell you how delicious the oxtails were." This let Mrs. Gold know in a hurry that Mr. Fleming and Mr. Gold had both accepted Bridget into the household even if she was another pretty Irish girl with red curls.

"Well, Bridget, you arrived at the worst time our family has ever had, I can assure you of that," Mrs. Gold said coldly. "May we have a minute in here to plan our meal for tomorrow?" she said by way of dismissal.

"Of course, ma'am, and my sympathy to you," Bridget said quickly, with barely a glance at Mr. Fleming to make sure it was all right, and left. She went into the kitchen and started helping Gilbert with the cookies he was baking. He had several different kinds of dough, some drop, some rolled out. They worked in silence and Bridget thought over what had just happened.

The woman had probably gone off to this country house of theirs and told her husband she never wanted another Irish or redhead or young girl or the like hired to serve in their home. Then Mary Martha had recommended her friend and they didn't know that Bridget was all those things until she got to the house. Most likely by that time Mary Martha had got wind of what the missus had said and that's why she'd been nervous yesterday. Then everything went to hell in a handbasket and they were forced to depend on Bridget, plus she got on with Mr. Gold, so they just ignored what Mrs. Gold wanted. Will Mrs. Gold fire me? Bridget wondered. Not for a few days, I'd guess. There must be somethin' about not firing folks during the mourning period. I'll just have to make myself indispensable, Bridgett resolved.

BRIDGET was putting all the cookies in tins when Benjamin Gold appeared in the kitchen. He was not at all what Bridget had expected. He looked a bit like a blown-up, bigger-than-life version of his father. You could see the family features but they were buried in flesh. Benjamin was a big man, over six feet tall and well over two hundred pounds. He was not the least bit formidable, though. Maybe it was because he was sobbing. He stood inside the kitchen door as if he were hiding from someone, rigid, straight, and tall, but crying hard out loud with the tears coursing down his cheeks. Bridget liked him right away.

Benjamin stood there another few minutes and Bridget tried to stay quiet and let him have his cry. He finally took out a big, white handkerchief and blew his nose. "Oh, my God, this is so hard. Seth, brother, what happened? I loved you even if you were a fool." He stopped talking to himself, put away his hankie, and acknowledged Bridget's presence with a little bow. He didn't seem the least bit embarrassed that she'd seen and heard him in such a state. "You must be the new cook. I'm Benjamin. I started to crack up upstairs, in the room with Seth's body and Dad. I made a beeline for the kitchen. It must have something to do with my childhood. Can I have some cookies?" he asked when he spotted what Bridget was doing.

"Bridget Heaney, sir, and you can have as many cookies as you need. Food always makes me feel better, too. Cooking it or eating it."

"Hello, Bridget, I can tell you're a good sort and won't tell my wife on me, will you? She insists I don't eat sweets between meals."

"It'll be our secret. I think you can have anything to eat that will help you get through this sadness, sir. I'm sorry for your loss."

Benjamin shook his head as he popped a chocolate-iced cookie in his mouth and then nibbled on a second. "My little brother. He was going through a rough period but I had faith in him that it would all smooth out. He had started working for Gold's a couple of years ago and the last time we had lunch he told me he was finally getting the hang of it. He said he had some great ideas for the business. He was excited. It doesn't seem possible that he's gone."

"So you decided not to go in the family business, eh?" Bridget commented as she opened a second tin of cookies, little pistachio ones, and offered them. This time Benjamin took a whole handful with a sheepish grin on his tearstained face.

"No, I'm the one who *did* go in the family business. My great-grandfather was one of the founders of the New York Stock Exchange, where I work. My father was the rebel who wanted to start his own department store. It turned out well for him, though."

Bridget was surprised. "I'm sorry, sir, me not knowin' these things. And what with all the commotion yesterday, I didn't have a proper time to learn all of it." She changed the subject. "How is your mother doin', sir?"

Benjamin looked surprised, then he chuckled. "My mother? Oh, Mrs. Gold isn't my mother. My mother, the first Mrs. Gold, died ten years ago. It was a fluke accident. A drunken, we assume he was drunk, carriage driver ran her over right in front of this house. Kept right on going. Estella was my sister and brother's nanny. I was in college then, at Harvard. I guess Estella moved up to a better job," he said with another chuckle that sounded sad.

You could have knocked Bridget over with a feather. Suddenly Mrs. Gold's youthful appearance made sense. It wasn't the face creams after all.

BRIDGET and Mary Martha were sitting on Bridget's bed. They'd been dismissed at nine and told to rest, as the burial was in the morning. Then friends would start their visiting and they could expect a houseful for a week.

Bridget and Mary Martha were exchanging news of their day. "So tonight Chef gives us the menu for tomorrow, after the burial. Mr. Fleming told me yesterday that the tradition is for eggs and bread and a family friend is supposed to cook it, but now the missus has ordered a fancy French buffet. Chef was in a pucker, I could tell. He has a prep list for us as long as my arm."

Mary Martha laughed. "The missus wouldn't give up a chance to impress folks, even if it's a funeral."

Bridget put both of her hands on her hips, even though she was sitting down. "Why didn't you tell me Mrs. Gold wasn't the children's mother?"

"I didn't have time to tell you anything, Brig. Who was to know that things would take a bad turn like this and you'd need to know all the family history? It took me six months to figure it all out. Sally's been here since she was thirteen. She's thirty-five now so she told me most things."

"Luckily Master Benjamin didn't take it wrong when I asked how his mother was doing."

Mary Martha grabbed her chest with both hands. "Oh, dear Lord. What did he say, pray tell?"

"That Estella, he called her that, was his sister and brother's nanny, and that when their mother died, she got a better job."

With that, Bridget and Mary Martha erupted in peals of laughter.

Bridget thought of another of her questions. "Why is she wearing around a torn bodice, I wonder?"

"It's the tearing of the clothing. It has an official name in their religion. That's what Mr. Fleming says. Mr. Gold tore his shirt as well. And now Mrs. Simon, although I don't think she's a relative. I think it's just to support her lady, Mrs. Gold, and because she's Jewish."

"By the way, Mary Martha, you failed to mention that Justin was a Negro." Neither she nor Mary Martha called black people the more common "nigger." That's because they had their mouths washed out with soap for saying that word at the orphanage. Not that the ladies allowed Negro children to live there. It was more that the Protestants were particular about how you talked. Bridget guessed it was a good habit to get in, talking polite. It taught Bridget that you need to talk polite and with respect to people whether you give a whit about them or not.

"Well, again, we went right from the frying pan to the fire yesterday and he wasn't here so I forgot you hadn't met him. And after you're around him, you forget about his color," Mary Martha said.

"He told me a bit about how he grew up working at Mr. Gold's parents' house but I didn't want to ask him—is he a freed slave of Mr. Gold's?" Bridget asked.

"Oh, no. First off, Mr. Gold has never had slaves. He's against slavery. He says no one in his family has ever had slaves, that the Jewish people were slaves for years and they should all know better. I heard him talking about this myself while I was serving dinner one night. He was glad last week when President Lincoln got reelected. Second, Justin is a free man, born and raised here in New York. He says they passed a law a long time ago that made slavery illegal here."

"How old is he?"

"I heard him say once he would be fifty one of these years pretty soon. I also remember he said that he and Mr. Gold were born the same year, but I don't know which one it was."

The two women fell silent with the mention of poor Mr. Gold. "I guess we better get to bed. Tomorrow will be hectic," Mary Martha said sadly.

"Oh, no, not yet. I have so much to ask you about," Bridget said. It was then she remembered the box in the closet and went over to get it out. "Mary Martha, did you ever see this before?" she asked as she brought the box over to the bed.

Mary Martha crossed herself. "It was Katherine's, it was. She said it had all kinds of recipes in it from hundreds of years ago. But all I ever saw were some spices. The chef laughed at it and told her to keep it up here out of the way of real cooks. She loved that box. She must have forgotten it."

"Why did you just cross yourself?"

"The box seemed like witchcraft to me. Still does. I never wanted nothin' to do with it. What if Katherine cast a spell on Master Seth with it so he'd die?"

"Oh, don't be silly. The box didn't shoot him twice with a gun," Bridget noted. She tried to open it but the lid didn't come off. The box had a paddle shape to it and she saw that there was a hinge of some kind on the narrow end of what would be the paddle handle, if it were a paddle instead of a box. She tried moving the lid across instead of up and down and it slid easily to the side. Inside, were all kinds of dried herbs and spices. The aroma was heady.

"Don't breathe it too much. It might make you drunk," Mary Martha cautioned, turning her head away.

"Silly, here's cloves and cinnamon and these star things that smell like licorice. These are common enough although I don't know about the dried herbs. Where are the recipes?"

"I don't know, Brig, but just put it up. We can fiddle with it some other day, after the, after tomorrow. I don't like it," Mary Martha said, pushing the box away.

Bridget slid the top back on the box and put it back on the shelf in the closet. "I think it's beautiful. It has carvings of women who cook on it. Someone a long time ago made that box for someone like me."

CHAPTER SEVEN

THE first thing Bridget noticed when they brought Master Seth down the stairs was how simple the coffin was. It was much nicer than the pine box she was able to buy for Da, but still, she had seen fancy coffins and this wasn't one. When she asked Mary Martha about it, they were all standing at attention in the entry hall, waiting for the coffin and the family to pass. Mary Martha shushed her, but after the procession was out the door, she informed Bridget that Mr. Fleming says everyone in the Jewish faith is supposed to get buried in plain clothes and with a plain coffin, so a poor person does not receive less honor in death than a rich person.

Bridget realized that she hadn't seen Seth since she found the body. She hadn't had any reason to go to the first or second floor since she took Mr. Gold his supper that first night. Now was her first glimpse of Master Benjamin's wife, too.

She was plump and tall, just like he was. They looked a good pair. Benjamin was crying again, his big face cracked open with grief and tears. Mr. Gold was walking right behind the coffin, one of his hands resting on it, like it was his son's arm. Mrs. Gold's head was covered with black veils.

The coffin passed Bridget and she lowered her head. Mr. Fleming had told the staff at supper last night that Jewish people don't get embalmed and they never have open caskets, thank the Lord. Bridget hated that part of the Catholic faith, having to walk by and look at someone you knew, all stiff and waxy. Mr. Fleming guessed the fact you don't get embalmed must have something to do with the fact that their religion requires prompt burial. Bridget had noticed little holes in the sides of the casket. Mr. Fleming had also said something last evening about the body having to come in contact with the earth. That was when all the other girls from the house crossed themselves. She guessed the holes were a way to be true to that rule without just pitching dead folks in a hole in the ground, no casket at all.

As soon as the family and the mourners left to go to the cemetery on Nineteenth Street, the household sprang into action. Mrs. Simon had gone to the funeral but then she was going to be the one who cooked the eggs and the bread for the family. Mr. Gold had insisted that they conform to the religious custom, which Bridget thought was strange for someone not religious. She still didn't quite understand the connection between being religious Jewish and being born Jewish. After the eggs and bread had been served, the fancy food that Mrs. Gold had ordered would be put out.

Bridget, Chef, and Gilbert went downstairs.

They'd reserved a worktable just for Mrs. Simon and had a loaf of Jewish rye, one of the egg bread called challah, a whole bowl of eggs, and a chunk of good butter all ready for her.

The three of them were working pretty well together by now. Bridget wasn't there only to clean out the icebox. Chef let her take her share of the prep list. She made a mousse with some of the smoked fish and some dried dill that was really tasty. Even the chef had remarked on it. Now she was making applesauce. Gilbert was baking a cake and Chef had a huge beef roast in the oven. That morning Bridget had made a mustard fruit compote of dried prunes, apricots, and figs to go along with the roast.

Today Mr. Fleming's rule about no deliveryman coming in the house was suspended. The iceman had already come and delivered another big block of ice plus some chipped off in a sack. The fishmonger was there with oysters and a whole salmon. He was leaving a man just to open the oysters. Chef put the long, narrow copper fish poacher on the stove and poured in a couple of bottles of white wine with a few sprigs of parsley and an onion that he split open. The kitchen was busy. Mr. Fleming had said to have the food ready by one. He thought the family would be back at noon and they could eat; then the callers would start arriving.

Bridget didn't mind spending her days in the basement, especially since there was some natural light. She was happy to let the others arrange the buffet today and even for Karol and Kate to take the food up. It was less work for her, and it didn't feel like they were trying to keep her from the important work just because she did her job a floor below the family.

She remembered how Justin had described his role and Mr. Fleming's role yesterday. It helped her understand. Mr. Fleming was their front man with the outside world. She was one of the unseen ones, like Justin. But she was needed, like all the rest who worked mainly out of sight.

Everything happened pretty much on time. A little after noon, Mrs. Simon came downstairs, put an apron on over her black taffeta dress, and made a big copper sauté pan full of scrambled eggs. Mr. Fleming put them in a fancy silver chafing dish and headed upstairs. Mrs. Simon left the kitchen without saying a word to anyone except Chef and Mr. Fleming, just giving Bridget a mean look once and totally ignoring Gilbert. She was sniffing and her eyes were red from crying.

Bridget accepted the fact that Mrs. Simon and Mrs. Gold didn't like her. She'd tackle them when all the hubbub was over. She could be mistaken, but she didn't think Mr. Fleming would allow her to be fired just because she reminded them of Katherine. After all, the son who was tempted by redheads wasn't around anymore, so why should he lose a good worker? She hoped that was the way he saw it.

Right now, Mr. Fleming was a nervous wreck. He had to deal with Mrs. Gold, and she had become hysterical sometime yesterday, crying and throwing herself on Seth's body. The mourning women were used to such actions, but they did not approve one bit. The rules of mourning were there to provide people with a full expression of grief without anyone behaving like a maniac. So they, the guardians of Seth's body, left Mrs. Gold to Mr. Fleming and Mrs. Simon to deal with. They were there for the dead.

Mr. Fleming also had to prevent Mrs. Gold from turning this into a seven-day party. He could tell by the amount of notes she'd dispatched that she was using this as a chance to pay back some of her social debts. On the other hand, Mr. Gold was experiencing the biggest loss of his life and really didn't want anyone around. Mrs. Gold was dramatic in her grief, but Seth was still only her stepson.

And so the day rolled on. By two o'clock there must have been a hundred friends and business associates crowding every room of the first floor, eating oysters as fast as they could, the men drinking whiskey and the women nipping sherry. All the managers from Gold's Department Store were present, come to pay their respect to their employer. Mr. Gold had sent word to close the store today, so this was the only day they could visit. It was exciting for most of them because it was a chance to see what the house looked like. When Mr. Gold entertained the managers, he did it at Delmonico's or a steakhouse, not at home.

Bridget kept busy arranging oysters on platters and filling crepes that Chef had made with chicken salad. When they were out of oysters, the shucker went back to the fishmongers and Bridget moved over to help Gilbert arrange platters of sweets: cookies and thin slices of tarts and cheesecake, and tiny cream puffs that Gilbert and Chef called profiteroles.

Mr. Gold and his son Benjamin came into the kitchen. They had their arms around each other's waists. It was the older Mr. Gold who had a tearstained face this time. "Hi, Bridget, we had to get away," Benjamin said. "I told Dad this was the place to come for cookies."

Bridget smiled at them and pointed at the tins of all the different varieties. "Help yourselves, sirs. Will it be a crowd like this every day, Mr. Gold?"

"I certainly hope not, Bridget. I'm not sure I know all these people," he said with a sad smile.

"Dad and I have something to ask you," Benjamin blurted out. He never had been subtle.

Bridget wasn't sure if she should stop working, giving them proper respect by listening, or if she should keep working, giving them proper respect by not wasting time they were paying for. "Ask away," she said, and kept putting cookies on platters.

"Will you go downtown and try to find out in the Irish community if Katherine has relatives?"

Bridget smiled. "There are more than two hundred thousand of us in New York City, sirs. I read that in the *Herald,* them saying we were worse than the plague. A last name would be a start. Did it happen to be O'Sullivan?," she asked, remembering the reporter and what he said.

Benjamin whipped out a piece of paper. "Yes, her name was Katherine O'Sullivan, and here's an address that Mr. Fleming got from her some time ago but he wasn't sure what the connection was. It could be a father or a brother. I just think people will be more forthcoming with you than me or my dad."

"You think her kin might tell another Irish if they killed your brother?"

"Of course not, but maybe you'll be able to tell by talking to them if they were ticked off at Seth or, by contrast, if they haven't seen Katherine in years and knew nothing about Seth. I don't know what we expect to happen, Bridget. Dad and I just can't go back to our lives and do nothing. And we need your help," Benjamin said as he crammed cookies in his mouth.

"We have no intention of taking the law into our own hands, Bridget. We will notify the authorities if we find out anything that implicates Katherine's relatives in Seth's death. But we also know that we, and that includes you, will have to do the work. The police will not find the culprit unless he comes into the station and confesses," Mr. Gold explained. "They really don't have a homicide or detective division."

Bridget was sorry she'd made fun of them. "I'd do anything to help your mind have some peace, sir. If you'll clear it with Mr. Fleming, I'll go downtown and ask around tomorrow," she said.

Just then Mr. Fleming came hurrying toward them. "Mr. Gold, your cousin from Washington is here. He just got your post about Seth and started up yesterday. He says he needs to speak to you."

And with that, a man came rushing in the kitchen. "Isaac, I can't believe this has happened. I should have come back and told you."

"Told me what?" Mr. Gold said uneasily. He wasn't expecting his cousin, who had just been in New York.

"Katherine ran away. We were almost in Baltimore and we stopped at a tavern to feed the horses, and ourselves too. She must have caught a ride with someone traveling on the highway. When we noticed she hadn't returned from going to the outhouse, we searched all around and asked folks. The thing is, she could have just as easily caught a ride going back toward New York as the other way. And she sure was upset, crying every mile of the way. Betsy, my housekeeper, who came with me to fetch her, tried to tell her how much better off she'd be in a place where no one knew she'd been, you know, with a man. She just kept saying, 'He told me he loved me,' over and over."

"So you're saying that Katherine could have been in New York the night Seth died?" young Master Benjamin asked.

"Yes."

CHAPTER EIGHT

"You don't have to do this, sir," Bridget said. She couldn't believe she was going down to the old neighborhood in Mr. Gold's carriage, with Mr. Gold himself along for the ride. "I'm not afraid. I did live down here before the orphanage, remember? It was much worse then."

Mr. Gold shook his head. "I'm glad for the chance to get out of the house. There must have been two dozen friends of my wife in that parlor. It was getting a bit—"

"They were sending up quite a chatter, not that I mean that as an insult," Bridget said. Oh dear Lord. She'd interrupted him when he was talking to say something negative about his wife. Unlike Mrs. Gold and her friends, Bridget didn't know how to chitchat; that was for sure.

It made her so nervous but also excited to be doing this bit of detecting work. Having to try to talk to Mr. Gold made her even more nervous. She guessed he didn't spot it, though. He looked happier than he had since Seth died. He most likely didn't like having to stay around the house, since he had a big, important business to run.

"You can just go on to your store, sir. I can take the bus on downtown. I'm sure you must have things that need signing."

Mr. Gold shook his hand dismissively. "I'm not really working during Shiva. Bridget, I won't embarrass you but I have no intention of leaving you alone. I'll stay in the carriage. Look at it from my point of view. You're going to talk to strangers who may be dangerous and you are doing it for my family and me. I'm sure you'll have to shade the truth a bit about your reasons. I would never forgive myself if some harm came to you. I could have sent Justin with you but I needed to get out of the house."

"You couldn't embarrass me, sir. And I thank you for coming with me," Bridget said, finally realizing she was making it worse. He must think I don't want to be seen with him in an Irish neighborhood, she thought. He's crazy thinking it would be better to be seen with a Negro.

She tried to strike up a different topic, something she was curious about. "Your son, Benjamin, said one of your kin started the New York Stock Exchange. I would appreciate if you would explain to me what it does sometime. But what Benjamin said gave me the idea your family didn't just arrive in New York recent-like."

"Oh, no. My family has been here a very long time. It's a strange story. I assume you came here because of the Irish Potato Famine?"

"Yes, sir, 1855. The potatoes had come back, but conditions were still pretty bad when we left. Not so good when we got here either, what with so many Irish coming to New

York and them not being in very good health or having any money." Bridget could see it now. How pathetic they all were as they left the ship, their legs barely holding them upright, not one of them with a real suitcase, their belongings in paper packages and knapsacks.

Curse the English for having them hauled away like debris from the fireplace grate. "I'll pay for you to take them to America," she'd overheard their glorious English landlord say. Bridget had just turned ten years old and Maggie was eight.

She turned her thoughts back to Mr. Gold. "What year did your kin arrive?"

"In 1654. Just to give you an idea of how early that was, the American Revolution was not until 1776."

"Where were they from originally?"

Mr. Gold looked out the carriage window with a distant stare. Then he came back to her. "It's funny you should use that word, 'originally.' We were just like our ancestors. We wandered the earth. My family's roots are in Spain. But we'd left there, the Muslims and the Christians both after our heads. Went to Amsterdam, then Brazil. Then it was Christianity that forced us to leave Brazil. We meant to go to the islands in the Caribbean but some of us got lost. Twenty-three of us ended up in New York Harbor. The governor at that time, Peter Stuyvesant, didn't want to let us stay but there were Jewish members on the board of the West India Company. That's the company he worked for in Amsterdam, the company that founded the first settlement here in New York Harbor, called New Amsterdam. They told him to let us stay."

"It must be funny to you, the Nativists with all their bragging about being the only true Americans, and all. And you settled here at the same time and no one ever mentions your people."

Mr. Gold's eyes glimmered. "Oh, yes. It's very funny, Bridget, if you have a black sense of humor. Ironic and funny. You and I have that in common. We weren't wanted here in America. Even though I have a great deal more money than you do, I'm still an outsider just as you are. Of course, I myself did not make that difficult ocean voyage as you had to. It was my ancestors, two hundred years ago."

Bridget patted Mr. Gold's arm, then realized she shouldn't do such a thing and jerked her hand back. "Your folks would be real proud of how you've done, sir. The devil take those that don't see that."

"Why, thank you, Bridget," Mr. Gold said and she could tell he meant it. Then she remembered Seth and felt foolish. All the money in New York City didn't make up for having your son killed.

BRIDGET enjoyed the rest of the ride. They were both quiet but it was comfortable. Bridget was thinking of Mr. Gold's relatives, getting kicked out of country after country. No wonder he'd said the other day how religion had caused trouble in the world.

Bridget looked around at the scene outside the carriage. The noise level had gone way up and the streets were clogged with carriages and omnibuses and mule carts. It was slow going just to get from one side of an intersection to the other. She liked all the ruckus. They were clear downtown now, in what used to be called the Five Points.

Bridget had relaxed about coming down here to the old neighborhood to do a little investigating for Mr. Gold. In fact, the truth be known, she was looking forward to pulling a little scam, no matter how simple. Just because she had a legitimate job, there was no telling when she might have to live by her wits instead of her cooking skills. It didn't hurt to practice lying now and then, to make sure you were still believable.

The carriage stopped. Johnny, whom Bridget had still only seen in passing, jumped down and opened the carriage door for her, like she was a real lady. "We're here," he said.

Mr. Gold took her arm and helped her out. "What are you going to say?"

"That I work at another house on the block. That we got friendly and Katherine gave me her home address. That I missed her and wondered after her. It was my day off so I thought I'd check her up." Bridget called this over her shoulder as she walked quickly away from the carriage. No lie would work if someone inside this slum saw the fine ride she was in. She'd heard Mr. Fleming ask Johnny to fetch the double brougham and it was as big as the room she and Da and Maggie had when they first came to America.

Bridget stepped gingerly over a pile of fish skins and skeletons and wrinkled her nose. Yes, Five Points was supposed to be cleaned up, not as big a dump, not as dangerous, the newspapers said. They had torn down the Brewery, a giant building in which you used to be able to do and be anything for a dime a night. Bridget glanced down the street at where it had been. She'd gone in there looking for Da a few times. She shivered. What was there now didn't look much better to Bridget, just smaller, more like the other slum tenements up and down the streets. There still were a few pigs rooting around in the gutters down here. She shivered again, remembering a time when the pigs outweighed her by a hundred pounds and she would have to compete with them for good scraps of food. It was no big deal then although the pigs had always scared her. Every kid in the neighborhood had hustled against the pigs for their next meal one day or another.

Bridget checked the address on her piece of paper and entered the building marked 24 Mott Street. She knew there would be no names neatly printed on a list, giving the location of the various tenants. She stopped at the first door, which was open. Three small children were crying and a tired-looking woman eyed her suspiciously.

Bridget smiled, hoping she didn't look like some social worker. Just because I have a clean dress doesn't mean I'm not one of you, sister. "O'Sullivan?"

The women turned to the stove, losing interest. "They're gone."

"For now or for good?"

"They cleared out. Of course, Timothy is still off at the war, taking photographs. His father, the old drunk, moved out two days ago," the woman said. There had been a tad of pride when she mentioned Timothy. That must be Katherine's brother.

"Have you seen Katherine around lately?"

"Not that I remember," the woman said, picking up the smallest child and slapping him on the face as casually as she would a puppy. He cried louder.

"Where does her father drink?"

"The Spotted Pig," the woman said without hesitation. It must have been a neighborhood favorite.

Bridget took a chance. "You don't know a Maggie Heaney from the Pig, do ye?"

The woman, out of words, shook her head. Bridget reached in her pocket and pulled out a dollar. Mr. Gold had given her twenty one-dollar bills to bribe her way through the neighborhood. She had told him twenty quarters would have done the trick, but Mr. Gold said he knew how much people down here needed the money.

Bridget remembered how proud the rich ladies were when they'd give out coins at the orphanage. They made you act so grateful for it, not that you weren't. She didn't want to do the same so she put the money on the kitchen table, along with a little card that Mr. Gold had wrote out today, with the address of the Fifth Avenue house on it. "Thank you for your help. If you see Katherine O'Sullivan, I sure would like to know she's all right. You can send a boy to tell me. I work at this house and I'll pay all the bus fare, tip him, plus another dollar for you."

The woman tucked the bill away in her skirts without comment. Bridget left the room and the building as fast as she could. For a place that was already cold as ice in November, Bridget felt oppressive heat. She pulled at her uniform collar.

At the carriage, Mr. Gold looked out the window hopefully. "Her da moved out on Monday," Bridget said quickly. "I'm going around the corner to The Spotted Pig. Wait five minutes, then pull around in front and make sure Johnny parks the carriage so they can see it through the window, if there is a window. Sometimes it's good to get a whiff of money," she said and started down the block.

Bridget didn't remember The Spotted Pig from her childhood but it could have been in business then. All the rum holes and taverns looked alike when you were a kid. There was a sign painted with a pink pig with black spots on it, no words, and she went into the storefront below it.

A bar before noon was a pitiful place. No matter how

well kept or highbrow it was, the stale smoke and remnants of drink commingled to produce a rancid odor. Time lost and ideas squandered were everywhere. Regret and remorse were tangible. The Spotted Pig wasn't crying over spilled milk, however. The patrons had started creating a new layer of smoke, beer, tears, and whiskey dreams over yesterday's layer of the same. It was already eleven o'clock in the morning, and the place had been open since six. Dozens of workers had come in for a snoot before they started their shifts. A few gents at the bar already had a buzz on. When Bridget walked in the door, they looked in her direction, but not with much interest. A young woman in service coming in for a nip wasn't all that uncommon. This wasn't the uptown world, where women were barred from drinking establishments.

The bartender moved toward Bridget, and his eyebrows rose in the unspoken language of the barroom: What'll it be?

"Do you know a drinker from around the corner name of O'Sullivan?"

"Timothy O'Sullivan's da? The boy is really making a name for himself with those war photos."

Bridget had no idea what he was talking about. "Have you seen him lately?"

"Why?" the bartender asked, suspicious now.

Bridget laid a dollar on the bar. The bartender's eyebrows went up again. "I'm a friend of his daughter, Katherine. She left her service and I was trying to keep up with her."

He took the money. "It was somethin' about Katherine he was mumblin'. Came in a couple a days ago. Said his daughter was in trouble. Haven't seen him since."

Bridget thought about yelling out to the whole bar but she knew the word would be passed soon enough. She gave him another dollar and one of the cards with the address. "Send a boy if you see him, or her for that matter. I'll pay the hack and there's another dollar in it for you."

She and Mr. Gold had disagreed in a friendly way about giving out the address. Bridget told him: no telling who would end up with that information, a sneak thief at the least. Mr. Gold told her: anyone walking by could look at the house and see it probably had things in it worth stealing. The address on a card wasn't going to change that, and Justin and Mr. Fleming would protect the property. Bridget said: like they did when Seth was delivered to the dough box? Mr. Gold said: that was different, and kept printing the address on these little ivory cards, calling cards he called them. He had some with his name engraved all pretty on them but Bridget said that would lead folks to the department store and that was no good so he'd printed just the address on plain ones. It was a compromise, he said.

The carriage pulled up outside. "I'd sure like to know Katherine's all right, so I'll thank you to let me know if you hear anything," Bridget said, and turned to go.

The bartender nodded and gestured toward the window. "Fancy ride."

Bridget shrugged. "I hitched a lift with Johnny while he took a message to the Stock Exchange," she lied, not that this bunch would know what the Stock Exchange was. Nor did she.

The bartender squinted at the cab of the carriage, trying to see Johnny. Bridget left before her story sprang a leak.

Mr. Gold opened the door from inside. "Well?" he said impatiently.

"They said her da hasn't been in for a couple of days but last time he said his daughter was in trouble."

"And he moved out of his apartment?"

"If that's what you call it," Bridget commented dryly.

"He's gone somewhere with her," Mr. Gold said firmly.

"Or to meet her," Bridget added.

"Good work, Bridget," Mr. Gold said. There was hope in his eyes and Bridget hated to see that. She looked out the window instead.

Bridget didn't see that they knew much more than they had before. They didn't know where Katherine was, or where her father was for that matter. It did seem Katherine had made it back to New York and was hiding out, and that led to the question, why? Bridget really hadn't considered Katherine as the killer, but she had to admit there were bits and pieces of facts that were incriminating. The fact that she had run away from Mr. Gold's cousin didn't look good for Katherine's innocence. "Could Johnny take me by one of the big newspapers, sir?"

"Why, what are you on to?" Mr. Gold said and at the same time he yelled an address out the window. The carriage turned at the next corner and headed west.

"Both the woman in the apartment building and the bartender mentioned a brother who was a photographer, taking war photos. I think we should see if his photographs are published. We can tell by the pictures where he is. Maybe his location will be somewhere close enough that Katherine and her da went to be with him."

"That makes sense," Mr. Gold said, excited. "You're a smart young woman, Bridget. You can put two and two together."

When they pulled up in front of a building with the words NEW YORK RECORDER painted on it, Mr. Gold opened the door and got out, extending his hand to Bridget. "I know the publisher. He will help us."

Bridget got out and looked around. "What's that big fancy-looking building over there?"

"City Hall. This block over here is where all the newspapers are published. It's called Printing House Square."

Bridget was excited. A newspaper office was an exotic, unknown quantity to her, although she loved reading them. To actually go to the building where they created a newspaper was something. She thought of that young reporter who had camped out at the back door. Wasn't the *Recorder* the name of the newspaper he worked for?

They entered a busy lobby. People were hurrying past with long sheets of newsprint. Men in long blue smocks were pulling and pushing heavy-looking pieces of equipment. A woman sat at a reception desk and looked up with a smile. "May I help you?" she said.

Bridget couldn't believe it. A woman was working in this world of men. She had on a nice dark brown suit and her hair was pulled to the back of her neck smoothly. She looked about thirty, not an Irish thirty, and still young looking.

"I'd like to see Mr. Brown," Mr. Gold said, giving the woman one of his engraved cards with his name on it.

"Carl," the woman called, and a young Negro boy appeared out of nowhere. She handed him the card. "To see Mr. Brown," she said simply.

Bridget and Mr. Gold watched the lobby activity for a few minutes and then a small man with bushy sideburns came from one of many doors—doors leading to where the important stuff was done, Bridget guessed.

"Isaac, I'm so sorry about Seth. I meant to get over to the

Shiva but this war keeps us busy. I'm about fed up with it. But it looks like Sherman is getting someplace."

"I hope it'll be over soon. Of course, the business is nice. The truth is, I wanted your help with something, Harris. Do you know a war photographer named Timothy O'Sullivan?"

Mr. Brown nodded. "He's done some great work. We've printed quite a few of his shots."

"Anything lately?"

"I think so. Just give me ten minutes. I'll have someone pull them. Give Mrs. Gold my condolences," he said, shaking hands with Mr. Gold and hurrying back through the same door.

In less than ten minutes, a man motioned them to follow him through one of the other doors. They were in a room with dozens of large oak file cabinets with wide, shallow drawers. People were consulting lists and pulling copies of old newspapers out of them. The man led Bridget and Mr. Gold to a large table where a pile of newspaper pages was lying. "Here you go," he said and scurried away.

Bridget and Mr. Gold leafed through the pages, carefully making a second pile of the ones they looked through as they worked. The first photo pulled was from June of this year. Timothy had been with Grant at Cold Harbor, where the Union general had lost 7,000 men in twenty minutes. The photographs were sickening. Bridget looked away and took some deep breaths.

The last three photographs showed neat rows of tents, horses being quartered, a pontoon boat of some kind. They were all shot in Virginia.

"So Katherine could have gone on toward Washington instead of coming back to New York," Mr. Gold said glumly.

"She must have wrote for her da to meet her, then maybe

they went to find this Timothy," Bridget said as she straight-ened out the last page.

"She's running like a guilty party," Mr. Gold said solemnly.

Bridget couldn't argue. But she wasn't sure just what Katherine was guilty of. She also realized she didn't want the pretty Irish girl with red hair to be the murderer.

THE carriage stopped. Bridget had been lost in her thoughts. Going to the old neighborhood, talking to that woman who wasn't much older than she was but seemed dried up, seeing photos of those dead bodies, it had all unnerved her. She looked up and saw that they were in front of Gold's Depart-ment Store. It was grand, with windows all along Broadway so you could see the beautiful dresses and yards of fabric draped real pretty and a whole window full of clothes irons of various types. She let out something like a gasp, at least a sharp intake of breath, and Mr. Gold smiled indulgently at her excitement. "I need to stop here for a minute and I thought you could be measured for your uniforms at the same time. Don't tell the ladies from the congregation. I'm not supposed to be working."

Bridget just nodded and stepped out of the carriage with Johnny's help. She was getting used to being treated like a lady. Mr. Gold followed behind. In an instant two managers were by his side. They must have been hovering around the door just in case he popped in, or maybe he sent word before they left the house. Mr. Gold talked briefly to them and one came over to Bridget.

"Don, here, will take you up to the uniform department. When you're done, ask them to direct you to the offices," Mr. Gold said, and was gone.

Bridget wished the trip to the fourth floor would never end. She trailed behind this Don fella, gawking at each and every department they passed.

He delivered her to a stern-looking woman in the uniform department who marched her into the dressing room and ordered her to take off her clothes.

Bridget slipped out of Katherine's uniform and stood there in her camisole and petticoats while she was measured every which way.

"So, you're the new one, eh? Poor Mr. Gold. We all feel for him, that's for certain," the woman said as she ran a tape measure around Bridget's bust line.

"Yes, it's a pity. I never met Master Seth. What was he like?" Bridget asked, trying to sound only vaguely interested.

"A spoiled brat I'd call him. No one here at Gold's had a bit of use for him. We were all aggrieved that it wasn't Master Benjamin that would take over the store. I don't know who will do it now."

"Well, it's a long time before Mr. Gold will be too old to work," Bridget said rather crossly.

"Thank the Lord for small favors," the woman said and then fell silent, concentrating on her measurements.

When Bridget came out of the dressing room, back in the too-big uniform, Don was waiting for her. He had two different black wool full-length capes on hangers in his hands, one with a shoulder capelet attached and one with bright red taffeta lining.

"Mr. Gold said your cape must be replaced, that you'll 'catch your death in that thin inferior garment,'" Don said, quoting Mr. Gold verbatim.

Bridget gasped for the second time today. She stood there

dumbly as Don and the uniform woman whisked one cape on her, then the other.

"What do you think?" the woman asked, more to Don than Bridget.

"The red lining, it's much more sophisticated," Don said, handing the rejected cape to the woman to put back on the rack in some other department. That task complete, he inclined his head toward Bridget. "Follow me. Mr. Gold will meet you in the ice cream parlor on the first floor."

Bridget didn't notice a thing on the trip downstairs. She didn't know what had just hit her. A new cape and now she guessed they would have ice cream, a treat she had tasted only once in her life, and had dreamed about ever since.

"WHAT flavor would you like?" Mr. Gold asked.

Bridget had walked up and down the cases that held round metal containers of ice cream twice now and changed her mind about what she wanted at every new choice.

"Chocolate, sir. Or vanilla. I can't decide."

Mr. Gold took charge. "Put a dip of each in a bowl, please."

The young man behind the counter nodded then looked at him expectantly. "Nothing for me right now, Joe, thank you."

Bridget was disappointed. "Sir, we didn't have to come here if you weren't hungry for ice cream yourself."

Mr. Gold leaned in and spoke to her quietly. "I would like three dips with hot fudge sauce all over them but I'm sure the rabbi would hear about it. Ice cream and mourning don't mix, I'm afraid."

"Then we shouldn't be sitting in your brand-new ice cream parlor, sir. But it sure is nice," Bridget added as she looked around. Manager Don had told her it was brand new. Mr. Gold, or whoever he paid to do such things, had created a fancy room right inside one of the Broadway entrances to the store. It had big mirrors all over the walls with fancy gold frames. There were dozens of ladies in there right now, all dressed up, eating ice cream and little cookies like the ones Gilbert baked. The ladies all wore beautiful hats. Their laughter sounded like the flute music Bridget had heard at Christmas, at the orphanage.

Mr. Gold had instructed her to leave her kerchief off when they left home so she wasn't so obviously in uniform. Now, with her new cape on, she almost passed for a real customer.

The young fella named Joe passed her bowl of ice cream over the counter top. Bridget took it but was unsure of what to do next. Mr. Gold was huddling with one of the several managers that swarmed around him, talking low again. He looked up at Bridget. "Shall we go? I thought you might enjoy eating your ice cream on the way home."

Bridget really wanted to sit down at one of the little marble tables but she understood that Mr. Gold couldn't be seen in the ice cream parlor with his cook. How could he know she thought about ice cream all the time? "Yes, sir, but what about the bowl and the spoon?"

"I'll bring them back with me next week," Mr. Gold said as they went outside. Next week when the Shiva is done and life goes back to normal, Bridget thought. But it never will.

TO say Bridget felt special would be an understatement. She savored every bite of ice cream, but also she worried about getting anything on her new cape and so took care with the drips of cream from the bottom of the spoon. This tickled Mr. Gold and they had a laugh. When they were several blocks from the department store, Bridget held out a spoon-ful to Mr. Gold. "Just take a taste, sir. It couldn't hurt your boy for you to just have a bite of something so good."

Mr. Gold took the spoonful and did just like Bridget, closed his eyes a little when the cold cream hit his mouth. "I spent a fortune to build that ice cream parlor but it was worth it. Now all the ladies meet at Gold's, in the ice cream parlor," he said. He looked right at Bridget, in the eyes. "The concept of denying yourself is out of honor for the dead. Seth will never again have ice cream," he said and Bridget could feel what she'd heard in that father's scream the first day ris-ing up inside Mr. Gold once more.

She nodded her head solemnly and, with a quick motion, sent the ice cream flying out the open carriage window. She put the bowl and spoon down on the bottom of the carriage next to her boot. "Thank you for indulging a selfish girl, sir. I can have ice cream another time. And thank you for a nice, warm wrap."

Mr. Gold nodded to her but couldn't get any words out. She knew he was fighting tears and the heartbreak that went with them.

They sat in silence the rest of the way home. Bridget was wondering what to do next to help Mr. Gold with the Seth business and Mr. Gold was wondering the same, what to do about the Seth business.

Throwing out the ice cream had been easy, she thought. Of course she'd already had a good plenty. Would she have been so noble if she hadn't even tasted it yet? The memory was still there of the cold, the sweetness, the flavor. So it wasn't so bad, doing something to show her respect for

Mr. Gold's beliefs, if not his son, whom she had never met alive.

But showing your respect was something you did for a friend and Mr. Gold was just her boss; she couldn't forget that. In her experience, Bridget had noticed that the boss was never really looking out for your best interests, only his. You had to take care of yourself. She couldn't let down her guard; it would do no good for either of them.

As they pulled up to the back door of the house, Mr. Gold came out of his reverie. "Thank you for that, tossing the ice cream. That was very sweet. And thank you for your efforts today. I'll have to determine my next step," he said as Johnny opened the carriage door and Mr. Fleming appeared immediately, holding his arm out for Bridget to grab. Bridget hesitated but Mr. Gold indicated she should get out first and she did.

"Sir, I'm afraid there's a dustup inside," Mr. Fleming said, getting right to the point. His forehead was beaded with sweat. "Mrs. Gold and Mrs. Simon are in a rather bad spat."

"Thank you, Mr. Fleming, for the forewarning," Mr. Gold said grimly as he hurried inside.

Bridget couldn't imagine what those two could have done to get Mr. Fleming so shaken. Normally he'd be proud to take care of it himself; she already could see that about him. It must be the whole terrible mess, the death, and the funeral, all of it, that had him off his game so the women got out of his control. She quickly followed behind Mr. Gold.

THEY could hear the voices clearly. They were probably standing in that marble foyer, Bridget thought, for all the echo. She knew she would get called down for going where she didn't belong but she couldn't help herself. She slipped off her new cape, folded it over her arm, and followed Mr. Gold to the first floor.

There were five Shiva visitors standing at various positions around the entry hall, each one looking more uncomfortable than the last. They obviously all wanted to leave but couldn't figure out a way to do so.

"You don't really care about Seth," Mrs. Simon said, her voice shaking with rage.

"How can you say that? I raised him. He and Rose were mine more than hers," Mrs. Gold said defiantly.

Mrs. Simon reached across and slapped Mrs. Gold with the same offhanded cruelty that the woman in the tenement had used to slap her baby.

Everyone in the room except Bridget, who had seen plenty of slapping in her day, gasped, even Mr. Gold.

"Rose hated you," Mrs. Simon said, not affected by the reaction of the bystanders. She had worked up a head of steam and was going to let loose. "She couldn't wait to leave here. As much as she loved her father, you drove her clear across an ocean. Seth only stayed because you slipped him extra money. You paid him to pretend to be a loving stepson to you."

"Enough," Mr. Gold said, walking between the two women. "How dare you behave in such a way at Seth's Shiva? I think you are overtired, Mrs. Simon. Go to your room and take a rest, please."

Even with the "please," the whole room heard a command, not a request, in Mr. Gold's tone. Mrs. Simon turned and stormed toward the stairs.

"She never cared about anyone but herself, Isaac. She

doesn't love you either," Mrs. Simon threw out over her shoulder as she went upstairs.

Mr. Gold gave a severe look at his wife, then turned and started greeting the visitors. He did not allude to the scene and the tension seemed to dissipate quickly. Mrs. Gold waited until the older woman was safely up the stairs to climb them herself. Bridget could only imagine the boohooing that Mary Martha would have to put up with this afternoon. She retreated below stairs where Sally, Karol, and Katie were gathered, listening to the uproar.

"Sally, is Mrs. Simon somehow related to Mr. Gold?" Bridget asked.

Sally nodded. "Oh, yes, she is. She's the sister of Mr. Gold's first wife, the children's aunt."

"So now she's the secretary of the second Mrs. Gold?"

"She already lived here when Mrs. Gold was killed. Her husband passed early in life and Mr. Gold took her in," Sally explained. "Then when Estella became Mrs. Gold, she somehow talked Mrs. Simon into taking this position. She said it would do her good to get out and have something to do, that she was too young to be just a widow. Mr. Gold fell for it."

"So he made Mrs. Simon take the job?" Bridget asked.

"Not so much made her as encouraged her to. Then, with the master behind it, Mrs. Simon felt she couldn't say no, what with all the good Mr. Gold had done for her. I don't think she had any money of her own."

"Why would Mrs. Gold, the second one, want a secretary who is more part of the family than she herself?"

Sally turned to go back to the laundry, the two other girls following her. "I think she liked, likes, making Mrs. Simon do lowly tasks for her. It makes her feel important."

* * *

"SO, what do you think, Brig? Do you think Katherine snuck back in town to knock off old Seth?"

Bridget and Mary Martha were sitting on Bridget's bed with their nightgowns on and their stockings rolled down around their ankles to keep their feet warm. Bridget had just recounted her trip to Five Points and Gold's Department Store.

"Not really. But I'll go around New York City in a carriage until Mr. Gold gives up."

Mary Martha nodded in response to this sensible attitude of Bridget's. "If not Katherine, who?"

"What about Mrs. Gold?"

Mary Martha looked horrified. "What are you talking about?"

"The other night I couldn't sleep and I'd gone to the loo. I heard Mrs. Gold yelling that she would have killed Seth herself before she'd see him with a tramp like Katherine. What if Katherine came back secretly to confront Seth, and Mrs. Gold caught them and killed Seth, and Katherine and her da are running for their lives?"

There was silence for a minute, then Mary Martha started giggling. Bridget joined in. "Okay, my theory is a little far fetched but she did say that, I swear."

"I believe you, Brig, but that's just something she said when she was out of her mind. She couldn't hurt her own boy, stepson or not, spoiled or not."

"And why didn't you tell me about Mrs. Simon being Mr. Gold's sister-in law? Did she ever come out of her room, by the way?"

"No, I took her some tea and she rushed me out the door,

tea and all, said she wasn't thirsty. I never even thought to
tell you about Mrs. Simon, one way or the other. Poor thing.
She always looks so sad. I didn't know about the connection
until this whole mess with Katherine and Seth started. She
sleeps down on the second floor, in the nanny's room, but I
was told that was so the missus could always get ahold of
her. Seth or Ben didn't address her as auntie, they called her
Mrs. Simon. She went in to talk to Mr. Gold in the library
sometimes when Mrs. Gold was in her suite, but that was
the only thing that made her different from the rest of the
household."

"How did you find out?" Bridget asked.

"What?" Mary Martha asked back, clearly confused.

"How did you find out that Mrs. Simon was wife number
one's sister?" Bridget asked impatiently.

"They had a row—but this one was in private, up in the
missus' suite. It was after the hoopla with Seth and Katherine came out. That's when Mrs. Gold decided to go up to the
country. Mrs. Simon didn't want to go, said they was needed
right here, said it wasn't fair to leave Mr. Gold with the
mess. Mrs. Gold said she should have kicked Mrs. Simon out
of the house the day her sister got struck down. Those are
cold words, aren't they, Brig?"

"Stone cold," Bridget said quietly, remembering the chill
she'd taken when she heard Mrs. Gold the other night.
What did Mrs. Gold mean she should have thrown Mrs. Simon out? Was she already so sure she'd be the next missus?

CHAPTER NINE

"**H**APPY birthday, Bridget," Mr. Fleming said.
Bridget was cooking bacon, and really concentrating on keeping the pieces straight, so she hadn't seen Mr. Fleming coming her way. Now she looked up and smiled. "Thank you, sir." Mary Martha must have told.

"The day you came to us, our schedule went awry," Mr. Fleming observed with understatement. "We never got around to arranging a day off for you. I've been told you are not religious so I was wondering if you would mind having Saturday off. It's a day the Golds are often in the country."

Bridget nodded. "Saturday would be fine, sir."

Mr. Fleming gave the stingiest of smiles. "But for this week, you can have the rest of your birthday off after breakfast. You're to report to the kitchen as usual tomorrow morning."

Bridget was surprised and a little uneasy. Sure, she'd

thought about what she would do on her birthday, if she were a grand lady and not herself. Go shopping at Gold's Department Store, buy a dress and a hat, have ice cream three or four times, eat dinner at Delmonico's in the Roman Room, meet someone, fall in love, open a little bakery.

In the past, her birthdays had been less than stellar. For the last three years, she'd spent every one of them the same, looking for Maggie, and then getting drunk. The lack of success in finding Maggie made for a lot of dark, disappointing memories. She shrugged and placed the last piece of bacon on a brown paper sack to drain. Maybe this would be her lucky year.

BREAKFAST was a jolly affair. The staff tipped their coffee cups to Bridget's birthday and they were all more animated than usual. It could be because they were on day four of the seven-day Shiva and a normalcy had returned to the household, however sad it was.

The days had a routine. Prayers were said for the dead. Bridget heard them call it Kaddish.

A group of people usually came to pay their respects around two and another group in the late afternoon. The amount of food offered was minimal now, tea and cookies, sometimes little open-faced cucumber sandwiches, and whiskey for the men.

Mr. Gold had not left the house again, and Mrs. Simon and Mrs. Gold didn't have much to do with each other. Mrs. Gold was still receiving guests and Mrs. Simon stayed busy writing thank-you notes to those who had already come to call, in the Golds' name, of course. She took stacks of them in for Mr. Gold to sign each evening. Mrs. Gold didn't appear to sign her own name. Perhaps he signed for them both.

As Bridget was cleaning up her cast-iron skillet, straining the grease into a crock and wiping it down with a cloth instead of putting it in water, Mary Martha slipped up beside her with two dollar bills. "This is not much of a birthday gift, but I know you haven't had a pay day yet and I thought you could use some mad money for today. Are you going to look for Maggie?"

"Yes," Bridget said helplessly, taking the money from her friend and giving her a hug silently. Mary Martha had explained to Bridget many times that she should accept the fact that Maggie was most likely dead. Bridget always said, yes, I know, but I can't give up hoping. Today, they didn't bother to recite those familiar refrains.

"Try around the new cathedral," Mary Martha offered. "There are people camped all around the construction site."

"Thanks to ye, Mary Martha," Bridget said. "I'll take the bus up there right now."

Bridget flew upstairs to change clothes. She put on her pretty white blouse and her only skirt, a serviceable navy wool one that the German landlady had sewed up for her. She counted out her coins, and with the two dollars Mary Martha had given her, she had almost four. That would do her. She opened the closet door and grabbed her cape, spied the carved box and hesitated, then closed the closet.

She'd examine the box closely very soon, but not now. It was her birthday and for a few hours she was free.

BRIDGET took the omnibus north up Fifth Avenue to Fiftieth Street. There it was: the cathedral that the Irish were building. It was still long from finished but Bridget couldn't help but be impressed. It looked like a fairy tale castle, a massive stone structure that stretched over the block. She'd heard about it for years.

Bishop Hughes, who had died earlier in the year, had been a stonemason himself, the newspapers said. He'd asked the few rich Irish Catholics in New York to all throw in a thousand bucks apiece. That cash hadn't lasted long, and ten years had gone by since they started Saint Patrick's. It looked to Bridget like there was ten years to go before it would be a real cathedral.

Construction had come to a halt during the war and now the site was littered with limestone boulders covered with moss. The entries to the structure were boarded up and chains with padlocks secured openings.

Bridget trudged east on Fiftieth Street to the back of the site. There was a shantytown of sorts back there, a wilderness of tents and shacks built from discards of years of construction. Garbage, small children, the residue of campfires, and human waste were all over the ground. Bridget approached the nearest dwelling, a hut made of wooden pallets wired together with a piece of tin over the top for a roof. By the neighborhood standards, it was a palace. There had been a fire going in front of it recently—pieces of wood were still smoldering—so Bridget guessed it was occupied. "Hey, there," she yelled and knocked on the side of the shack.

"Go away," a hoarse female voice croaked. A male grunt from inside made it clear she wasn't alone.

"Do you know a Maggie Heaney?" Bridget asked.

No one responded to her question, only a few giggles from the feminine voice. Bridget moved on to a nearby tent.

And so it went. In a short hour the ordered reality of the house at Thirty-Fourth and Fifth seemed to recede from Bridget's consciousness. That was only a dream, where young Irish girls could have their own bedroom with a window and earn twelve dollars a month. This was the real New York, where children wandered around looking for parents who didn't come home, women sold their body for a drink of something alcoholic, and there were thieves stealing from these poorest of the poor. It sucked at Bridget like the muddy ground did at her old boots.

Bridget had come across a group of five children, guttersnipes they called them, the oldest probably ten, rolling a sleeping drunk over so they could check the back pockets of his britches. They looked at her with blank stares when she asked if they knew a Maggie Heaney. The tallest boy said, "Go fuck yourself," as calmly as you'd expect a "how do you do."

Maybe Mary Martha was right and Bridget would be smarter to count her sister among the dead. Wouldn't it be a better thing for Maggie than living in this uncertain hell? Bridget had to admit she never imagined her sister happy with a good job or a husband and kids of her own. She never went to legitimate businesses looking for Maggie. Why was she so sure Maggie had ended up in trouble somewhere?

Because Bridget remembered the last time they were together, how angry and defiant Maggie had been. How determined to show everyone they were right, she would never amount to a hill of beans. Bridget had to fight those feelings in her own heart and soul every day. A worthless child from Ireland, what could you possibly deserve?

Bridget knew these searches were some kind of penance. She had always kept a good job, however lowly, and she was getting to do what she loved. In contrast, her sister hadn't found her place in the city after the orphanage. So part of the quest in foul-smelling taverns and tenements was to assuage her own guilt for having made it out of there.

She walked back to Fifth Avenue and caught the next omnibus south.

THE Spotted Pig wasn't one of Bridget's haunts. Neither her father nor her sister had drunk there. In fact, she had never been in the Pig until she'd visited it for Mr. Gold the other day. She was surprised to find that she'd ended up at the door.

Bridget took a place at the bar, in the second tier behind those that were seated. It was the same bartender. He must be the owner. "You again?" he spat out, eyebrows up in a question.

"Irish whiskey, please," Bridget replied, not wanting to bother with explanations.

Bridget took the jigger of whiskey when it was offered and gulped it. She gave a dollar to the bartender. "Another, please."

They played their roles. He filled up her glass and gave her change. She handed him a tip and looked at the other participants. It was still a daytime drinking crowd but not quite as desperate as the morning folks. It was well into the afternoon, a perfectly respectable time to tipple. A group of carpenters were right in front of her at the bar, laughing among themselves. A fair Irish lad winked at her. Bridget winked back, then thought better of it and started walking to the door.

"They were back," the bartender called out.

She turned. "Katherine's da?"

He nodded. "And Katherine. Yesterday. Sat at a table. Seemed real nervous. I mentioned folks had been asking after them. They didn't tell me nothin', only that they were waiting for someone. A fella came in, sat with them a while, and they all left together."

"Did you know the fella?" Bridget asked.

"Not from around here. Blond hair, blue eyes, one hand bandaged, a dandy sort," the bartender said, then the eyebrows went up again. Bridget recalled what she'd promised and reached for the other dollar in her pocket. This was going to cut in to her birthday fun. She gave it over.

"Send a boy next time. And thanks to ye," she said and went on outside, only looking over her shoulder at the carpenter once. He was watching her.

Bridget considered her options. She still had enough money to get good and drunk. Sex with a stranger was possible. She only had to wait for the carpenter to come out of the tavern for that. Her heart just wasn't in either of those choices.

She took the omnibus up to Gold's Department Store, went right in, and headed for the ice cream parlor. This time she ordered a hot fudge sundae and sat down at a table to enjoy it, eating slowly, letting each spoonful melt in her mouth before starting another. Every bite made her happy. Still, a roll in the hay might not be bad either. Bridget thought back to the little tavern and realized it hadn't even been a serious option. Maybe she was getting too old for such foolishness.

Bridget stayed in Gold's until the store closed, at six. She tried on hats, looked at the French lingerie, smelled the new shoe smell in the shoe department. The linen floor, with all the sheets and towels, was amazing. When they dinged a bell and announced ten minutes to closing, Bridget started for the door with all the other customers.

"Miss Bridget, Miss Bridget," a voice called. It was Don, the manager who had selected her cape, hurrying toward her. "I saw you trying on hats and I wondered if you could possibly take some papers home with you to Mr. Gold. It will save me two hours," he said. "Day off?"

Bridget thought about telling him to take the papers himself, that she wasn't going back to the house yet, but she didn't. How could she deny the favor when she was wearing a fifty-dollar cape on her back, fifty dollars for heaven's sake—she saw one on the rack with a price tag—courtesy of Mr. Gold and picked out by Don himself. He could have chosen a cheaper model. "Of course, sir. I'm ready to go home right now."

Don had a big manila envelope in his hand. He shoved it at her and looked relieved. "Thank you, Miss Bridget. I can have supper with my kids now."

Bridget put her hand on Don's arm to check his flight. "One thing, sir, that I was curious about. Where did Master Seth work?"

Don blinked and gestured toward the stairs. "Up in the offices with his father."

"No, I mean what department? What did he do?"

Don nodded, finally comprehending her question. "When Seth came on, it was to manage the uniforms."

Bridget didn't move or speak, indicating now she didn't understand.

"Oh, you must not know. Gold's provides many of the uniforms for the Union Army. We have a whole factory downtown. They've lost so many soldiers this year that we can't keep up. Some replacements have to wear dead men's clothes."

Bridget could hear Mr. Gold saying to that publisher gent, "We're glad for the business," and the uniforms surely were what he meant. "That must have kept him busy," she said, turning toward the door again.

"He spent most of his time down there, at the factory," Don said, hurrying toward the stairs.

BRIDGET was embarrassed to be home so early on her day off, and it being her birthday to boot. There was no sneaking in, at least not that Bridget knew about, so she rang the bell and soon Mr. Fleming stood there quizzically.

"I was havin' a bit of ice cream at Gold's and Mr. Don, one of the managers, asked me to bring some papers home to Mr. Gold," Bridget explained.

Mr. Fleming held out his hand. "Thank you for bringing them. I assume you have other plans for the night."

Bridget nodded her head, even though she didn't. "Oh yes, sir. But if I could, I'd like to talk to Mr. Gold myself. About those inquiries he asked me to make."

Mr. Fleming hesitated a second, then nodded and opened the door, handing her a single key that he slipped off his key chain. "When you come home tonight, here's a key so you don't have to wake Justin. Now come with me," he said as he led the way to the library.

Mr. Fleming knocked lightly and entered. In a moment, he returned to the hall and nodded at the door as he passed Bridget. "Go on in," he said as he hurried on down the hall.

"Hey there, Mr. Gold. I mean, hello, sir."

"Happy birthday, Bridget. Thank you for taking time

out of your birthday to bring these to me," he said, indicating the envelope. "I'm honored that you spent part of your day at Gold's."

Bridget bobbed her head up and down. "I had a hot fudge sundae and it was grand. But I also had a shot of whiskey at The Spotted Pig. The bartender remembered me and said that Katherine and her father had been in there yesterday. They sat at a table and waited for a gent. Then all three of them left together." She didn't think it was necessary to tell him that it was two shots of whiskey, not one.

"A description?" Mr. Gold asked anxiously.

"Not much of one. Blond hair, blue eyes, a dandy sort, and a bandaged hand. That's all he said."

"This is exciting, isn't it?"

"I wouldn't get my hopes up, Mr. Gold. We don't know where they are and we don't know that it was Katherine or her da who killed your son."

"But now we have proof that she is back in the city. And out of all the Irish, two hundred thousand you told me, we found them."

"We do have that, sir. Perhaps your friend that publishes the newspaper could tell us where this Timothy O'Sullivan is right now. Then we would have a better idea of whether or not they're planning to meet him. Also, I don't think it would hurt to go by the father's address again. I just took the neighbors' word for it that they were really moved out. I should'a seen for myself."

Mr. Gold stood up and paced the distance to the fireplace and back to his desk a couple of times. "Thank you, Bridget. I think we're getting somewhere. Now please go enjoy the rest of your birthday."

Bridget wanted to tell him the truth, that she didn't

have anywhere to go and ask if she could please just go upstairs and take a long, hot bath, but she didn't. It was too
pathetic and she didn't want his pity for being a poor Irish
without friends or family, at least not ones she could celebrate with. "Thank you, sir," she said and left the room.

As she slipped out the back door, she heard the ruckus in
the kitchen, platters banging together, Chef talking French
to Gilbert, the girls trilling. They were all in there, getting
ready to serve dinner and kiddin' with each other. It sounded
nice.

Now Bridget was in a fix. She had to find something to do
for at least two hours. It was dark and cold so she couldn't go
for a walk. Most restaurants didn't allow women and she
didn't have the money for one if they had. The five-cent
movies were way downtown.

"Hey, red, where are you going so late?" a voice asked.
The reporter fellow appeared out of the shadows.

"It's my day off and I just had to bring some papers to
Mr. Gold," Bridget said with more pride in her voice than
she would have liked. She was a busy woman helping an important man. "What are you doing sneaking around the
house in the dark? Justin will whip your behind."

"Justin, that's the Negro fellow, isn't it? When I get put
on these stakeouts, I get to know the staff by name. Mine's
Michael Murphy, by the way, in case you don't remember.
Everybody calls me Murphy." Michael Murphy looked expectantly at Bridget, hoping she would tell him her name
now. She was so pretty and young. "I'm the reporter. Gave
you my card the other day."

Bridget started walking down the carriage path to Thirty-
Fourth Street, this Michael Murphy right on her trail. "You
didn't give me your card, you threw it in my shopping bags,

rude-like. And you were talking the most ridiculous rubbish I ever heard. Master Seth was not cut up in pieces."

Murphy hurried to walk by her side. "Did you personally find him? That's what Johnny says. By the way, did you see my story about Seth two days ago?"

Bridget turned toward Fifth Avenue and presently got on the omnibus going north. Michael Murphy hopped right on with her. "We aren't allowed to have the newspapers until the mourning is over," Bridget said stiffly. "And now I see why. You've been writing nonsense about Master Seth. I happen to know that your publisher, Mr. Brown, is a personal friend of Mr. Gold. He shouldn't let some no-account reporter dirty the reputation of a good man," Bridget snipped. "And Johnny was clear up at the country house when it happened so I wouldn't be puttin' much stock in what he tells ya."

Murphy grinned. "You don't understand how the newspaper business works. The publisher doesn't tell the editor what to do and vice versa. It's like the judicial and executive branches of the government, separate but equal. Where are we going, by the way?"

Bridget was trapped. "Saint Patrick's Cathedral, if it's any of your business."

An appreciative whistle came from the reporter. "I hear it's dangerous up there at night. What would make a pretty young maid go to Saint Pat's after dark?"

"I am not a maid for your information. I'm a cook, and a good one, too." Bridget hated herself for responding to Murphy's teasing. "What did your article say?"

"That the death of Seth Gold could be connected to a family scandal involving a member of the household staff."

"Oh, so that's it, is it? You think I'm the silly-headed nitwit that got herself involved with the young master?"

Murphy looked down at his notepad and shuffled the pages. "No, that would be Katherine O'Sullivan and if I'm not mistaken you are Bridget Heaney, just newly hired on at the Golds' mansion. You're the replacement."

Bridget hated being referred to like that. She tried to not rise to the bait so easily this time around and just nodded. "That's me and so now I guess we've officially met as we know each other's names. What you think you'll be finding outside the Golds' door, I just can't figure. He's dead and buried. Katherine is gone. It's over."

"Maybe, but I ran into some pretty interesting facts when I was researching this. Did you know young Mr. Gold was in charge of manufacturing most of the uniforms for the Union Army?"

"And why not? Gold's does all kinds of custom work. It might as well be the one to sew up for the Army," Bridget said, a tad defensively.

The omnibus stopped on the corner of Fiftieth and Fifth. Bridget got off and so did Michael Murphy. "Seriously, why are you here?" Murphy asked as he glanced around uneasily.

Bridget marched toward the bonfires in the back of the site. It was much more intimidating at night. "I'm looking for someone."

Murphy tagged along. "Katherine O'Sullivan?"

"No, I don't know the girl."

A group of prostitutes started yelling catcalls at the couple. They were plying their trade in the shadows of the church foundation, God help them. Murphy looked straight ahead but Bridget walked right up to them.

"Do you know a lass about eighteen name of Maggie Heaney?" Bridget asked and prayed they didn't. Even for whores these girls looked rough. They had on only camisoles and petticoats, underthings that used to be white but weren't anymore. Their breasts fell out of their tops and they were shivering with the cold.

"We don't give away anything, even information," one of them said smartly.

Bridget hesitated. She wasn't prepared for this, mainly because she hadn't been planning to visit Saint Pat's again today.

All of a sudden, out of the corner of her eye she saw a dollar bill floating toward the lead girl. It was in the hand of the reporter. Michael Murphy had their attention.

"Now here's a lad that knows how to treat a lady. What do you want, brother?" the young woman said.

"If you answer the lady's question, and a few of mine, there will be another of those for you to divvy up, ladies," Murphy said in his best reporter's voice.

"Maggie Heaney doesn't sound familiar to me—does it to you, girls?" the ringleader said, wanting to get this over with as quickly as possible. It was only a dollar, after all.

Bridget looked right in the girls' eyes as they all answered in the negative, trying to determine if they were telling the truth. She remembered what Mr. Gold had told her about looking people in the eye to see what kind of character they had. She didn't sense an outright lie from any of them but she was touched by what she did see. In this group of girls, Bridget didn't think a one of them had turned twenty; she didn't see one sign of life, one sign that the body around the eyes was still hoping for something out of each day. Was Maggie dead inside like that?

She looked down. "Thank you for that, and thanks to you, Mr. Murphy. Now you best be askin' your questions," she said and moved swiftly away. Let him try to get out with his trousers on, she thought.

Michael Murphy weighed the situation and decided not to run after Bridget. He knew where she lived and he'd find out sooner or later whom she was looking for. Maggie Heaney was probably a relative.

He had an idea for an exposé. LIFE OF CRIME IN THE CATHEDRAL. He could see the headline now. "So, ladies, who ventures up here at night and what for?"

Bridget had no intention of going back into the depths of that shantytown tonight or any other night. It had been difficult enough for her to swallow in the light of the afternoon. It brought back too many memories of how desperate her own life had been, in Cork and then worse when they got to New York.

She cut across the street and caught the bus going south. She'd been gone long enough to tell a good lie about it. Her feet hurt. It had been a long day. "Happy birthday, Bridget," she said out loud to herself.

CHAPTER TEN

BRIDGET was peeling potatoes. Today she was going to make her potato rolls for the first time here at the Golds' and she was just a little nervous.

It was Gilbert's day off so he had made up some little tarts for the mourning visitors and left before breakfast. Bridget would make some cucumber sandwiches to go with them later. She wondered what other people did when they had free time—Gilbert, for instance. Was there a place he could go and speak to other French folk?

Justin Morgan came in the kitchen with a long box. "Bridget, here are your uniforms. Will you kindly run and change, and place the four uniforms that belonged to Miss Katherine in this box. The boy from the store is waiting. Evidently they have a thriving resale business in these uniforms."

"Yes, sir, just let me put these potatoes on the stove," she said and looked around for Chef. She knew you weren't supposed to leave the kitchen without telling him. She knew this not because he'd said anything but just from good common sense. When the girl who helped her in the kitchen at the boardinghouse went out back to gossip with the maids from next door, without letting her know, it irritated her plenty. She put the potatoes on the range and stepped into the dry goods room. He was there, pulling down some dried beans from the top shelf.

"Chef, Justin brought me my uniforms. I have to go change so they can take Katherine's back to the store."

Chef nodded from his short ladder.

Bridget slipped back out to the kitchen and was disappointed to see Justin had left the box and resumed his duties. Bridget hadn't had another good talk with Justin since the first one. Having constant company in the house for a week, and for such a sad purpose, was sure a strain on Justin and Mr. Fleming. And having Mrs. Simon and Mrs. Gold not on speaking terms didn't make it any easier. Mrs. Gold relied totally on the two men now.

Quickly she ran up the stairs just as Mr. Gold was coming out of his rooms. "Bridget, can we run those errands today?" he asked.

"I can't leave today, sir. It's Gilbert's day off and it wouldn't be fair to Chef."

Mr. Gold was visibly disappointed. Bridget was afraid he was going to order her to come with him and the Chef be damned. That would cook her goose downstairs. She changed the subject. "Got my uniforms, sir. That was quick work."

Mr. Gold's expression changed to resigned. "I guess it would be better if we waited until Shiva is over," he said, then looked at the box Bridget was carrying and realized what she'd said to him. "Oh, good. I hope they fit," he said and went on down the stairs.

Bridget was nervous and in a hurry. She knew Chef would keep one eye on the potatoes but she didn't like to leave food cooking unattended. And what you put on the stove, you were responsible for; that was just it. Her new uniform fit perfectly as she knew it would. That woman had been very thorough with the measuring.

As Bridget swept the other uniforms out of her closet, the spice box on the shelf somehow dropped to the floor with a sharp bang. A drawer in the bottom of the box slid open. Bridget picked up the box and pulled the drawer out. "I wonder how you open this," she said out loud. The drawer was filled with paper of all types. There were rolled-up scrolls and some were single sheets that were laid flat. They all looked so old they would crack or turn to dust if you touched them. There was writing on them; Bridget could see that. But it was not in English.

She put the box carefully on the bed, hoping the drawer wouldn't magically close up while she was busy downstairs. Then she folded the other uniforms quickly to put them in the box. A sheaf of dollar bills came out of the pocket of one skirt. It was the tip money Mr. Gold had given her when they went on their downtown trip. "Oh, Lordy. Mr. Gold will think I kept his money," Bridget said to herself. She did keep a dollar, putting it in her clothes chest, to pay herself back for the bartender yesterday. A working girl couldn't afford tips like that. The rest she stuffed in her pocket, closed the box, and tore out the door.

Bridget went to the back door and found the messenger. Just to use the chain of command, she went to Justin's little office and stuck her head in. "May I give these to the lad?" she asked.

Justin nodded his head, deep in his ciphers of an invoice.

Bridget gave the boy the box and ran back to the kitchen, not knowing if Justin had tipped him or if he got a salary from Mr. Gold for working at the department store. She couldn't worry about it with potatoes on the stove.

The potatoes were just tender and she took them to the sink and drained them in a big colander. Next she got down the ricer from the big cabinet that held kitchen equipment that wasn't used daily. She pushed the cooked potatoes through the narrow holes in the ricer into another bowl, steam rising up in her face. She whipped some butter in them, then set the potatoes aside to cool and started her yeast. The secret to Bridget's potato rolls was buttermilk and she set two cups' worth into a saucepan to heat up a bit. When it was just warm, she took out a bit and added yeast and sugar to it in a big bowl. When the yeast started bubbling, Bridget added the rest of the buttermilk, the potatoes, a couple of eggs, and a dash of salt. Then she started adding flour. Soon she was lost in the pure pleasure of kneading and punching her dough.

She'd be so glad when all this trouble here in the house calmed down. She wanted nothing more than a nice, clean kitchen to cook in and those that wanted to eat good food to appreciate what she cooked.

IT was near eleven o'clock when Bridget finally went to her room for the night. She had forgotten about the box. There it was on the bed, the hidden drawer still open and over-flowing with papers.

She sat down and took her shoes off. That was the first thing she had to buy when she got paid, a new pair of ankle boots. Hers had come from a used clothes peddler that worked the corner by the boardinghouse. They never had fit right. It would be a real pleasure to have boots that had an arch support.

Bridget turned up the gaslight to high, then pulled the box to her lap. First, she turned the box all the way around, examining the carvings. She was right about them. They were all of women and food and also the act of cooking. The woman getting ready to kill the sacrificial lamb or goat, she couldn't tell which, was a powerful image but she didn't agree with Mary Martha that it showed some kind of demonic rite. Of course, Mary Martha was religious and she, Bridget, was a cook. They both leaned toward an explanation that was more familiar to them.

Bridget turned her attention to the drawer full of writing. Each piece of paper seemed to have a different type of writing on it. Bridget could make out one thing on all of the papers. There were lists such as would appear in recipes. She was excited. These must be the recipes that Mary Martha had heard about but never seen herself. The writing was in different languages. She looked at them for a long time, trying to decipher words that she recognized. One sheet of paper was in what Bridget was sure was Chinese, another in some other strange characters, not the letters of the English alphabet. There was also one in German. Bridget recognized that language from the boardinghouse Bible and also all the street signs in Kleindeutschland.

By tinkering with the drawer, Bridget found the catch that released it in the handle-shaped end of the box. She opened it and closed it a few times to make sure she knew how, then closed it up and put the box back on the shelf. What in the world was the box and how had Katherine come to have it? She could ask Mr. Gold or someone more worldly to take a look at it. Maybe they could read some of the recipes.

As Bridget fell asleep, she realized she only had more questions about the box, no answers. It was like everything else this last week.

MR. Fleming stuck his head in the kitchen. "Are you ready? Mr. Gold is in the carriage already."

Bridget had whipped up tomato aspic for lunch and now she put it in the icebox to set up. It was the first day after the seven-day Shiva and the house was anxious to go back to a normal schedule. But today couldn't be normal because Mr. Gold was determined that he and Bridget were going to return to the Lower East Side and the newspaper again. She'd tried to get ahead with her work before they left.

Bridget nodded and slipped off her apron and headscarf, put them on a peg in the staff dining room, and took her cape from another peg.

When she hopped in the carriage, Mr. Gold was tapping his fingers impatiently. He turned toward Bridget, eyes flashing. He was chafing at the bit for action. "I think we should start at the newspaper, then head over to the apartment."

Bridget wanted to explain to him that this wasn't an apartment in any sense of the word but she didn't. She herself had been in an apartment only once. One of the ladies from the Friendless had invited the girls who were graduating, that's what they called it, to her house for tea and cookies. The apartment had three rooms, plus a kitchen and a bathroom and running water. The girls were very impressed.

"Whatever you think, sir. That'll be what's best. By the way . . ." She reached into her skirt pocket and pulled out the dollars that she'd transferred from uniform to uniform for days. "I still have the money to buy answers."

Mr. Gold smiled. "I'd forgotten all about that money, Bridget. You could have kept it and I would have given you more today."

"That wouldn't have been honest, sir."

"No, I guess it wouldn't have been. But many employees would have told me that they spent the money on bribes and tips last week and then asked for more."

"Well, that would have been trying to pull the wool over on the boss. That would be shortsighted of them, wouldn't it?"

Mr. Gold nodded. "Very," he said.

Bridget got the idea that Mr. Gold could show a completely different side of his personality if you crossed him.

Soon they pulled up in front of the *Recorder* building. Johnny came around and opened the door, and as they went in, Bridget turned to Mr. Gold. "So we ask what?" she wondered out loud.

"If Timothy O'Sullivan has sent in any pictures lately. If they know where he is."

"Got it."

The same routine. The same receptionist who intrigued Bridget with her public job. She recognized them, Mr. Gold gave her his card, she called for the boy, and the boy ran to find Mr. Brown.

In five minutes, Mr. Brown came scurrying out to the reception area. He looked uncomfortable. "Isaac, how are you holding up?"

Mr. Gold shook hands. "I'm sorry to bother you again but I need to know where Timothy O'Sullivan is right now. Have you received any photos from him in the last few days?"

Mr. Brown was relieved. He wanted to avoid making an enemy of Isaac Gold. Isaac was a big advertiser for the newspaper. When they called him to the front desk to see Mr. Gold, he was afraid there would be angry words about the recent article. "I just happen to know, Isaac. He's been sent to cover Sherman's march to Savannah. The Union Army is fairly certain that Sherman will make it to the ocean before the New Year," Mr. Brown said.

Mr. Gold looked and sounded disappointed. "So he's already in Georgia."

"Yes, I think so," Mr. Brown. "What's this all about, Isaac?"

Mr. Gold shook his hand. "Thank you so much for all your support this week, Harris. I'm just trying to find out why my son was killed."

Mr. Gold took Bridget's elbow and guided her out the door.

"So, Katherine and her father most likely are not on their way to meet the brother who is in the midst of the most important campaign of the war," Bridget said dryly.

As they waited for Johnny to pull up the carriage, someone reached out a hand and squeezed Bridget's shoulder. She jumped and Mr. Gold spun around, ready to defend her against a threat of the street. Michael Murphy quickly released his hold and raised his hands, palms up, grinning.

"Well, Bridget, you left me in the lurch the other night," he said. "Welcome to Printer's Row." He turned to Mr. Gold, offering a hand. "I'm Michael Murphy, Mr. Gold, a reporter for the *Recorder*."

Mr. Gold stepped close to the young man, ignoring the outstretched hand. "I know who you are. I've seen you outside my house, and at a time when any decent person would respect our grief. A colleague sent me the article you wrote, feeling that I should know what was being printed about my family. What are you doing accosting a member of my staff?"

Bridget's heart started pounding. Somehow she was going to be indicted for knowing this clown.

Michael Murphy grinned again. He seemed to be enjoying himself. "Just doing my job. Your family is news. And as for Bridget, she led me on a merry chase away from your house. Pretty clever to have someone work as a dupe. Good to see you again, Miss Heaney. Wait until you see my new article about Saint Patrick's." He bowed his head slightly and went in the building.

Bridget felt slightly better. She was surprised Murphy even tried to get her off the hook.

When they were safely in the carriage and edging through the heavy traffic crosstown, Bridget and Mr. Gold started talking at once.

"Mr. Gold, I can explain . . ."

"What was Murphy talking about . . ."

Bridget fell silent and Mr. Gold held up his hand. "Please, continue."

It came spilling out in a torrent. "The truth is, sir, I haven't been able to locate my sister these last years. On my birthday I always look for her. I really didn't have anything to do after I came back to the house but I was embarrassed to say so. I left again and the young man, Murphy he calls himself, followed me, so I went on the bus up to Saint Pat's, where I'd been earlier looking for Maggie. I kinda left him there, surrounded by professional girls."

"What does the cathedral have to do with your sister?"

"No building work is being done on it because of this war, sir. So people who don't have nowhere else to go have built a sort of shanty town there. Guttersnipes and prostitutes and whatnot."

"And that's the kind of place you think you will find your sister?"

"Most likely, sir," Bridget gulped. "Now can I ask you a question?"

Mr. Gold nodded, curious about what it would be.

"If you did see the newspaper article Murphy wrote, which I have not by the way but Murphy told me there was one, why didn't you yell at your friend Mr. Brown right now for publishing it in his paper? What kind of friend is he?"

"There were also stories in six other papers so we must assume it was a newsworthy tragedy. Mr. Brown hires editors to collect news and tell the public about it. The article, no matter how reprehensible, wasn't filled with falsehoods. If you are well known in the community, that's really all you can expect."

"That makes sense, I guess."

"Now I want to ask you a question, about your sister. Do you check with the police?"

"Once in a while, Sir. Not as often as I should."

"Do you have a systematic approach to searching?" Bridget wasn't sure what that meant. Her silence indicated as much to Mr. Gold. "I will be glad to help you list all the possibilities, then we can begin a proper investigation," he said.

Bridget couldn't believe it. She and Da had looked for

Maggie together once in a while. It was one thing they shared that usually didn't end in an argument. She had never mentioned her sister at the boardinghouse for some reason. And since Da was killed last year, she had no one to talk to about Maggie. Old friends like Mary Martha were sympathetic but they would never have thought to say, "Let's begin a proper investigation." Bridget felt such relief she wanted to weep. She gave a smile instead and said, "I sure could use the help, Mr. Gold. But first let's find out who killed your boy."

When they got to Mott Street, Bridget had an uneasy feeling. "Would you please come in with me this time, Mr. Gold? I'll still do the talkin' and all but sometimes it's good to have a man along."

"Of course," he said and they both got out of the carriage. Bridget felt a wave of hopelessness surging out of the door of the building. It slowed her down and made her legs feel like they weighed a ton. It was so strong she could hardly drag herself up the stairs toward it.

They walked down the hall, and as before, the first door was open. Bridget knocked on the doorframe. "Hey there, how ye doin', do ye remember me?"

The woman was in there with her children. Mr. Gold came into view behind Bridget and her eyes went from one of them to the other. "They came back," she stated flatly.

Bridget's heart skipped a beat. She heard Mr. Gold's sharp intake of breath behind her.

"Katherine and her da?" Bridget asked, trying to sound casual.

"I saw them yesterday or was it the day before?" she said vaguely. The baby crawled over to Bridget and pulled herself up on her skirt. Bridget picked her up and sat her down in the middle of the room. She started bawling.

"What's their number? Maybe we'll go check," Bridget said at the same time she put down two dollars on the table.

"Three-thirty. Third floor in the back," the woman answered as she went over to the table and took the dollars. She turned away and her other two children silently moved toward the door to watch Bridget and Mr. Gold.

Mr. Gold traded places with Bridget as they went deeper into the building, taking the lead. The worst thing about these stacks of humanity was the array of smells. Nothing was harder to stomach than the aromas caught in the tenement halls: urine, cooked cabbage, whiskey, vomit, feces, and just plain stale air. And the halls were dark, even on a sunny day. When they started up the stairs, groping in the dark, Mr. Gold held out his hand for Bridget and she didn't even hesitate or debate whether it was proper. She held on tight. As they reached the third floor, another odor joined the usual mix, but one that Bridget or Mr. Gold didn't recognize immediately. "Dear Lord, somethin' is really foul up here," Bridget commented, trying to hold her air as long as she could between breaths.

Mr. Gold took a handkerchief out of his inside coat pocket and put it over his mouth and nose, silently leading Bridget toward the back of the building. There were others living on this floor—children were running back and forth in the hall, and mothers were walking down the stairs with big baskets of laundry, going who knows where to hang them to dry. They all seemed oblivious to the smell, their noses desensitized by all the spoilage in their lives.

Bridget and Mr. Gold stopped in front of the last door on the left, the only one on the floor that was closed. Bridget knocked and yelled, "Katherine. Katherine O'Sullivan, are you in there?" There was no sound from inside. Bridget knocked again, and when no one responded, she tried the door. It was unlocked and she boldly turned the knob. The door opened to a scene that would have caused her to faint two weeks before. But she was made of sterner stuff now.

Katherine's and her father's bodies were on the floor, one near the window, and the other in the corner. Both of them were dead, and from the looks of it, both of them had been shot. Two bloody spots near Katherine's right breast marked the entry wound. Her father was hit in the forehead. A rust-colored pool circled Katherine where she was frozen in death, cowering in the corner. The rust was dried blood, Bridget supposed, but it seemed instead like a pool of questions poor Katherine was floating in. Did she beg for mercy, for her life, as the killer came toward her?

"Oh, Lordy," Bridget gasped.

Mr. Gold put down his handkerchief and let loose of Bridget's hand. She hadn't noticed that they were still holding on to each other. He gestured toward the stairs with a resigned sigh. "Go get Johnny and both of you hurry to the police station down the street. Someone's killed the very people we needed alive. I'll wait up here."

Bridget didn't argue.

CHAPTER ELEVEN

BRIDGET sat there in the carriage for a few minutes but it didn't make sense. She wasn't sure Mr. Gold was streetwise enough to be alone up there. She got out with a bad feeling in her gut and started back up to the third floor.

The building was thick with patrolmen running in and out. So far they hadn't brought down the bodies.

She and Johnny had hightailed it down the street in the carriage and she had run into the precinct house and asked to see whoever was in charge of murders.

Everyone on duty had a big laugh about that. Ignoring their crude manners, she insisted someone come with her, that she had found two people shot. Reluctantly, two policemen came with her in the carriage. She led them up to where she and Mr. Gold found the bodies.

The police asked her a couple of things on the way over from the station. Bridget answered them.

"You say you were looking for this O'Sullivan woman. Why?"

"I was just helping my employer find a former member of the staff. He needed to ask her a couple of questions. We found them dead," Bridget stated primly.

"Did you have a beef with the O'Sullivans?"

Bridget shook her head. "I personally never met Katherine O'Sullivan or her father. Mr. Gold didn't tell me what he wanted, just thought an Irish girl would do better on these streets." Not the whole truth but not a lie, either.

When she and the police reached the room, Mr. Gold was standing in the hall with the door closed, talking to several small children who wanted to know what he was doing there. Bridget realized they were fortunate it was daytime and most of the menfolk were out of the building. An outsider discovering two murdered Irish in this neighborhood might have been in a dangerous predicament.

When the police saw what the situation was, they sent one men back to get additional help. It was then that Bridget quietly told Mr. Gold about her conversation with the police so they could keep their stories straight. Mr. Gold told her to wait downstairs and turned back to Mr. O'Sullivan's room. He was preoccupied and gloomy, pale and sweating.

Now, as she returned to the crime scene, she thought about this latest turn of events. Bridget was still not convinced that Katherine or her father was the murderer of Seth Gold. But they were involved in something that had ended their lives. Bridget hoped there would be a clue of some kind upstairs in that tiny room full of death. A note from whoever they'd met at The Spotted Pig was what she was hoping for. And she wanted to be the one to find it, not the police.

When Bridget reached the third floor, there was an argument going on. Three civilian men were trying to get in the O'Sullivans' room. They were arguing with the police, belligerent and probably more than a little drunk. The police seemed uncomfortable and nervous around the local men. The Draft Riots last year had pitted Irish cop against Irish workingman and neither side wanted a repeat, especially the cops, who hadn't relished shooting their countrymen.

Bridget couldn't see Mr. Gold. Surely the police could protect him. She went to the door and acted much more confidant than she felt. "The sergeant wanted to question me," she said to the patrolman guarding the door. She just hoped there was a sergeant around so she wouldn't be found to be a liar right off. The patrolman stepped aside and Bridget crowded into the cramped space.

As she passed, she overheard one of the men, a big, burley fellow with a beard, say, "He come down here and killed one of our girls, and her father, too, and we want you to lock him up." It was already worse than she had imagined.

Although it was cold enough to see your breath in the room, the presence of all the warm, living bodies was not helping the two cold, dead ones. The temperature in the room was rising. The smell was overpowering and Bridget almost gagged.

No one looked at her, no one but Mr. Gold, who was sitting on one of the plain wooden chairs with two policemen standing above him. His demeanor had gone from disappointed to confused. Could the police believe the same thing those fellas outside did? "Can I be of any help, gentlemen?" she asked innocently. "Me and my boss, here, Mr. Gold, he's the gent that owns Gold's Department Store, were looking for poor, dear Katherine. Seems we found her too late."

The cop that rode in the carriage with Bridget looked over at her. "Gold's Department Store?" Then he turned his attention back toward Mr. Gold. "Was it your son that was killed just lately?"

"Yes, it was. Katherine worked for me until recently and she and my son were friends. I was hoping she might know something that would help identify the killer."

"Friends?" the cop repeated scornfully. Who had ever heard of a servant and the master of the house being friends?

Mr. Gold nodded. "Sometimes young people who work in a household know more about what's going on than the grown-ups. I am desperate for information."

"Maybe she had some information all right, and that's why she's dead."

All the time this interrogation was going on, Bridget was looking around for something, she didn't know what. The room was empty except for two chairs with a small table between them and a mat on the floor for sleeping. Any personal items had already left with Mr. O'Sullivan the day he moved out. Bridget guessed he had paid until the end of the month and not bothered to let the landlord's agent, now there was a low career, know he was leaving. So the room had been available when he and Katherine needed it. They'd most likely waited here until they met the blue-eyed man at the Pig, a man Bridget believed had something to do with their deaths.

Under the leg of Mr. Gold's chair she did spot something, just a scrap of paper. She'd have to get it or let Mr. Gold know to pick it up, without being obvious. A coughing fit might work. Bridget started out with a couple of small coughs. She was interrupted by a commotion in the hall. The door swung open.

"There she is. That's her," a voice said.

Two policemen were holding on to the arms of the woman from the first floor. She pointed in the room at Bridget. "She came over here the other day, asking about Katherine. Came back today with the gent."

Bridget could feel the interest of the policemen turn away from Mr. Gold and toward her. She continued the coughing. Mr. Gold stood up and offered his chair to her. "Bridget, are you all right? Sir, I would like to take Miss Heaney home now."

Bridget faked a real little spell, sliding the chair over to loosen the piece of paper before she sat down. She fanned herself and acted pitiful. "I think I'm going to be sick," she said.

"Yes, of course," the lead policeman said sarcastically. Mr. Gold held Bridget's elbow solicitously to help her be seated. She had intended picking up the paper off the floor so she now had to try to do so with his hand on her arm. The result was so obvious the copper couldn't help but laugh as he reached the piece of paper before she did. "Is this yours, maybe something you dropped when you shot these two?"

Bridget had no choice. She took the piece of paper boldly from the policeman and glanced at it, memorizing the address on it, knowing she couldn't have possession of it for long. "No, I thought perhaps it had fallen from Mr. Gold's pocket. It's not mine."

The policeman took it back and held it out to Mr. Gold. "Is this yours?"

Mr. Gold shook his head without even looking at the paper. "I didn't even notice it," he said, and then took a look. "Oh my God," he said quietly.

"What?" Bridget demanded, her coughing fit halted.

"That address, Ten Broom Street. That's the factory."

"Your factory?"

"Yes. That's where Seth manufactured the uniforms for the Union Army."

"So you are telling me that the one scrap of paper in this stinking little room is the address of a factory you own?" the policeman asked.

"Officer, what is your name?" Mr. Gold asked.

"O'Malley, sir. Sergeant O'Malley."

"Sergeant O'Malley, I am just as concerned about this as you are. However, my employee and I just found a pair of dead bodies. They are moldering over there on the floor and I suggest you presently concentrate on them. I will be glad to answer any additional questions you might have." He gave the Sergeant a card with his address. "Here is where you can find me, or at the store. I am sure you and I will both investigate what possible connection the O'Sullivans have, had, to my uniform factory. Now may we leave, please?"

O'Malley wanted to haul them both down to the station but he could always do that later. Mr. Gold sure couldn't up and leave town very well. He'd talk to the boys uptown about the young Mr. Gold's death first. And he'd check out the girl. Bridget Heaney. The name sounded familiar. "Yes, Mr. Gold. I'll be in touch shortly," he said. He turned to his fellow Metropolitans. "Boys, two of you accompany Mr. Gold and the lady downstairs. Don't let the local troublemakers out there get a hand on them."

Bridget and Mr. Gold were hustled down the stairs. Although there was some bellyaching when the crowd realized they weren't in handcuffs, it wasn't really clear to those in the hall that they weren't being taken to the police station, so they were satisfied. When they reached the sidewalk, the two patrolmen watched them get in the carriage and the carriage pull away.

"Mr. Gold, thanks to ye for getting us out of there. I thought we was goin' to the lock-up there for a bit," Bridget said as Johnny turned the carriage to go north.

Mr. Gold held his temples for a moment. "I can't believe any of this. First Seth, now Katherine and her father. She lived with us for two years."

"As upsettin' as it all is, sir, I think we need to make one more stop before we go back to the house."

"To the factory," Mr. Gold said.

"Yes, sir. Maybe someone there saw Miss Katherine."

"I know you're right but I just want to go home and think it all through." He seemed to gather his strength. "We'll go to the factory, though." He sighed, called out to Johnny, then sank back in his seat.

Bridget was as confused as Mr. Gold sounded. They had come downtown for a second look, found two dead people and a scrap of paper with the address of Mr. Gold's factory. For the first time, Bridget had to concede that Katherine might have been involved in Seth Gold's death.

Ten Broom Street was a long, low building with transom windows all around. Bridget and Mr. Gold entered into a bustle of activity. Long racks on wheels, full of uniforms, were being pushed through the entry hall. They stepped into the main room and saw row after row of sewing machines operated by women whirring away. The foreman hurried toward them, surprised to see Mr. Gold.

"Mr. Gold, what can I do for you, sir?" he asked nervously.

"Erasmus, I hope you can keep a hold on this place for a

few days more. I haven't gone back to the store yet. I'll send someone down to relieve you in a couple of days."

"No problem, sir. We're getting along just fine and dandy. Have a shipment going out tomorrow."

"Erasmus, I need you to tell me the truth now. You can't protect Seth anymore."

"Yes, sir. I never told you false, sir."

"And I will not belabor the point that sometimes not speaking is as damaging as telling a lie. That's all history now. Did a pretty young woman name of Katherine ever come here to my son? Red hair, young?"

The foreman looked over at Bridget. "Yes, sir."

"Think, man. When was the last time you saw her here?"

A look of panic crossed the man's face. "Well, sir, I'm pretty sure it was the day before Master Seth was killed. They had a row."

"Did she come down here often?"

"Well, sir, not so often but more than once, that's for sure."

"Did you hear what they were arguing about?"

"No, but Master Seth seemed surprised to see her. I guess I figured it was the end of a little fun that the boy had been havin' and she was pretty upset about being thrown over."

"So she left?"

"Well, after a bit the two of them seemed to kiss and make up," Erasmus said.

Neither Mr. Gold nor Bridget had expected that. "What makes you think they made up?"

"Just as I said, sir. He had his arm around her. They kissed. She smiled up at him like he was the sun and the moon," Erasmus explained. "They left together, sir."

It was the last thing they had expected to hear.

* * *

BOTH Mr. Gold and Bridget were quiet on the way home, mulling over the surprises of the day.

"Do you think we'll be arrested?" Bridget asked.

Bridget always amazed him. "I wouldn't' think so, Bridget. There has to be someone on the police department who will realize that those two have been dead quite some time, whereas we just showed up a couple of hours ago."

"I hope you're right, sir. The Metropolitans aren't known for thinking things through. But aside from us, this doesn't add up. If Katherine and your son did make up, there'd be no need for her father to kill Seth, now would there? And sure that's no reason for someone to kill Mr. O'Sullivan, and Katherine, too."

"You're right about that, Bridget. We're back where we started, only there are two more dead bodies."

The carriage pulled up at the back door of the house. "I've got to get back to work, Mr. Gold. It's already four. I'll be lucky if Chef doesn't make me wash dishes. But I'll be thinkin' about what we learned, or didn't learn," she said as she jumped out of the carriage.

Bridget hurried into the kitchen, trading her cape for her apron, which she'd left on a hook in the downstairs dining room.

Chef and Gilbert, and everyone else, were puzzled by Bridget's frequent absences. They'd all talked about it at lunch. Mr. Fleming, who was very strict about such things, had been vague about Bridget's reason for going off with the boss. But he had been clear that it was not optional behavior, that Bridget must follow Mr. Gold's orders.

At first Chef and the rest of the staff wondered if Bridget

was Mr. Gold's girlfriend, planted in the kitchen so Mrs. Gold wouldn't realize they were carrying on. But Bridget was a good cook and had carried her weight during the mourning period despite having to go on these "errands." They didn't think she would be so competent and hard-working if she was just a plant. Mary Martha swore she'd grown up in the orphanage with her; that she was a professional cook but she was also helping Mr. Gold solve Seth's murder. They thought Mary Martha was exaggerating about Bridget's helpfulness, but this made as much sense as the theory of Bridget and Mr. Gold being involved romantically.

The jury was still out on Bridget, but as long as she worked hard to keep up her end, the rest of the staff, from Mr. Fleming to Justin to Chef, was satisfied. And Mary Martha had been right about those potato rolls. They were delicious.

The Gold household, like much of New York, was in a transition period about their meals. All over the city, the noonday meal had been designated "dinner" for years, and was the largest meal of the day. Men came home from work, stores closed, and children left school to eat dinner. Evening food was usually leftovers of the noon meal and had been called "supper." But the war had strained the labor pool, made working hours longer, and many folks didn't get enough time off midday to go home. This had turned dinner into lunch in some parts of the city, where it was just a quick meal to sustain a man or woman through the afternoon. Additionally, the upper crust seemed to be taking on a new idea of entertaining friends at home for the evening meal. So, working folks kept the habits of eating dinner and supper—unless they didn't receive enough time off to go home for the midday meal, and had to eat lunch on the run from a saloon or an oyster cart. Rich folks had adopted lunch and dinner as their meals.

In the Gold household, these changing habits translated into different meals upstairs and downstairs. When life was normal, Mr. Gold and Seth rarely came home for lunch. Mrs. Gold entertained her lady friends for lunch, or went out to one of their houses to eat. The household staff ate their largest meal at one or two, after they had served upstairs, earlier if no one was at home.

The nighttime meal was dinner at the Golds', the main meal of the day whether there was company or not. Benjamin and his wife came to dinner often, and Miss Rose, when she was in town, always seemed to have a houseguest. The staff ate a supper of leftovers from the Golds' table most of the time, or something made from their own noontime dinner. It was an efficient way to use all the food they purchased and cooked.

TONIGHT the Golds were having roast duck, a favorite of Mr. Gold's and a great deal of work for Mr. Fleming. He had to present the ducks on a great platter with a fig and port sauce on the side and fresh figs artfully garnishing the patter. Then he had to take the whole thing to the sideboard and carve the ducks, which meant slicing some breast meat off and topping it with the sauce. Mr. Gold usually asked for a leg as well so Mr. Fleming would have to try to gracefully carve one off, not that easy to do in the dining room when you can't grab ahold of the bird with your hands.

But the staff loved duck nights because there was a lot of meat left on the carcasses and they had a grand supper with them. Bridget had made Brussels sprouts the way she'd learned from an Italian woman at the market near the boardinghouse. She blanched the sprouts, then pulled apart the leaves, sautéing them in butter with chestnuts she sent Harvey down the street to buy from a street vendor. They went well with the duck. Even Chef gave her a compliment on them and said he wanted to serve them upstairs sometime soon.

Bridget knew she had to tell them now. It would be in the newspapers tomorrow and they had worked with Katherine, knew her, cared for her even if they disapproved of her actions. But she put it off until they were almost done with their meal and Mr. Fleming was talking about cleaning projects for tomorrow. Lord knows, they wouldn't have an appetite after she got done with them. She'd barely touched her food.

"I've got some bad news," she said.

The worst moment of telling bad news is the one before you spill the beans, when everyone is imagining what you're going to say, their own fears taking over their mind for a minute. Bridget saw that in the faces of these good people. She ducked her head so as not to make eye contact and hurried on. "Mr. Gold and I found Katherine and her da today," and the table was immediately in an uproar, everyone asking a question, their eyes bright and shining again. Bridget took a deep breath. "I'm so sorry to tell ya, but they were shot dead, like Master Seth."

Those around the table stopped talking and moving, frozen in an eerie tableau. The look of fear reappeared in their eyes. Bridget wished she could say something that would banish the thoughts she saw flitting around from

Sally to Karol to Mr. Fleming, thoughts that she was sure had a shape and form to them, a big negative cloud, but that was impossible. She was scared and unsure, too.

In a moment the questions started again and Bridget did her best to answer them. Finally Mary Martha, with tears in her eyes from the shock of it all, said, "Will ya tell them, Bridget, so as we all know, why Mr. Gold has been askin' you to go around places for him?"

Bridget shrugged. "It's not because I'm so smart or good at talkin'," she said modestly. "It's because I'm Irish and I'm someone Katherine didn't ever lay eyes on. Back when he was thinkin' she, Katherine, got her da to kill Master Seth, she not layin' eyes on me was a plus. I could ask about her in the neighborhood and she wouldn't spot me for someone from the Golds'."

That seemed to pacify this group. They went on to imagine what set of circumstances would lead to the death of both a member of the Gold family and also Katherine and her father. Shortly they all had to get up and resume their duties and Bridget went in the kitchen to roast some bones for Chef. He was making stock tomorrow. As she struggled with a baking sheet full of bones, carrots, celery, and onions, trying to open the oven door and not drop the whole heavy thing, she heard a tap on the kitchen window.

Michael Murphy was squatting down, his face up against the window. When he saw Bridget, he smiled and motioned for her to come outside. Bridget looked around the kitchen. Gilbert and Chef were in the pantry. Elsie and Harvey were washing the dishes. No one was paying her any mind. She shoved the bones in the oven and headed down the hall. When she opened the door, she put a kitchen towel between the door and the locking mechanism and pulled it almost shut. That way she would be able to get back in without bothering Justin, or him knowing she was sneaking out.

Murphy was waiting for her in the shadows. "Murphy, what do ye want?" Bridget barked. "You'll get me in trouble for sure. You heard Mr. Gold."

"I knew I should have tailed you two today. I don't know why I didn't follow my instincts. Every newspaper reporter in the city will be out here in the morning so just tell me about it, please."

"I cannot talk to any reporters; you know better than that. Go away."

"Bridget, you could have got yourself killed, just like the O'Sullivans. What are you doing traipsing all over town with this man? I thought you were a cook."

Bridget's eyes flared with anger. "The reasons I'm helping Mr. Gold are none of your business, Mr. Murphy. Why don't you go down there to the stinking hole on Mott Street and poke around?"

"I've already been there. The police are very interested in you and your boss as the murderers, did you know that? They have some theory that Katherine was responsible for Seth Gold's death and now she and her father have been killed in some kind of revenge slaying. And you know who will hang if they continue to go down that road, don't you? It won't be the rich merchant, Isaac Gold. It'll be the poor Irish cook, Bridget Heaney."

"Well, then, we will have to find the real killers, won't we, Murphy?" Bridget snapped and turned to go back in the house.

She ran right into Justin, who had come outside to see

why the door was open a slit. When he realized who was out in the dark, he decided to listen in. Now he bowed his head slightly at Bridget, then turned his scornful glance on Murphy.

"Justin, Murphy was banging on the kitchen window so I came out to chase him off," Bridget said defensively.

"It sounds like Mr. Murphy is trying to scare you into telling him some nonsense that he can print, Bridget. Congratulations to you for not succumbing to his meager charms," Justin said as he moved swiftly over to Murphy and picked him up by his lapels. Murphy's shoes were flapping in the air as he tried to regain purchase on the ground. "You are tiresome, young man. And rather like a dog with a bone, unwilling to let go. If you like your fingers unbroken and able to hold a pencil, please leave now."

Murphy tried to retreat with a modicum of dignity. He backed up a couple of steps and tipped his hat toward Bridget, then turned and hurried away down the drive.

They stood there watching until he hit Thirty-Fourth Street, then Justin and Bridget slipped inside. She was sure Justin was going to call her down so she paused to get her scolding.

"Bridget, it concerns me what Mr. Murphy said about you and Mr. Gold. A police investigation is never good, I've observed. Is there any danger that either of you could be implicated?"

"Not if the coppers realize that Katherine and her da were killed long before we arrived on the scene."

Justin shook his head. "This is dangerous business, Bridget. Mr. Gold would never let you take blame for something you didn't do, but Murphy is right about one thing. A rich merchant or an Irish cook? Which one is more likely to see the rope?" He turned back to his office. "Be careful. And don't leave the door open again."

Try as she might, Bridget wasn't worried like she knew she should be. She finished up her prep, taking the roasted bones out of the oven and storing them in the icebox plus making the dough for cinnamon rolls, then went up to bed an hour or so after everyone else.

Her mind was on something else, or someone else. Michael Murphy. He sounded like he was concerned about her, maybe even liked her a bit. Bridget was smiling as she drifted off.

CHAPTER TWELVE

BRIDGET heard them before she could see them. Two women were crying and Mr. Gold was yelling, or at least talking loud.

Bridget rushed downstairs from her room to the second floor and peered over the stair rail. In the entry hall, Mrs. Simon, Mr. and Mrs. Gold, and Mr. Fleming were standing, or the first three were standing and Mr. Fleming was working, piling up a stack of luggage and boxes.

"How could you do this to me?" Mrs. Gold shrieked.

"Easily," Mrs. Simon snapped. "You said you wanted to throw me out years ago, the day my sister was killed. Now I'm going. I won't even inquire as to the reason you think my brother-in-law would have allowed such action back then."

Mr. Gold reacted. "And I would *not* have allowed such a thing to take place. Estella has forgotten that she was in no position to order anyone around at that time. You cannot go, Mrs. Simon. I will not hear of it. You have been a member of this family and household for many years. I wouldn't let my son or daughter wander off without my guidance as to where they were going. I won't let you."

Mrs. Simon bristled. "I am a grown woman not requiring a keeper, thank you very much. I've worked like a dog for Mrs. Gold for years now and received little praise or thanks for it. I appreciate what you did for me when Herman died but I have paid for my room and board many times over. I am not honoring my husband's memory by staying here another day. He would not want me to do what I do."

"What do you mean by that?" Mrs. Gold said, holding on to her husband.

"Some things are obvious," Mrs. Simon said and she grabbed a carpetbag and walked out.

Mr. Gold knew better than to argue with an angry woman when her mind was made up. He turned toward his butler. "Mr. Fleming, go with her and see her to her new lodgings. Do you happen to know where she is moving, by the way?" Mr. Gold looked like he was going to split a gut, Bridget thought as she watched from up above.

"No, I do not, sir," Mr. Fleming said formally.

"Are you sure you didn't know about this, Isaac?" Mrs. Gold asked. Her fingernails were digging into Mr. Gold's wrist.

"Mrs. Gold, if you want to discuss this further, let us do it upstairs in your dressing room," Mr. Gold said. His tone was smooth and icy. Bridget had never heard that tone of voice from him before. She felt as if she were listening to a stranger.

Katie and Karol came up the back stairs talking a mile a minute, unaware another drama was unfolding. They looked

at Bridget, question in their eyes. Bridget shook herself out of
the spell that the Golds had cast, them and Mrs. Simon. She
went down the stairs the girls had just come up, ignoring
their inquiring eyes, eager for the simplicity of the kitchen.

What a consolation cooking was for her. Cooking was
hard enough physical work to make you aware of your body,
that you were alive. It was also creative enough to satisfy
your soul. Bridget wasn't sure what a soul needed, not trusting a priest to tell her or having much time to think about it
herself. But she honestly felt that making food was like religion to her. You did it and felt like a better person afterward.

For the rest of the morning Bridget cooked, first making
biscuits and waffles, then working up a beautiful chicken
salad for lunch. She thought about her own precarious position with the police and Mr. Gold's position as well. Then she
tried to guess what had really happened this morning to drive
Mrs. Simon out the door. How would she live, and where?

Justin strode through the kitchen, looking to talk to
Chef about some wine invoices he had folded in his hands.
He saw Bridget deep in thought, the edges of her mouth
turning down slightly. He paused and went over to her
worktable. "A penny for your thoughts, young lady."

Bridget was glad to see him. "What will become of Mrs.
Simon, Justin? I heard the dustup in the hall this morning.
What happened to send her out on her own like that?"

"I think she made a decision about her life when she and
Mrs. Gold had that flap last week. Sometimes you just get
to the point you can't take it anymore, whatever 'it' is in
your particular case. In Mrs. Simon's case it was that unpleasant scene during Shiva for Seth. She waited until the
Shiva was over to leave, out of respect to her nephew. And as
for what will happen, I would be very surprised if Mr. Gold

did not pay her living expenses quietly through the store."

Bridget was relieved to hear that. "I knew he wouldn't let her go for wont, her being his sister-in-law. Mr. Gold has a good heart, and he can afford it, can't he?"

Justin smiled thinly. "Both of those things are true. He does have a good heart and he can afford it. Now may I ask you something?"

Bridget knew what was coming. More questions about her finding all the bodies. "Tit for tat," she said.

"As you have the most information and firsthand experience, what is your opinion on these tragedies that have befallen our house?"

Bridget couldn't help being pleased. Justin was asking her opinion on something and he seemed to be doing it just as serious as could be. "Well, sir, the fella at the factory, Erasmus, I think it was, said Miss Katherine came down there to see Master Seth the day before he died and they made up and was all lovey-dovey."

"You went to the factory?"

"After the tenement. There was a piece of paper with the factory address on it so we went over to see what was what. Didn't find out enough."

"So Katherine runs away from her new employers, Mr. Gold's cousins, on the way to Washington. She shows back up at the factory to confront Master Seth and they reconcile. Then what?" Justin asked.

"I think she and Seth were to meet here at the house or the factory the night Seth was killed and she saw something. She either saw the murder or saw who was bringing the body here to dump it. She found her daddy and together they trumped up a scheme of some kind that got them killed. The bartender at The Spotted Pig told me they were in there that night with a blond, blue-eyed fella and they all three left together. Next thing that happens, they're dead."

"Yes, that would make sense. But then we don't know who this fellow is or why he killed Master Seth in the first place or if he did."

Bridget had never been good at holding anything back. Since she couldn't talk to Mr. Gold about this, Justin was another smart person whom she respected. "No, we don't, sir. But there's another idea I had. It's just terrible, but I had it anyways."

Justin tilted his head and looked expectantly at Bridget. "Would it help to talk about it?"

"Well, on that first night, when you weren't back yet but Mrs. Gold was, I heard her yelling at Mr. Gold that she would rather see Seth dead than with that tramp. What if she meant it?"

Justin held up a finger to his lips. "Shhh. We can't even consider that. Mrs. Gold was in the country, remember?" Just then Chef came out of the icebox and Justin gave Bridget a look and went on about his business, talking to Chef about the wine orders and such. Bridget could hear them talking about normal household things. She was thinking about the look Justin had given her. It was a warning; she was sure of that. She must put that theory in the back of her head and keep it there.

But she could see it happening. Mrs. Gold comes back to town and goes directly down to the factory to talk some sense into Seth. Mrs. Gold and Seth have a big fight. Lord knows the woman has a temper. She shoots Seth and goes back to the country. All this at an hour when Erasmus and the seamstresses weren't around.

Bridget had to laugh to herself. A combination of a little

knowledge and a lot of imagination was what she had always relied on. Sometimes she couldn't even sell herself on her wild theories. Bridget knew that she hadn't met Mrs. Gold at the best time to gather a true opinion of her. If Mr. Gold liked her, there must be something more to her than the spoiled brat Bridget had seen.

And certainly ladies like Mrs. Gold didn't have to resort to murder to solve a silly family problem. That was the kind of violent thinking Bridget had been brought up around; it wouldn't be for ladies like Mrs. Gold.

Still, Bridget had heard Mrs. Gold say ugly things to Mr. Gold, and she had sounded very sincere at the time.

Bridget marveled at how you were judged by the things that you said. Here Bridget was stuck with the impression that Mrs. Gold had made on her, that she was a hateful, spiteful woman. And Mrs. Gold was stuck with Bridget's impression of her that she didn't even know about. Words sure were important. Once they were out of your mouth, you had no idea what trouble they could cause, or good for that matter.

Bridget worked busily for a few hours, her imagination concocting various possible scenarios that could solve all the murders in a nice neat package. When both Mr. Fleming and Justin turned up in the kitchen, she was jolted out of her own mind and back to the world around her.

"There's a Sergeant O'Malley with another officer to talk to you and Mr. Gold. Of course, Mr. Gold isn't here and so I sent Harvey to fetch him at the store. I felt it would be better if they didn't go interrupting him there. The gents say they'll talk to you first," Mr. Fleming said in a harried tone of voice. Would things never get back to normal?

Bridget couldn't move. She stood looking at the dough

on her hands. Finally she walked silently over to the sink to wash up.

"THIS here's Sergeant Morgan. He works up in this ward and is in charge of the investigation for young Mr. Gold. Bridget, how do you suppose you're the one who found all these bodies?" Sergeant O'Malley asked. His eyes were green with glints of gold shot through them. "Cruel" was the word that popped in Bridget's mind when she looked at those eyes.

"Wrong place at the wrong time, I suppose," Bridget said, trying not to be fresh. They were sitting in the staff dining room off the kitchen, the three of them.

"Since I didn't hear your story the day you discovered the body, let's run over it now," Sergeant Morgan suggested.

Bridget shrugged. "Nobody heard my story because no one asked me nothing straight to my face. I guess Mr. Fleming said a cook found the body and they were done with it," she said a tad defensively, then realized pointing up the weak detecting procedures of men who worked for Sergeant Morgan was not a way to start the interview. "It was my first day to work here. I was making bread and I went to put the dough in to rise." She pointed in the direction of the dry goods room. "He was in there, his body that is, in the dough box. I told Mr. Fleming and Chef. That's it."

"If it was your first day, how did you know who it was?"

"They all had talked about how Master Seth was gone missing. He looks like his father. I guessed it was him. All I knew for sure was that there was a dead person in the dough box where he didn't belong."

"And since then, you've become quite the little helper to Mr. Gold, haven't you, Bridget?" Sergeant O'Malley asked.

"I work for him."

"I bet you do. Why do you think he asked you to go downtown looking for a girl you never met?"

"That's why. Because she'd never seen me. Mr. Gold was thinking that Katherine had something to do with Seth's death at that time. He wanted a stranger and an Irish one if possible. That was me."

"Sounds like your boss was out for blood," Sergeant Morgan observed.

"My boss wanted to find out who killed his son. He did what he thought best," Bridget said, knowing how uppity it was of her to speak for her boss but not being able to stop herself.

"And that was to set a cook out on the streets of Five Points searching for a woman he'd sent out of town. Doesn't make sense."

"None of it does. Turns out she wasn't out of town. She ran off and came back here to New York and got herself killed."

"Yes, she did. Did she get killed because you found her for your boss, told him where she was, and then led him right to her plus her old man?" O'Malley challenged.

"I'm sure you could tell an old corpse from a new one. Those bodies weren't freshly shot," Bridget parried.

"You two could have easily slipped up there, killed them, then returned because you forgot something, like a piece of paper with an address. That particular tenant building isn't like the Astor Hotel, where the comings and goings are monitered."

"You really think us fools, do ye? That we'd be so proud as to think we could kill two human beings then sashay back in the next day to tidy up?" Bridget tossed back at them. A slight quiver had developed in her voice.

Mr. Gold stepped in the room, angry and flush. "Officers, what is going on here?"

"Sit down, Mr. Gold, we were just talking to Bridget about how she keeps finding dead bodies. And why a cook like her would be out and about with an important man such as yourself," Sergeant Morgan said. "By the way, I'm Sergeant Morgan. I'm working on your son's murder."

Mr. Gold put down a stack of newspapers he had under his arm. Bridget could see the top one had a headline about Katherine and her father. REVENGE KILLINGS IN FIVE POINTS? it said. "I would prefer to talk to you upstairs in my library and for you to let Miss Heaney get back to her duties. I can assure you she did nothing but assist me on a line of inquiry that was my idea from start to finish."

"You happen to have a cook who knows that neighborhood well," Sergeant O'Malley said, malice getting the better of his thin veneer of good manners. "I thought I remembered the name 'Bridget Heaney.' I asked around the station, and she and her sister Maggie were some of the best little thieves in Five Points. Maggie either flirted or played innocent and Bridget here emptied their pockets." The two officers stood up. "I'd watch me silver if I was you," he said to Mr. Gold.

"Miss Heaney has proved her trustworthiness to this house. Please follow me," Mr. Gold said severely with just a tiny glance toward Bridget as the men went up to the library.

Bridget sank back down in a chair. Her cheeks were burning, on fire with shame. O'Malley was just downright mean. He could have brought up her past to shake her up at the beginning of the conversation, but he'd waited until Mr. Gold was there to hear it as well.

The coppers always tried to get the ones on the same team fighting against each other. They used to do that with her and Maggie: try to get one to tell where they kept their stash or accuse the other sister for some type of crime such as selling dope or child sex. Bridget and her sister never went for that, committing other crimes or the confessin'. They never gave up their hiding place and they never got sent away, until the city passed that law about you couldn't stay by yourself younger than fifteen. In fact, Bridget couldn't remember a time when they had been caught in the act. The most that happened: a mark would accuse them, would be sure they had lifted his wallet or her purse, but no one had ever proved it by finding the lost merchandise on the girls.

Bridget pulled the newspapers over in front of her and looked at the front-page stories about Katherine and some about herself, too, hinting that she was a paid assassin or worse. The most shocking coverage was a photograph of the dead bodies on the second page of the *Herald*. She guessed even that rag, couldn't put dead bodies on the front page. She anxiously shuffled through to find the *Recorder*. WAR PHOTOGRAPHER'S FAMILY SLAIN was the headline with a byline by Michael Murphy. Bridget couldn't help but smile a little. Murphy had slanted his story away from Bridget and Mr. Gold and toward the fact that Katherine's brother was a well-known photographer who wouldn't even be able to bury his father and sister because he was off at war, not being shot at like most Irish, but at war nonetheless.

Mr. Fleming hurried into the dining room to retrieve the newspapers. Bridget gave them over and stood up. "Sorry, I got distracted by these, sir. There's something I need to tell ya."

Mr. Fleming was impatient with this latest bother. "More bad news?"

"The coppers spotted me as a lifter when I was a kid. My

sister and I picked pockets to stay alive. That's a fact. They told Mr. Gold."

Mr. Fleming brushed it off. "We all have a past. Do you think I'd be working here in New York instead of Boston if I didn't have one?" He took the papers and hurried away.

IT was late but Bridget didn't want to leave the kitchen. She made up some bread dough and put it in the icebox until morning to bake. She made some dumpling dough and cooked a couple of chickens that needed to be used up. She strained the broth and picked the meat off the bones, storing them separately. Tomorrow they could have chicken and dumplings for lunch in a jiffy.

Lunch today had been a chaotic affair, what with the police questioning Mr. Gold and Bridget plus Mrs. Simon moving without telling anyone beforehand. The staff couldn't decide on a topic, jumping back and forth between the two rather grand incidents every other sentence. Bridget did her best to seem unconcerned with one and noncommittal about the other. "Mr. Gold won't let Mrs. Simon starve or him and me go to jail," was her standard retort.

Bridget was marking time, avoiding bed. Her mind was so full she couldn't possibly sleep. She'd expected a call to go up and talk to Mr. Gold but it hadn't come. Dinner was over upstairs, and supper down.

As she cleaned up her workspace, Bridget succumbed to out-and-out despair for a few minutes. She imagined Mr. Gold was furious with her for not telling him she used to make her living as a pickpocket, even though he had been kind about it. Worse yet would be if Mr. Gold were not furious, just disappointed in her for not telling him this. She couldn't blame him for either; sure there was many a time in this city where a good-for-nothing was hired by a family to help and ended up hurting them instead.

The police had to find out the answers to three killings and she was the closest thing to a criminal involved. She felt herself losing her grip on a life that was turning out to be too good to be true. Bridget lowered the gaslights in the kitchen and went up to face a sleepless night. As she climbed the back stairs, Mr. Gold came out of his library. "Bridget, come in for a minute. I know it's late but I brought home some work from the store, and the next thing I knew, it was eleven. Are you just getting through?"

Bridget wanted to dance down the hall. He sounded normal. "Oh, yes, sir, I was just doing a little ahead to get ready for tomorrow," she said as she went down the hall and into the library.

Mr. Gold indicated she should sit in the same leather chair as before, and this time she didn't even feel guilty. She patted it a little on the armrests. "What did the police say?"

Mr. Gold frowned. "They asked me the same questions I assume they asked you, why were you and I down there, what did Katherine have to do with Seth, why was she leaving our service, why did I send her out of town, why did she run away and come back to New York, so many things I don't know the answer to."

"Sir, I would like to talk to you about what the police said about me and my sister. Of course, your son's death is more important, but I have to tell you the truth."

"Please."

"It's true, it is. We were pickpockets, sneak thieves, whatever you call it. We usually took money and jewelry off folks, but if we got the chance, we would take things out of people's homes, too."

"And did you get arrested?"

"Brought in, yes. Arrested and found guilty in court, no. They never found any goods on us. We had a smart hiding place. When we took something, I made for our stash place as fast as I could, dropped the goods off, then picked them up later."

Mr. Gold smiled. "I wouldn't have expected you to be sloppy. Was this before or after the orphanage?"

Bridget was shocked. Did he think she'd picked pockets as a grown-up? "Oh, before, when we were little and living alone. I wasn't exactly truthful about our father, sir. He wasn't much of a provider at his best. When we came to America and my ma died on the way, after that we saw him very little. Da got us a room for a few months, did some day work, then didn't come home for two weeks. That first time when he came back, he paid the rent for another month. We didn't see him for three months after that. We were able to keep the apartment by doing, you know, stealing. When the landlord came around, we'd give him the rent, tell him it was from da. Da showed up one day and stayed home for four months. We were thrilled. He tried, but more and more we, Maggie and me, was making the lion's share of our expenses and he just took it for drink. He up and left again and we didn't see him for six months. Ran into him on the street and he was all ashamed with a million excuses. I wanted to pick his pocket but Maggie said why risk it when he wouldn't have a dime," Bridget blurted out, ending with a chuckle that sounded more like a sob.

"What a sad story," Mr. Gold said, ignoring Bridget's attempt to treat the sordid story lightly. "Too many Irish

immigrated at the same time and none of you were in physical or financial condition to do so. Our city just couldn't
support all of you with jobs."

"And most of us Irish were poor country folks, all of a
sudden in the midst of this big, bustling city."

"Well, I'm sorry you had to exist in such a way, Bridget."

"There was worse that others had to put up with, sir."

"Now I understand why we need to find your sister. She's
your only family and she was your partner in crime, so to
speak. It must have created a very deep bond. If you survived
that terrible time, I bet she's still alive somewhere. I have
good instincts about these things. We'll start tomorrow."

"Mr. Gold, I did not mean to . . . I did not mean to mis-
lead you by not telling you about Maggie and me."

"You were eleven years old, a child for heaven's sake. The
fact that you paid your own rent is remarkable. And Chef
and Mr. Fleming are very pleased with your work. So am I. I
apologize for the implications about you and me that some
of the newspaper reports printed."

Before Bridget could reply, the door to the library flew
open and Mrs. Gold entered. "My, my. You two have been
busy, haven't you?" She held the batch of newspapers in her
hand. "Isaac, may I speak to you, please?" She turned her head
toward Bridget for the first time. "Isn't it a little late to be up
for someone who must prepare breakfast?"

Bridget got up and made it to the door in one move-
ment. "You are right, Mrs. Gold. Good night then, sir," she
said as she stepped out into the hall.

He was in for it now, Bridget thought as she went up
to bed.

CHAPTER THIRTEEN

"Mrs. Gold wants to see you," Mr. Fleming said ominously. He rolled his eyes but gave Bridget no other clue. "In her morning room," he said by way of instructions and hurried out of the kitchen as fast as he'd hurried in.

"Chef, the missus wants to see me," she called. Chef looked up and smiled, then said something to Gilbert in French. Bridget could tell they were amused by the possibility of Mrs. Gold letting loose on Bridget. It wasn't that they especially wanted any bad to come to her; they certainly didn't want her fired as she had really picked up the slack in the kitchen. But surely she deserved a small amount of grief for lollygagging all around New York City with Mr. Gold.

Chef and Gilbert were picking three wild turkeys that had been delivered that morning. Mr. Gold had insisted they stay in town for Thanksgiving, which was coming up in three days. Mrs. Gold had pouted about that but Mr. Gold was adamant. They were still in the thirty-day period of mourning. There were to be no parties or celebrations and so they would stay home and have only the family to Thanksgiving dinner.

Bridget ran up to the second floor, hoping to catch Mary Martha around somewhere before she went in to see Mrs. Gold. Mary Martha would know what mood she was in. The hall was empty so Bridget had nothing left to do but knock on Mrs. Gold's "morning room" door.

"Come in, Bridget," Mrs. Gold said, sounding friendlier than Bridget had expected.

Bridget opened the door and then walked into the room just a few steps. "Mr. Fleming said you wanted to see me, ma'am," Bridget said demurely, her head down. I'll play the cowed puppy, I will, she said to herself.

Mrs. Gold was reclining on her chaise lounge, noisily leafing through the newspapers. She didn't stop or look up. "Bridget, as you know, Mrs. Simon has left our employ. Mr. Gold tells me you are very good at running errands, so I am offering you the position of my secretary."

Bridget couldn't believe her ears. It was a trick, but she was already in the middle of it. There wasn't a thing she could do now. "Thank you so much, ma'am, for asking me. I am sure that this is a real compliment. But I can't accept because I am a cook. It's what I love doing. It's my calling, I guess. I wouldn't be good at anything else."

Mrs. Gold threw the papers on the floor and stood up, her attention suddenly all on Bridget. "Then, if you are destined to be a cook, perhaps you should do that and stop running around with Mr. Gold on this ridiculous, unrealistic quest of his. This is New York City, for God's sake. Unless someone is caught in the act, crimes go unsolved, as will Seth's murder. The sooner Isaac gets that through his head, the sooner he will be able to heal. I'm sure you want the best for Mr. Gold. So now that you have declared your rightful place is the kitchen, stay there."

Mrs. Gold was good, Bridget gave her that. Not only had she made it impossible for Bridget to investigate Seth's murder, she was also unknowingly messing up Bridget's chance to have help in finding Maggie. "Yes, ma'am," Bridget murmured and left the room.

Mr. Fleming was standing there in the hall with a list in his hands. He looked at her with a terse smile. Bridget supposed he had heard their conversation or knew ahead of time what was going to happen. "We're having your Brussels sprouts upstairs on Thursday, you'll be glad to know. Now take this list, which I would normally give to Harvey, and go shopping. One of your stops is Gold's Department Store. Mr. Gold wants to talk to you."

Mr. Fleming was trying for stern and cross in his attitude. He was about out of patience with everyone in this household but it really wasn't Bridget's fault. She was only a pawn in the Golds' marital chess game, so he relented and gave her one roll of the eyes toward Mrs. Gold's room. "Don't worry. Harvey couldn't have done the shopping for this. It's Thanksgiving and we require some special ingredients. A cook should go. But under the circumstances, you should use a hack, not Johnny. If the missus wants the carriage and you're in it, heads will roll," he said. He gave her the list and a wad of money, and turned away.

Bridget sat mooning in the carriage, fiddling with one of her boots. Her feet already hurt and she had lots of walking to do. It wasn't as enjoyable traveling without Mr. Gold.

She felt a devastating sense of loss over this that she hadn't expected. The thought that they wouldn't be able to continue their investigation of Seth's death, or start one for Maggie's life, was just awful. When she arrived at Gold's, her first stop, she wondered what to do. She shouldn't have been concerned. Manager Don spotted her right away from the mezzanine and hurried over.

"I was up there watching for you," he said, indicating the balcony where people could watch the main floor of the store. "Mr. Gold wants to speak to you. But first we have to get you some new boots. 'Get her out of those abominations before she breaks her leg' were his exact words."

Bridget didn't even argue. She knew the manager would follow Mr. Gold's instructions and her boots were uncomfortable. She briefly wondered what the man thought about the free cape and new shoes Bridget received as a job bonus. But then, the newspapers had painted a picture of Mr. Gold and Bridget that, if not inferring a sexual relationship, certainly painted one of a partnership of some sort. She was stuck with it. She might as well have shoes that fit.

When Bridget walked into Mr. Gold's office twenty minutes later, she felt as if she was dancing on air.

The man in the shoe department asked her what kind of work she did, then was back in a jiffy with three different pairs of shoes and boots. Bridget chose ankle boots in soft black leather with a squat heel.

"Bridget, here's where I spend most of my time. Please come in," Mr. Gold said from the open door of a frosted glass box of an office in the middle of a large room with men and women sitting at desks writing in ledgers. The walls didn't go up to the ceiling, just up far enough so he could talk in privacy. Bridget guessed you didn't want anyone to hear you fire someone, or at least a nice man like Mr. Gold wouldn't.

"You have women working here as clerks?" Bridget asked in wonder.

"Yes, we've found that they are excellent employees. However, there is resistance to having them on the floor, with the exception of alterations and seamstresses. I'm sure sooner or later women will be salespersons at Gold's. These things take time."

There was a wooden chair with a back and a leather seat. Mr. Gold indicated Bridget should sit down and she did. "Mrs. Gold asked me to be her new secretary," she blurted out.

Mr. Gold tilted his head and looked resigned. "And what did you say?"

"That I was a cook and cooking was my calling. I don't know why Mrs. Gold would want me to work for her. She doesn't even like me."

"Mrs. Gold was embarrassed by the amount of press you and I received for finding the bodies of Katherine and her father. She felt it made her lose face, that you were out in the carriage helping me, instead of her. I can assure you, though, that she would have declined had I asked her! So she devised a way to make it difficult for us to continue our work. I assume she said if you didn't want to work for her, then perhaps you should stay in the kitchen, cooking?"

"Yes, sir, something like that."

"Bridget, we will continue. You are just going to have to do some things on your own. I will help you as much as I can, but you'll have to do most of the legwork by yourself. Can you do that?"

"Yes, sir."

"Today I think it prudent if we don't stir up the muddy waters of my son's investigation or the O'Sullivans'. Let the Metropolitans have a chance to find someone other than us to blame. Today you begin looking in earnest for Maggie Heaney. I have already sent a messenger down to City Hall and received a reply. A friend of mine runs the Hall of Records. Now, this will be difficult for you, and I wish I could be there to help. You must go through the death certificates today, Bridget. It is the first thing we want to cross off the list."

Bridget felt a little queasy. "Yes, sir. But what if Maggie didn't have any identification? What if her body was just tossed in the river or some such?"

Mr. Gold looked at Bridget sternly. "I heard all the love in your heart and soul when you talked about your sister last night. You must be brave. We can never be one hundred percent certain that she didn't die an anonymous death. But what we will know today is that in the official deaths recorded in New York City, either she will or will not be listed. That is more than we know now."

"I guess I'm a little scared," Bridget admitted.

"Of course. That is natural. Remember, I have faced death before, when my first wife was killed. You will survive. What I have done is asked my friend to bring out the letter H death certificates for the last five years. Does your sister have any scars that would be noted?"

"Yes, sir, she has a long scar on the inside of her upper right arm. When we were on the ship, she slipped on a ladder and it had a nail sticking out that caught her arm. It never healed up right. She never liked to show her arms."

"Very good. I also told him to bring out the anonymous death certificates of young females for the last five years.

That scar surely would be noted as an identifying mark. Can you do this, Bridget?"

Bridget had asked for help. Mr. Gold had the connections; now she had to use them. She got up. "I can do this, sir. It will be easier in my new boots, which I thank you for. Mr. Fleming sent me to do the shopping for Thanksgiving as well. Can I stop by to tell you what happens at City Hall?"

Mr. Gold shook his head. "You better go on home. I'll check with you this evening."

Bridget was disappointed she couldn't report to Mr. Gold but she knew they were pushing it as it was. The shopping crowds were busy this holiday week at the food stalls. She'd have to move fast. It would be no good if she was gone more than four hours total, and one of them had past already.

By the time two hours were gone, Bridget had her food-stuffs all bought and stashed in the coldest parts of the carriage she'd hired. Now they pulled up in front of City Hall and she gave her instructions to the driver for the second time. As she went up the imposing stairs, she took a look across the street at the *Recorder* building. Michael Murphy was nowhere to be seen.

Bridget had a bit of trouble finding the office that kept the death certificates. It was down in what could be called the basement of City Hall, back in a corner filled with oak file cabinets. There were two fellas doing what she guessed she'd be doing, going through files with bored expressions.

A man with bushy sideburns came up to the front counter. "Yes?" he said in a flat tone of voice.

"Mr. Gold, the gent who owns the department store, sent me down to check on a death certificate for a Maggie Heaney?" She had decided to play it like she was Mr. Gold's personal assistant or secretary or something and tried to think how that person would talk. She decided a real secretary would feel entitled to all the information the city had.

The clerk seemed mildly irritated. It had taken him almost an hour to accumulate the files that his boss, a Mr. Wilson, had requested for this woman. But at least she'd shown up and it hadn't just been an exercise in futility. The insurance gents were bad about coming down, demanding files pulled and then not showing up again for days. And they didn't tip, though he supposed this girl wouldn't either. He opened the swinging door at the end of the counter for her and stepped aside as she walked in.

"First table. I brought you out a chair," he said and held it momentarily for Bridget. She whisked a dollar out of her skirt pocket and slipped it to him.

"Thank you, sir," she said, trying to sound as if she worked like this every day. She was disheartened by the height of the stack of the files. She knew it wouldn't be easy reading, descriptions of the cause of death had to be grim, but she plunged in, grabbing the first file off the top. Haase, Alice.

When she stood up more than an hour later, she was elated. Her sister had not been officially listed as dead in the City of New York in the last five years, nor had any Jane Does, as they called them, had a scar on the arm like Maggie's. To celebrate, she gave the clerk another fifty cents and hurried out to her hack driver.

She'd have to make up a story to cover how long she'd been gone. How about a thief at the green grocer who made them all wait for the coppers to ask them to identify the boys who'd run away with the onions? Yes, by the time she got home, she could have that tale in shape to tell. Mr. Fleming had told Chef she wouldn't be back until after lunch anyway. She'd finished up the chicken and dumplings for them early this morning.

BRIDGET was excited. She had made brioche for the first time.

Chef had helped her along, and Gilbert, too. They said it was fine to make it ahead of time. They would use it for French toast a couple of times this week and then for the dressing on Thursday. It certainly had a different texture than regular bread—that was from all the butter and eggs—but it was delicious, and Bridget was proud that she had accomplished something French. She even made two of the classic-shape brioche, the ones that looked like giant muffins with a topknot like a nipple. The rest of the dough she baked in Pullman loaves. She was covering the nipple ones with a cloth so they could be used for breakfast when Mr. Gold and Mr. Fleming stuck their heads in the kitchen. The rest of the staff had gone up to bed already.

"How did it go today at City Hall?" Mr. Gold asked.

"She wasn't there. Not in the H's or in the Jane Does. That's what they call them," Bridget said cheerfully. "Look, I made brioche for the first time. Chef said I had a nice crumb. That's the texture of the bread in the middle when you cut it." She whisked off the towel to show her work.

Both Mr. Fleming and Mr. Gold couldn't help but smile. "It looks delicious. I'm happy about the results with the death certificates. I told you I don't think she's passed away. Mr. Fleming and I are going to struggle with the accounts with Justin. Good night, then," Mr. Gold said and the two men went on down the hall.

Bridget put her brioche in the pie safe and broke off a hunk of rye bread that she'd bought at the kosher bakery today. She went into the icebox with a paring knife and sliced off a wedge of soft cheese Chef called Brie. She wrapped them both in a towel and turned down the gaslights, going up to the third floor.

Mary Martha was waiting for her in her room, reading a pocket novel, snuggled up in Bridget's bed. "Hi, Brig. It's great to come in here to read. I can't read late in with Sally, the light bothers her. I don't think Sally reads too well."

Bridget handed the bread and cheese to Mary Martha, then slipped out of her uniform and into her nightgown. She hurriedly unlaced her new boots and kicked them in the closet. She wasn't ready for Mary Martha to question her about them. In a few days they'd be scuffed up, and if she did notice them, Bridget could say she'd bought them with her first month's pay, which she didn't have yet but would soon.

"Mary Martha, I went to City Hall and went through all the death certificates and Maggie wasn't there," she said happily.

"You're kidding. What made you think of that?"

"Mr. Gold told me to go there, that it was no sense worrying when you could find out the facts. Of course, I know lots of people are killed and thrown in the river. But at least officially Maggie isn't dead."

"Oh, Brig, I'm sorry I always have been so sure Maggie was gone. I just hated seeing you so wrung out about her."

"The point of it is, I haven't been making a 'systematic investigation,' as Mr. Gold puts it. I've just been checking with the police once or twice a year and visiting bad parts of town, asking if anyone knows a Maggie Heaney. What are the chances of success with somethin' so willy-nilly as that? I have to make an effort, then we'll see."

"Well, let's just hope no death certificate means no death. Bridget, may I ask when you did see her last?"

"We'd been out of the Friendless less than a month. I was workin' at Delmonico's hard hours. We had a room in a tenement on Broom Street. Days would go by and I wouldn't see Maggie. She was wild as a stray cat. When she was home, she was asleep. I was doing it all, paying for the room, a bit of food, keepin' the place straight. One night she came home drunk, right about seven o'clock. I'd just come in the door myself and I was bone tired. There wasn't a bite to eat and the place was a wreck, clothes and bed things thrown around. I let her have it, told her she was acting just like our da. She laughed at me and said she was just like her da and all that learnin' to read and doin' numbers and cleanin' and cookin', maybe it had stuck on me but not on her. She said she'd been picking pockets and had a nice stash already and that's the life she wanted, that she'd get her own place rather than hear me whine about it."

"And then what happened?" Mary Martha said, her book forgotten on her lap.

"I said something proud, told her to go then, be a drunk like him," Bridget said. "And by glory, she left then and there. I was too mad and tired to run after her. I was so sure she wouldn't leave me, that she and I were a team forever. We had gone through so much I didn't take it serious. After two days I started to get worried, started asking folks, looking in the bars. I even run down Da at his pub. I thought maybe she'd moved in with him. He hadn't seen her nor had anyone else."

"Oh, Bridget, what a puzzle."

"Seems like we have plenty of 'em, don't it?"

"But there's one puzzle that I know and you don't," Mary Martha said proudly.

"What?"

"Where Mrs. Simon is. Mr. Fleming told at lunch."

"Well, spill it out."

"Kleindeutschland. She already had paid for a room in a German Jewish boardinghouse for ladies north of Houston. Mr. Fleming said it was real nice."

"Mrs. Simon isn't German, is she?"

"No, but she can speak Yiddish, which is some combination of German and Hebrew he said, and so do they. It seems she talked to the ladies who were here sitting with the body after she and Mrs. Gold had that flap and they recommended this place. It isn't exactly her kind of Jews. Mr. Fleming called them long names. It seems the Spanish ones and the German ones must believe somewhat different, like the Lutherans and the Church of England do. But Mr. Fleming said there aren't many of the Spanish kind even though they were here first, so Mrs. Simon has to stay with the German Jews."

"How was she, did Mr. Fleming say?"

"Sally asked if she was crying and carrying on in the carriage. Mr. Fleming said no, she was downright chipper. When they got to the place, she introduced him around and told him not to worry about her, that she should have done this years ago, that she promised herself she'd stay until her sister's children got raised and now that Seth was gone, she could leave."

"Families," Bridget sighed.

Mary Martha got up and padded to the door. "They seem a big lot of trouble when you've never had one yourself. But I wish I did," she said, waving goodnight and heading down the hall to her own bed.

CHAPTER FOURTEEN

THE Thanksgiving dinner came off without a hitch. Mr. Fleming did up some flowers, lilies that made the table look grand. Sally had washed and ironed a heavy ivory brocade tablecloth with matching napkins. The entire staff complimented her on it. Master Benjamin and his wife had come, and in accordance with the mourning period, there were no other guests. Mrs. Simon did not make an appearance. Chef had worked hard at creating an elegant meal, wanting to make up for Mr. Gold's heartache in a small way. The family sat down about two in the afternoon.

There had been oysters on the half shell, a creamy soup made of cauliflower that Chef called Madame DuBarry, a striped bass with a mushroom sauce, the turkeys, dressing from the brioche, Brussels sprouts, Potatoes Anna, which were one of Chef's specialties and were these big, puffy potato slices, squash puree, a breast of roasted veal, potato rolls, and lots of choices for desserts—cakes and pies and a pumpkin pudding that Bridget had never tasted before but took a real liking to. She'd learned a lot working with Chef and Gilbert on the meal and had contributed the Brussels sprouts, the squash, and the rolls out of her own repertoire.

Bridget was in the kitchen, transferring the vegetables from the polished silver to plain white bowls for the staff meal. In walked Benjamin Gold, his face covered in a new beard. "So, sir, you decided to grow some whiskers? Happy Thanksgiving to ya," Bridget said. She was glad to see Benjamin.

"Hi there, Bridget," Benjamin smiled and grabbed a piece of crisp turkey skin. "I can hardly wait to shave this scratchy stuff off. Dad and I can't shave for thirty days. It's part of the mourning. Didn't you notice Dad's is growing longer? Now let me in on the scoop. I hear the lovely Estella offered you the privilege of serving her."

Bridget nodded. "She was upset because Mrs. Simon quit and all the newspapers were making up tales about Mr. Gold and me. I told her my place was in the kitchen."

"And I bet she told you to stay in the kitchen then?"

Bridget laughed. So did Benjamin. "You sure know how Mrs. Gold works."

"Tell me about finding Katherine."

This sobered Bridget's mood. "We went back downtown. The barkeep at the pub told us she and her da had been in and met up with a fella the day before. Then we find them both shot in her da's old room. It was a sight."

"And now you two are suspects?"

"Well, hopefully the coppers will figure out that we discovered the bodies long after they were shot. But we found a piece of paper near the bodies and it was the address of your dad's uniform factory. So we went there, and the fella down there told us that Katherine and your brother made up, left the premises lovey-dovey." Bridget gulped for air.

Benjamin looked over the leftovers. "This is big news," he said as he slathered butter on a potato roll. "Seth didn't let me in on the reconciliation."

"It happened the day before he died. He probably didn't have a chance." Bridget had an idea but the whole staff was gathering in the other room. She had to go. "Master Benjamin, I have to go to dinner. How long are you staying?"

"The ladies have retired for a nap, then we usually have leftovers for supper and I happen to know there's a surprise on the way for Dad."

"Will you stop down here before you leave? There's something I want to show you," Bridget asked, nervously edging toward the dining room while she talked, her arms full of bowls.

Benjamin took two of the bowls and walked with Bridget in where the staff was gathered. "Great meal, everyone. Leave us something for supper. Chef, the soup was superb," he said, nodded at Bridget, and waved as he left the room. "I'll be back down here for the dessert my wife won't let me have upstairs."

Sally smiled slyly. "Bridget, the Gold men can't stay away from you, can they now? Sit down so we can eat," she ordered. Everyone laughed, Bridget included.

AROUND five the back door bell rang and Justin slipped out of his office to get it. A great commotion ensued, bringing Bridget out of the kitchen to the hall. She was slicing up the turkey and the veal for the next meal. Most of the staff was still resting. The Golds weren't having supper until six or six-thirty and there was nothing new; they liked leftovers on Thanksgiving, Chef said. She had made stock with one of the turkey carcasses already, in case they needed to make soup with bits of vegetables and meat to make it all last another meal for the staff.

"Oh my goodness, Miss Rose, your father will be so happy," Justin said in his sonorous voice, the voice that Bridget was thrilled and frightened by.

So that was the surprise that Benjamin was talking about.

One day at lunch Mr. Fleming had explained that Mr. Gold had sent his daughter word of Seth's death but had instructed her to stay in Spain as her school didn't break for holiday until December, although Mr. Fleming said he could tell that he, Mr. Gold, missed her terrible through all these sad days. Justin, who sat at the table like everyone else but Harvey, had made them all laugh when he said they should thank the Lord for small blessings. Bridget got the impression that Rose was a handful.

Now she was here. Bridget's curiosity almost killed her during the rest of the evening. Those who worked the evening meal, which was definitely supper today, were all abuzz with comments about Miss Rose's chic Spanish clothes, the way her hair was done, this and that. Bridget was dying to see her in person. But she kept in her place for a change, and stayed in the kitchen until well after the staff had eaten their supper. She did dash up to the third floor once and was disappointed to not run into a single person. She had no idea what fancy clothes they wore for Thanksgiving.

There had been plenty of veal and dressing and vegetables left so Chef said to make stock with the other turkey carcass and they would have soup tomorrow. She was struggling with a stockpot full of broth, pouring it through a strainer into another stockpot, when suddenly Benjamin appeared with his sister in tow. Bridget couldn't stop what she was doing and just gape at Rose but that's what she felt like. Rose was the most gorgeous creature Bridget had ever seen.

"Hello there, Bridget, this is my sister Rose, who came home to surprise Dad. I've been filling her in on how you've been helping us try to discover Seth's murderer. She wanted to meet you. Is there any pie left?" Benjamin said.

Bridget nodded and kept her eyes on the broth. "Yes, sir, just let me get this stock transferred and I'll go fetch them for you. I saved back a piece of that chocolate torte for you as well." She stood straight now, her task complete. "I sure am glad to meet you, Miss Rose. It has been sad times here. I know you will be a balm to your father's soul."

Rose was as dark and exotic looking as Bridget was fair and, to her thinking, ordinary. She was wearing a silk dress that seemed to be burgundy red one minute and shiny silver the next. Her hair was pinned up in an elaborate chignon. She smelled good and had on beautiful red lipstick. She certainly didn't look like she'd been on a ship for two or three weeks. Of course, Bridget reasoned, her passage to America and Miss Rose's were the difference of ten years and lots of wealth. She supposed it was possible to get across that terrible ocean in comfort if you could pay for it.

Still, Bridget was impressed.

"My brother and my father, to some extent, are hard to fool. They say you are a good cook and a smart detective. I believe those are two skills a modern woman needs no matter what her career is. So I'm happy that you are here," she said and extended her hand toward Bridget.

She wants to shake my hand, of all things. What in the world? Bridget awkwardly met the hand with her own and shook it. She added a silly little half curtsy and smile so she wouldn't appear to think herself an equal. No sense in starting things off on the wrong foot.

"And I to meet you, ma'am."

"Now feed my brother his secret sweets. I'm going back to deal with Estella." With that she swept out of the kitchen leaving a delicious, sweet perfume smell behind her.

Bridget hurried into the pantry and icebox, bringing Benjamin an array of choices. He quickly filled a plate and headed for the staff dining room. "Rose is something, isn't she? Come sit with me, Bridget, while I enjoy doing something my wife wouldn't approve of, not that she isn't right. I need to lose a few pounds."

"I'll be right there, sir. I have something to show you." Bridget rushed into the dry storage room to retrieve the box. She took it into the dining room and sat down across from Benjamin. "This was in my room, which was Katherine's room before. Mary Martha said she talked about these old recipes but they're in some other language. You going to Harvard and all, I thought you might recognize some of it." While she talked, Bridget had opened the top compartment with the spices and now slid open the drawer with the recipes.

Benjamin put down his fork and pulled the box over toward him. "Italian, a sauce recipe; French, something with lamb; Ladino, a stew of beef and apricots, I think I've eaten that," he commented as he shuffled the pages.

"What's Ladino?" Bridget asked.

"It's what our ancestors spoke. It's a mixture of Spanish and Hebrew. The Sephardic Jews took the language around the world with them. Not many Jews in New York speak it. I don't, but my grandfather spoke it and wrote it. That's how I recognize it." Then he unfolded a small piece of paper and looked over at Bridget. "You don't have to have a Harvard education to recognize this one. It's from my business, not yours."

Bridget looked at the page in his hand. On it was written only one line. VERWLco 50,000. "This isn't a recipe, that's for sure."

"No, it's the abbreviation we use on the trading floor for Vermont Wool Company. Surely Katherine couldn't afford to buy fifty thousand shares of Vermont Wool Company. That would've cost a pretty penny even before the war."

"What does the war have to do with it?" Bridget asked.

"Vermont Wool Company is the company Dad buys the wool from, for the uniform material, for the Union Army. The stock has quadrupled in value since the war started."

"So what do you suppose this piece of paper with the stock abbreviation was doing in there with all the recipes?" Bridget wondered out loud. "I agree Katherine probably wasn't buying any stocks, or shares, whatever you call them, herself."

"You know, Bridget, I think you should come down to the Exchange tomorrow. I'll show you what we do and I'll also ask around about Vermont Wool. Surely someone will remember a big trade like fifty thousand shares."

"Maybe Seth bought this stock?" Bridget offered.

Benjamin shook his head. "If he knew that Gold's Department Store was going to place a big order with Vermont Wool and then bought stock ahead of that order, that's an ethical problem. Our family wants to prevent that kind of trading. I know my brother was a bit of a rounder, but he would have talked to me if he was going to do something like that. I would have put a stop to it."

"Maybe that's just the reason he didn't go to you."

Benjamin finished his pie and started in on the chocolate torte, still shaking his head. "Believe me, I would know. No other trader would touch this but if, just if, they had, they would have told me, Bridget. When you see how the trading floor works, you'll understand."

"I can't come until Saturday. That's my next day off."

"The exchange isn't open on Saturday. I'll speak to Mr. Fleming and see if you can't switch your day off this week."

"You really think this is important, don't you, sir?"

Benjamin stuck the tip of his finger in a dollop of whipped cream left on his plate and then in his mouth. He stood up. "That was even better because I snuck it. I came down here a lot and hung out in the kitchen when I was a kid. And yes, I think this stock thing might be important to finding out about Seth's death. I've got a little bit of a queasy feeling about it. And a knot in my stomach. But that could be the multiple desserts."

They walked into the kitchen, turning the gaslights down in the dining room as they left. "Then if you can square it with Mr. Fleming, I'll be there tomorrow. We know one thing. Something about this piece of paper made Katherine hide it in her most prized possession, this box. Something about it is important."

"I can see the headlines now," Benjamin called as he walked down the hall to rejoin his family upstairs. "COOK SOLVES CRIME."

Bridget couldn't help but smile. She took her box, turned down the lights, and headed up to bed.

* * *

SOMETHING about a holiday makes us feel either all filled up at the end of it, or desolate and empty. As the house settled down for the night, everyone was reflecting on the day.

Mr. Gold sat in his library, more content than he had been in he didn't know how long. His daughter and son had conspired together for her to come home. Benjamin must have telegraphed Rose as soon as they found Seth. The hole in his soul was still there, but having Rose home helped. Now if he and Estella could just reach out for each other. They had been so far apart for so long.

MRS. Gold paced around her bedroom with the lights out. She didn't want Isaac to approach her tonight so she had pretended to be asleep. Instead, a tempest blew inside her. Now that Mrs. Simon had finally left, good riddance, that loathsome daughter had popped up unannounced. She should have known Benjamin would pull something guaranteed to make his father feel better and her more irritated. She'd never been close to Benjamin; he'd been too old when she was hired. But she and Rose had had a good time once, before Rose grew into such an independent girl. Why couldn't she be shy and demure and easily controlled? Isaac had been easy to dominate for years but she could feel that bond loosening. He was not so easy anymore.

ROSE was glad to be home, of course. Her old room felt cozy and familiar. And she'd missed them all, Dad the most. But this was a serious crimp in her lessons, in the progress of her singing career. If it weren't for the fact that Dad and Benjamin would never rest until Seth's murder was solved, she wouldn't have come back to New York. She'd just have to make sure they solved this so she could go back to Spain in January.

MR. Fleming drank some Scotch whiskey in his room. Thanksgiving certainly was simpler when you couldn't have guests, although he'd have guests every night if it would bring back Seth. Not that the boy was his favorite. That would be Benjamin, then Rose. No, Seth had actually been a troublemaker, what with his constant harassing of the female staff and his dishonest ways. But it hurt him to the core when Mr. Gold hurt. The man was a prince. Thank goodness he wasn't religious. If they had to keep a kosher kitchen and such, someone else would be the butler, someone who knew about such things. Thank goodness for the New Yorkers who needed to buy a little polish by having a butler.

JUSTIN Morgan turned out the light in his office and went into his bedroom. He was glad the day was over. The food had been very good and Miss Rose surprising her father was a plus—first, because it made Isaac happy and, second, because it made Mrs. Gold furious. If this whole tragic situation allowed Isaac to see Estella for what she was, then Seth, the spoiled brat, would not have died in vain.

* * *

BRIDGET tossed and turned. When she thought of the food, she figured everything had gone pretty well. The Brussels sprouts could have used a minute more blanching, but everyone liked them. The potato rolls had been near perfect and her squash puree was better than mashed potatoes. Nothing she was ashamed of. That made it a good day, she supposed.

CHAPTER FIFTEEN

BRIDGET was busy. She'd made waffles for breakfast upstairs, heating the cast iron waffle iron on top of the coal-burning stove. They had one of each, of course, wood and coal burning, but Bridget favored the coal burning one if you needed an even heat. She'd made extra batter so she would have enough to make waffles for the staff. That's what she was doing now. At the same time she was heating up her turkey stock in a big soup pot and chopping little bits of veal and turkey left from yesterday plus some other leftovers from the Thanksgiving meal.

She'd pour the batter in the hot iron and close the lid, chop for three or four minutes, lift the waffle iron lid and fork the waffle onto a plate, then pour some more batter and go back to chopping.

"Smells good," Mr. Fleming said as he tore off a piece of waffle and nibbled at it.

"Good mornin', sir. Did Master Benjamin speak to you about changing my day off?"

"Yes, yes, he did. But Miss Rose had other ideas. She insists that she was going to ask her father if you could accompany her to visit Mrs. Simon in Germantown, since you are familiar with that part of town. When going to Wall Street was mentioned, she said that she would like to see her brother in action. She said you two would go to the Stock Exchange, then stop off at Mrs. Simon's on your way north. There was something about shopping at the store and the new ice cream parlor but I told her you had to get back to work."

Bridget, thinking of ice cream, protested. "But if it's my day off . . ."

"Oh, no. Miss Bossy Britches said these trips are part of your job so why make you use up your precious free time on family business. You still have Saturday off."

Bridget grimaced although the whole arrangement seemed very fair to her. "I bet the missus didn't like that one bit."

Mr. Fleming was already walking away, one more arrangement complete in a life of arranging. "She wasn't present. The Gold children were having a private conference with their father. Get ready for the New York Stock Exchange."

BRIDGET had to admit to herself, if to no one else, that she was excited. Here she was watching the New York Stock Exchange do whatever they did, which she wasn't clear on yet. They were on a mezzanine, like at Gold's Department Store, where you could watch the "traders" down on the "floor." Those were terms Miss Rose used when she was explaining everything to Bridget. Master Benjamin was a trader and he was down on the floor right now.

"Did you come here to visit as a child?" Bridget asked. People here seemed to know Rose Gold and treated her very deferentially.

"Yes, all the time. My grandfather was still very active here until he died of a heart attack right down there on the floor six years ago. He was eighty."

"When did your great-grandfather start all this?"

Rose waved down at her brother who had spotted them. "In 1792. He and twenty-three other brokers. He was a grown man already. My grandfather was eleven or twelve. You can tell I've been steeped in the family history, can't you?"

All of a sudden a big commotion started on the trading floor. Everyone was yelling and they were all congregated around one of the many small podiums that were placed throughout the room.

"What's wrong?" Bridget asked.

Rose laughed. Her laugh sounded like tinkling bells, really pretty ones. "Nothing. That's what happens. Someone like Benjamin, a broker, has an order for a certain stock."

"Like Vermont Wool Company?"

"Yes. Like that. Every company whose stock is traded has a place around the floor where you go to transact business for that particular stock, at one of those podiums. There's a transaction handler, a specialist they call them, for each stock. He tries to put together a broker wanting to buy and a broker wanting to sell the same stock. If more than one broker wants to buy or sell, it becomes an auction. That's what all the fuss is about."

On one side of the mezzanine men dressed in blue smocks were writing numbers on a big blackboard affair the size of the whole wall. There were dozens of letters strung together like the ones Bridget and Benjamin had found in the spice box. Beside the abbreviations the men were constantly changing numbers. Young boys acted as runners, bringing the sign fellas new sales as they happened. The sign fellas had rolling ladders so they could climb to all the letters and figures on the board. Bridget noticed all the brokers on the floor looking up at those numbers while they jumped up and down and waved their hands.

Suddenly Benjamin was up on the mezzanine, standing beside them, kissing his sister. His forehead had sweat glistening on it, which he was now blotting with a handkerchief. Bridget thought he was so cute in a "pinch his fat cheeks" way. "Hi, sis. Are you showing Bridget the ropes?"

Bridget answered for Rose. "Miss Rose is very smart about what's going on. She's teaching me. You sure have an exciting job."

Benjamin agreed. "Rose cried and carried on for days when Granddad explained to her that no woman could be a stockbroker. She'd talked about working on the floor our whole lives."

Rose pushed the tip of a finger against her brother's ample chest. "And you always said girls weren't allowed and I didn't believe you."

Benjamin shifted back from brother to stockbroker. "I've got to get back. Bridget, the specialist remembered that trade you wondered about, even though it was in the first few months of the war. It was a large transaction for a company that didn't make much noise. And then suddenly, that same week, Vermont Wool got the contract with Gold's for the uniforms.

"Who bought the stock?" Bridget asked.

Rose shook her head. "The specialist wouldn't know that. Most stock is bought in the name of the brokerage firm;

they call that the street name. Individual customers don't usually put the stock in their name because it makes it harder to sell in a hurry, should they want or need to."

Benjamin gave his sister another peck on the cheek. "Wow, sis, very good. I'll find out who bought that stock. It just might take a little time," he said and hurried away.

Rose and Bridget watched the proceedings in silence a few more minutes. Rose sure looked as if she regretted she wasn't down there on the floor.

Bridget was fascinated with this unfamiliar world. Now that she knew each podium represented a different company's trading station, the chaos made a little more sense. She wondered what area was for Vermont Wool. As her eyes circled the trading floor, she saw a young man who gave her a start. He wore his flaxen blond hair long, curling over his collar. His eyes were an intense shade of blue. When he looked up at the price board, he turned toward Bridget and Rose and looked right at them. Bridget had never seen eyes so blue. She didn't want him to spot her looking at him so she lowered her own eyes. That's when she saw his right arm. His hand and forehand were bandaged.

"Come now, Bridget, let's go see Mrs. Simon," Rose ordered, but in a friendly voice.

Bridget followed, her head swimming with the possibility that the man on the trading floor, who must be a stockbroker like Benjamin, was the man who met with Katherine and her father the last day of their lives.

It wasn't until they were well away from the Stock Exchange in the brougham that Bridget regretted she hadn't pointed him out to Miss Rose. She seemed so acquainted with the place, she might have known who he was. She'd ask Mr. Fleming's advise. Maybe she could send a message to Master Benjamin. "Did you really want to be a stockbroker?" she impulsively asked Rose.

"Since I was eight years old," Rose admitted.

"When they told you it was men only, what did you think?"

"That my grandfather was a powerful man and he would make an exception for me. I was used to getting my way, as you can imagine."

Bridget smiled. "So now you're in school in Spain. What do you study? I'm guessing it's not stockbroker learnin'?"

"I'm studying singing. I'm going to be an opera star."

Bridget had only the most rudimentary knowledge of what the opera represented. "Like at the building on Irving Place?"

"Yes, that's the Academy of Music. And there's a new opera house being built, to be called the Metropolitan. But I won't get my start in New York. Opera is very popular all over Europe. Hopefully next year I can start singing small roles in Germany or Italy."

"You're never coming back to New York to live?"

"Who knows? But my career is in Europe right now."

The carriage stopped and Johnny jumped down and opened the door. Rose put her hand on Bridget's arm to indicate that she wasn't to get out yet. "Wait. I want to hear your version of the story. Why did Mrs. Simon leave? What does the staff say?"

Bridget launched into her version of events. "One day during the seven-day mourning period . . ."

"The Shiva," Rose corrected.

"They really got into it. Mrs. Simon said you moved to Spain to get away from her, Mrs. Gold I mean. She said the only reason Seth was still around was because she, Mrs.

Gold, paid him under the table to stay at home. Mrs. Gold said she should have kicked Mrs. Simon out when her sister, your real mother, died. Then your father broke it up and they didn't speak much after that."

"What did Justin and Sally and everyone think of the fight?"

"At supper, staff supper that is, we thought the whole house was out of whack what with Seth being killed, that the two were going to make up soon as things got back to normal, or not normal, because I don't think things will ever be normal for your father, but you know . . ." Bridget wasn't expressing herself very well. She blundered along. "The remark about throwing Mrs. Simon out bothered folks."

"Because it inferred Estella had the power to do so?"

"Yes, ma'am, if 'inferred' means made it sound like she had the power. Not that any one of us believes your father would do anything improper. It sounded like Mrs. Gold might have had designs on your father, that's all."

"I think she did, but we'll never know, will we? Thanks for all the information, Bridget. Dad didn't mention the details of the tiff to me, of course. He never tells me anything that makes Estella look bad. Did Mrs. Simon leave then?"

"No, no. She waited until the Shiva was over. The very next day after, she was all packed and that's when she left. Mrs. Gold was madder than a wet hen about not having a secretary. Mrs. Simon said she pledged to your father to stay until you kids were grown, and she should have gone sooner. She'd already rented this place."

Rose peered out the open door. "What is this Germantown?"

Bridget shrugged. "The Germans that had some money

when they came over bought their houses together and
started businesses like back home. I worked in a boardinghouse just down the street. Most of these folks don't have to
talk a bit of English. They go to the German butcher, the
German shoemaker, they read German newspapers. Even the
street signs here are in German."

"So why is Mrs. Simon here? My mother didn't and she
doesn't have a drop of German blood."

"The ladies from your congregation told her about this
place, that it was for German Jewish ladies. And Mrs. Simon
knows something called Yiddish."

Rose pursed her lips. "I don't know how the ladies from
my congregation would know. We are Portuguese-speaking
Sephardim. These people are German-speaking Ashkenazim.
We have been here for two hundred years. They came last
week." Rose got out of the carriage and Bridget followed.
"I'd ask her to come back, to make sure my father is all
right, but I can't blame her for not wanting to be Estella's
whipping boy."

"Do you think there's something the matter with Mr.
Gold?" Bridget asked anxiously.

"Beside having a broken heart?" Rose said coldly as she
rang the doorbell. Bridget remembered that soul-wrenching
scream when Mr. Gold saw Seth, and couldn't argue with
Miss Rose about whether or not there was something
wrong.

A large, severe-looking woman opened the door.

"Hello," Rose said pleasantly. "May we please see Mrs.
Simon?"

The woman inclined her head, then asked in German if
they spoke Yiddish; at least that was what Bridget gathered.
She could understand German fairly well but her tongue

stumbled over speaking the words. She was about to tell Miss Rose what the woman had said when Rose answered, apparently understanding on her own.

"No, I'm afraid we have no Yiddish and very little German," she said in English.

The woman nodded, gave them just a hint of a smile, led them into a parlor, and then disappeared, leaving them to seat themselves.

"You understand German?" Bridget asked.

"Operas. I know a little Italian, French, German, and more Spanish. Portuguese, of course. That's our family language."

Mrs. Simon appeared in the doorway, holding out her arms. "Rose. Isaac said you weren't coming home until December."

Tears ran down Rose Gold's cheeks. Bridget thought she looked beautiful crying. Some women could do that, look lovely when they cried. Bridget had seen herself in the mirror when she cried a few times and she considered herself to be the other type, the women whose face cracked into a million splotchy pieces.

Mrs. Simon and Rose held each other for several minutes, sobbing. It was as if each had been holding in her grief, waiting for the right time to let it go, and that moment was now.

Bridget was uncomfortable being in the same room with such a personal outpouring. She also knew Mrs. Simon didn't much care for her and would sooner or later realize she was witness to their grief. She tried to concentrate on the figures on the table, the pattern of the carpet, the hang of the drapes. The drapes weren't as luxurious as the ones at the Gold's house, of course, but they were of fine quality.

The furniture, the rug, and all the other furnishings in the room, including a silver tea set and many porcelain animals, all seemed to be real nice. The boardinghouse Bridget had worked in, clean and pleasant as it was, was pretty austere compared to this one.

Eventually the two women unclasped. "Would you like to see my room?" Mrs. Simon asked Rose.

"Aunt Slim, please think about Dad," Rose said urgently.

Bridget couldn't take it anymore. As curious as she was about the inner thoughts of the two women, she didn't want to be part of this. "Miss Rose, I'm going to go back to the house now. I'll get a hack on the corner. You're fine here and Johnny can bring you home."

Mrs. Simon acknowledged Bridget for the first time. "Bridget, have you made any progress in finding Seth's murderer?"

Bridget would have to say they had, if eliminating possibilities was progress. "I'm trying to help Mr. Gold, ma'am, as best I can and still do my other job. Right now it's cooking I better get back to."

"Thank you for accompanying me, Bridget," Rose said as a way of dismissal. She made no mention of their other errand.

Rose and Mrs. Simon walked toward the stairs. "After you see my room we shall have some tea, and will you sing something for me?" Mrs. Simon asked with tenderness.

Bridget slipped out the door. Rose had called Mrs. Simon Aunt Slim, a perfect nickname for someone so tall and thin. Yet Bridget had never heard her referred to as anything but Mrs. Simon. How difficult to live the life of an employee when you're really a relative.

Bridget would bet a week's pay the current Mrs. Gold had had something to do with that.

* * *

BRIDGET was cooking Italian pasta for the first time in her life. Chef had appeared with boxes of these dried strips of dough that reminded her of the German egg noodles she'd learned to make at the boardinghouse, except these were already formed, dried out, and in various shapes. And they didn't have egg, Chef said.

One of the fancy food purveyors had sent word he had just received a shipment of dried pasta directly from Italy. Chef had left the house immediately to purchase some personally. The wholesaler had given him printed recipe cards that the spaghetti manufacturer in Italy sent along so folks would learn to use their products. They were in Italian, a small marketing error, but it was easy to tell what the ingredients were.

Chef and Gilbert had been fussing over the sauce all afternoon. Chef had sent Gilbert out twice, once for dried mushrooms called porcinis, which they soaked in warm water, and once for some hard cheese Gilbert grated into a tall pile. Bridget didn't get the name of the cheese.

Chef fussed around the stove as Bridget boiled a pot of water and put some oil in it as he had instructed. Then she added the long, thin pasta and stirred the water around with a big wooden spoon. The idea was to keep the strands of "spaghetti," as Chef called it, separate. Chef should have cooked it himself for all his nervous advice. He took out a piece of the pasta, now limp in his hands, tasted it, and pronounced it ready. Bridget took the pot off the stove and drained the pasta in a big colander.

"Work quickly," Chef snapped. "Put it on this platter, then drizzle it with oil so it doesn't stick together."

When Bridget got the pasta situated, Chef placed fat chops on top of it, then poured sauce over the pasta and meat.

"What's all this, Chef?" Bridget asked.

"Veal chops with a mushroom Marsala sauce," Chef said proudly as he sprinkled the grated cheese on the top. He placed a large silver dome over the platter, then turned to Karol. She struggled with the weight of the platter, then got the hang of it and started walking upstairs. For some reason, the Golds' home did not have a dumb waiter to transport food to the main floor. Mr. Fleming complained about this often.

In a few minutes, Mr. Fleming came downstairs, fuming. "Of all the dishes in the world to re-create, you had to choose that one," he fussed.

"They didn't like it." Chef was crestfallen.

"On the contrary, they were delighted, especially Master Benjamin's wife. Just last week she heard her girlfriends talking about this new food from Italy, pasta. She felt very in vogue."

"Master Benjamin is here?" Bridget asked. Perhaps she could ask him about the blond man on the trading floor.

Mr. Fleming ignored her, intent on making his point with Chef. "No, it is I who am not happy with this new dish. How in the devil am I supposed to serve it from the sideboard. Every damn strand of the slimy stuff is covered with sauce. They go this way and that, throwing sauce all over my shirtfront. And when I managed to get it on the plate with some sauce still on it, chop on top, the family didn't know how to eat it. They asked me. Of course, I didn't have a clue. I said to cut it up to fit on a fork."

"No, No," Chef wailed. "You're supposed to twirl it on your fork."

"Thank you for informing me of that after the fact," Mr. Fleming said tartly as he left to return to the upstairs dining room. Sally was going to have her hands full in the laundry tomorrow.

It was funnier later, when the staff took their turn twirling spaghetti. Bridget cooked another pound or two; there was plenty of sauce left and four chops. Chef took the meat off the chops and added it to the mushroom sauce. Everyone got hit with flying sauce at some time in the meal. The biggest laugh came when Chef's full fork came unwound and a mound of spaghetti landed on his jacket. They were in the middle of a good laugh about this when Master Benjamin appeared at the doorway of their dining room. Mr. Fleming stood up.

"Sit, sit," Benjamin said. "I'm just here for another piece of that Italian cream cake to go, if you don't mind, Bridget. This whole Italian meal made my wife very happy. Now she can brag about having pasta."

Mr. Fleming sat down. Chef muttered a "Thank you, sir," and Bridget hurried into the kitchen, where Harvey was fighting his own fight with the spaghetti.

"Why, I wonder, does Justin get to eat in the dining room but Harvey doesn't," Benjamin asked.

Bridget's eyebrows darted up. "I wondered that same thing. I asked Mr. Fleming. He said Mr. Gold gave him strict orders when he first got this job that Negro members of the staff were to be treated like the rest of us. If you know Justin, you know he's one of the smartest and most interesting people, and you wouldn't want to have supper without him if he was around. Harvey is just a kid, and if he eats with us he has to say yes, ma'am, and no, sir, and act interested in what we're talking about. If he fills his plate and eats in the kitchen, he can go out back and smoke before Elsie needs him."

Bridget had cut two big slices of cake while she was explaining this point of downstairs life. She wrapped them in the parchment paper Gilbert used to bake with, then a linen towel. "How are you going to sneak this home?" she asked.

"I'm taking it out the back door to our Cabriolet right now. I have news. I just told Dad."

"What?"

"That big purchase of Vermont Wool stock was made by Harriet Simon, my Aunt Slim."

"Did your father know about it?"

"No, and I could see he was upset."

"I'll try to talk to him later. Thanks for digging that up. There's something else, sir."

"What is it, Bridget?"

"I saw a fella I thought looked familiar when I went with your sister. He was down on the trading floor. Blond longish hair, real clear blue eyes. He had a bandaged hand."

"Oh, you probably saw him at the Shiva. He's a friend of Seth's, and mine too. Ian Strong is his name. Did you think him handsome like all the other girls do?" Benjamin asked in a teasing tone. He was walking toward the back door, she back to the dining room.

"Too much a dandy for me, sir," she said, hoping she sounded lighthearted to Master Benjamin's ears.

BRIDGET, holding the spice box in her hand, knocked on the library door. She'd come downstairs from her room on the chance that Mr. Gold might be up and available. She couldn't worry about the niceties, like Mr. Fleming announcing her and asking permission.

"Come," he said and Bridget stepped in.

"I just wanted you to know what's happened lately," Bridget said hesitantly.

Mrs. Gold had been somewhat successful with her play to keep Bridget from actively helping Mr. Gold. The thread had been torn between them, at least temporarily. The bond that had been forged in the emotional days right after Seth's death was weakening in light of their positions in the workaday world.

As far as Mr. Gold was concerned, no day would ever be "normal" again and he had trouble relating to the expectations of society. If his cook could help him solve Seth's murder, or do anything else for him he might ask, who could say that was improper? He especially resented Estella, who was concerned not because she felt Bridget would do harm to him, but because the situation made her lose face in her own shallow, narrow world. As a former employee who became his wife, you would think she would be nervous of someone seeking to replace her, but that was not the case. She was afraid someone would think less of her for her husband being seen about with the cook, as if they were on an equal social basis.

Bridget, on the other hand, had come into this household at a time of crisis. She was feeling her way as far as what was really "normal." She liked it better when she got a chance to use her natural curiosity to try to help out, but she really had no rebuttal when she was reminded of her lowly position as a cook. The other had been a gift, to get to do some investigating, see other parts of New York. And Mr. Gold, well, right now she felt he was more a friend to her than a boss, but she knew he had the power of putting her out in a minute, as he had done with Katherine. When they became too bothersome, young Irish girls could be replaced, even smart ones who made potato rolls. She never forgot that.

So she stood in front of him, and they both longed to replace that that had been lost between them.

"I suppose Rose and Benjamin have kept you up to date?"

Mr. Gold looked better, she'd have to give that. His eyes weren't so dead. Having Rose home must have done wonders for him.

"Sit down, Bridget. Let me see this box of yours."

"Well, it's not really mine. It's Katherine's. It was in my closet when I moved into that room. Mary Martha said Katherine treasured the box, rest her soul. It gives Mary Martha the willies. She thinks it's pagan or witchcraft or such."

Mr. Gold looked at the carvings closely with a magnifying glass. "Amazing. This certainly must be valuable. It seems to be depicting women consecrating and using food, but actually cooking, not just harvesting. It's like the difference between eating an apple off a tree and baking an apple cobbler. The carving is almost reverent. Alchemy, Bridget, that's what you cooks do. And where is this secret drawer Benjamin told me about?"

Bridget didn't ask what alchemy meant, although she intended to find out later, she released the drawer. He finally motioned for her to sit while he looked at the pages carefully. "You can see by the different papers that these were from different time periods. It's practically an education in the history of papermaking."

Bridget was pleased with Mr. Gold's interest in the box,

but right now there were more pressing matters to discuss. "This is where Benjamin and I found the paper with the stock written on it, sir. Vermont Wool Company. Fifty thousand shares. Benjamin says that's a lot."

"Yes, and Benjamin tells me the specialist for that stock remembers the transaction as coming right before we placed our first big order for uniform material. Someone made a bundle," he said icily.

Bridget wondered why he hadn't said, "Mrs. Simon made a bundle." She supposed he would get to that. She still wanted to understand the importance of the stock quote. "Why do you think Katherine kept that piece of paper, sir?"

"Did you enjoy going to the Stock Exchange today, Bridget?"

Now Bridget was truly puzzled. He was talking in circles not his usual direct self. "Why, yes I did, sir. It was just like an Irish wake, what with everyone yelling and trying to get the attention of the other fellas down there. But then Miss Rose explained to me how it works and it all started to make sense."

"Poor Rose, she so wanted to trade," Mr. Gold said.

"I think she still does, sir."

"Well, Bridget, I'm guessing Katherine never saw the Stock Exchange in action like you did. So, what do you think might have compelled her to hide that slip of paper in her most important spot?"

Bridget had actually considered this. "I think she either thought the paper was important and would be useful to her, or Seth asked her to hide it for him."

Mr. Gold nodded. "I concur with your conclusions. If it was the latter, that Seth asked her to keep it, when he was killed it became the former, something useful to her."

Bridget was struggling to keep up.

"Now what do you make of the new information that Mrs. Simon was the buyer?"

Bridget shrugged. "I don't know enough about the stock buying and selling, sir. But my guess is: You and Seth were thinking of buying lots of wool from someone. That would make the price of their stock go up, whoever you chose. Seth gave his aunt the money to buy the stock you picked, it did go up in value, and they sold the stock and split the profits."

"Which makes me an unknowing partner in this unethical business. Seth was adamant about using Vermont Wool. I was leaning toward New England Wool. I let him have his way because I was happy to see him take an interest," Mr. Gold said bitterly.

"Mr. Gold, Benjamin said your family was against trading on knowledge that no one else would have. How come you can still do it?"

Mr. Gold tapped his fingers on the rim of the magnifying glass. He had long, slender fingers, Bridget noticed. Beautiful fingers like the rest of him. "It's just a matter of time before it is against the rules of the Exchange and perhaps against the law. For years, men have thought nothing of making millions by buying and selling stocks that they had special knowledge of. This is just a small example but perhaps you'll get what I mean. Seth knows he is going to place a big order with Vermont Wool. He buys the stock low, and when Gold's places the order, the stock goes up. Seth sells the stock and makes some cash."

Bridget was stuck. "That's what I just said. What's so bad about that?"

"Think about it, Bridget. The people who sold their stock to Seth in the first place. Do you think they would have sold it for, say, five dollars a share when next week, after our order, the market would offer ten dollars a share for the same stock?"

"I see. By having more information than the poor fella who sold to him, Seth took advantage of him."

"Exactly," Mr. Gold said with conviction. "Seth and Mrs. Simon were wrong. But the greed of these men, bankers and railroad men and brokers, knows no bounds. My father wanted to outlaw that sort of trading at the New York Stock Exchange, but he died and then war broke out. That war was a good reason to keep the status quo, and get rich quick."

"Is this why you got out of the stock-tradin' business?"

Mr. Gold groaned. "It might have been one of the reasons, but I got into something just as shady, retail. Do you know, Bridget, that Gold's is the first department store to put the prices on the merchandise? Until us, the customer was supposed to bargain for everything and the salesclerk made up a price according to what he thought he could get, not what the item was worth. Isn't that ridiculous?"

Bridget had never thought about it before. She just always assumed she was getting gypped. To think otherwise was for fools. "That's real fair of you, sir, when you could get more money from some folks than from others. You've made me think about the right and wrong way of doing things. Thank you for that. Since you believe it's wrong to do this kind of stock business, are you angry at Mrs. Simon?"

Mr. Gold turned the spice box slowly, deep in thought. "No, I blame myself. I didn't realize how much her position with Estella rankled her. I thought they enjoyed each other's company. I'm sure Seth offered her a percentage of the profits and she saw it as a way she could make some money of her own. She never wanted for anything, but she didn't have the resources to leave, which she obviously wanted to do. I had put her in an untenable position."

"You have such a kind way of looking at things, sir."

"Getting angry at Mrs. Simon or the Stock Exchange or even the other store merchants for all their greed isn't going to bring Seth back," Mr. Gold observed sadly.

"Speaking of that, there was a man on the trading floor that looked like the description the bartender at the Pig gave me: blond, blue eyed, with a bandaged hand. Benjamin said he was Ian Strong."

"Ian. No, that's not possible. There must be dozens of people in New York that meet that description."

"With the bandaged hand?"

"A bandage is a temporary thing. The man in the pub could have removed his bandage the very next day. Ian could have just applied his yesterday. Hardly a reliable identification."

"He a friend of yours?" Bridget asked, ignoring all the protestations.

"Certainly a friend of the boys. His family has held a seat on the Exchange for years. He had an interest in Rose. I guess he could have met Katherine at some time if she and Seth went out in public together. But Ian is something of a snob. I can't imagine that he would set foot in The Spotted Pig."

"I think we should ask him, sir."

Mr. Gold stood up and handed her the box. "I agree. But let me think about how to approach the whole subject."

Bridget stood up. "Sir, tomorrow is my day off. I could use some ideas about searching for Maggie."

Relief flooded Mr. Gold's face. Your heartache, not mine. Easy. "Next you must go to the old orphanage, the Friendless place."

"It's not run by the Protestant women anymore. Mary Martha told me the nuns run it now."

"Go anyway. They may have old records, or Maggie could have stopped by there."

Bridget knew he had a good point. "Yes, sir. The Friendless. Anything else?"

Mr. Gold held up his hand. "Yes, but do not go there after dark. Go between three and five in the afternoon, late enough people will be up and early enough you won't be accosted."

"Where are you talking about, Mr. Gold?"

"Greene, Mercer, and Howard. Oh, and Wooster, just over from the store on Broadway. The best brothels are there. Don't argue with me about this and don't say your sister wouldn't do that. Hunger erases ethical positions, on occasion. Here's more tip money. You won't get information for free there." He opened a drawer of the desk with a small key and counted out twenty more one-dollar bills, handing them to Bridget.

Dozens of images flew through Bridget's mind. She didn't want to imagine her sister in a whorehouse, high class or not, but she had made it through the death certificates so she could do this. She knew if she complained, Mr. Gold would remind her how much he wished he could go fish Seth out of trouble again, because it would mean he was still alive.

"Yes, sir, thank you, sir."

She turned to go.

"Bridget, I wish I could go with you. Be careful."

"Yes, sir."

Chapter Sixteen

There was a moment as Bridget left the house, knowing she didn't have to be back until bedtime, when she felt lost again. A home, even one that isn't your own, is like a lifeboat. Wind and waves, blinding rain, rocky shores, but you have a chance to climb out and dry off and walk away. She looked around, half expecting Michael Murphy to pop out of the bushes, and found that she was terribly disappointed when he was nowhere in sight. With nothing to impede her departure, she hurried down the path to the street.

As Bridget boarded the omnibus heading downtown, she was conflicted. Her idea was to stop off at the boardinghouse first and have a word with Mrs. Simon. Was she just postponing her own unpleasant business? Did she dread going to the orphanage? The only answer she could come up with was yes, she was willing to put it off as long as possible. Today was the day but it didn't have to be this minute.

Mrs. Simon first, the orphanage second, the high-class whorehouses third.

Bridget knew she was overstepping her bounds with this visit to Mrs. Simon and she knew not to expect a warm welcome. But she figured if anyone had a chance of getting useful information out of Mrs. Simon, she was it. Mr. Gold felt guilty for letting his wife bully his sister-in-law. The kids, Rose and Benjamin, saw her as the last connection to a long-lost mother and would never want to see her in a bad light.

When Bridget arrived at the boardinghouse, close to Union Square, she was greeted by the same unsmiling woman who deposited her in the same austere parlor. She didn't have much time to reminisce about her years cooking in a house much like this one, only not so far north and less affluent. The farther north in Kleindeutschland you traveled, the richer the households. Mrs. Simon hurried in with a worried look on her face.

"Is something the matter with Rose or Benjamin?"

Bridget rose from the uncomfortable chair she'd been sitting in. "No, ma'am, as far as I know, they are both just fine. I came down here for your help, ma'am."

Mrs. Simon pulled the pocket doors of the parlor shut. "What is it?"

Bridget decided to keep it simple. "I found a box that belonged to Katherine in my room. It had a note in it about a stock sale. Vermont Wool. Fifty thousand shares. Benjamin asked around about it around the Stock Exchange. He found out it was you who bought that stock, ma'am, then sold it after Gold's gave them a big order and the stock went way up. What I was wondering is, why would Katherine have hidden a piece of paper with that information on it? Why would she find it so important?"

Mrs. Simon involuntarily raised her chin and put her hands on her hips in a confrontational stance. "I suppose Benjamin and Isaac didn't approve of Seth and I investing in Vermont Wool."

Bridget agreed. "No, I suppose they didn't. But Benjamin and Isaac both said it wasn't against the Stock Exchange rules, although Benjamin wants to change that. He says in five years it will be against the regulations. That's a part I don't understand. If it wasn't against any rules, why didn't Seth just buy the stock in his own name?"

"Isaac believes deeply that profiting from any prior knowledge that you have is unethical. He would have fired Seth, or that's what Seth believed."

"And you? Do you think it's unethical, Mrs. Simon?"

"I can see Isaac's point of view, of course. But in my case, there were other factors to consider."

"Do you mind letting me in on what they are?"

Mrs. Simon gave Bridget a long, appraising look, and gestured for her to sit down. Bridget did, perching on the edge of one of the horsehair settees. "Seth came to me with this scheme. He gave me the money to buy the stock and then we divided the profits. I got twenty-five percent. I saw a way to get a little nest egg so I wouldn't have to work for Estella for the rest of my life. You work for her—you can understand that."

"I surely can. I have nothing to look forward to but working for the rest of my life. It can get you down if you let it. And since you once had a husband and all, it must be hard to take care of someone else's life."

"And someone so appreciative, like the second Mrs. Gold," Mrs. Simon said dryly.

"Tell me true, Mrs. Simon. Do you think your Stock Exchange purchases could have anything to do with Seth's death?"

Mrs. Simon looked her right in the eyes. "It wasn't the only time Seth dabbled in the market. He continued throughout the war. I wasn't the only person who bought stocks for him and split the profits later. There was a lot of money."

"Do you think Katherine and her father were in on it?"

"Yes, I do, not that Seth ever told me that. That would have meant acknowledging their relationship."

"I guess it's safe to say Benjamin didn't act as broker for any of these sales."

"Oh, my goodness, no. I knew, and of course Seth did, Benjamin felt just as his father and grandfather did. I think whoever the broker was might have put up the money for all the transactions. But that's just a guess. Seth was very secretive about it with me."

Bridget got to her feet. "Well, what's that saying, a means to an end. It looks like you have a real nice place here. Are the ladies good people?"

Mrs. Simon, her lanky frame so angular and graceless, got up and walked with Bridget to the door. "Anyplace would be better than the Gold mansion. It just had too many bad memories."

BRIDGET walked up to Twenty-Ninth and Madison, where the Home for the Friendless had been. What was the appropriate response to seeing the place again? Fondness, dread, fright, relief?

She always told herself the ladies—the Female Guardian Society, she would always remember that name—gave them an education and that was a real plus. Lots of the relief societies that took in spare children just worked them hard until they were fifteen. So the Friendless didn't have to teach them to read, write, and do arithmetic. Kids at the Friendless got an education if they paid attention.

Then there was the cooking. Bridget wasn't sure the other girls who worked in the kitchen, when she did, saw it the same way. She thought it was glamorous. She thought it was her future. She wanted to become a great cook. Most of them never got better with practice at their appointed duties. She remembered how a girl named Betty burned the oatmeal every time. Then there was Shannon, who never could get the hang of chopping up carrots and onions so they were all the same size. And Polly couldn't make a pie crust that you could put a fork to; hers was like a rock.

Bridget had now walked back and forth in front of the entrance four times. She slipped a ragged photograph out of her pocket and looked at it for the first time in months. She had brought it along to prove she had been an inmate of the place. When she put it in the pocket on the inside of her cape, she'd made a point of not looking at it. Now she did.

There they were, little girls in all manner of getups, fancy and plain. They wore the castoffs of the Protestant women's church congregations. She and Maggie were in the first row, hair parted down the middle and smoothed back in a headband, then a mass of curls in the back. Everyone in the front rows at least had their hair combed and their Sunday clothes on. No one was smiling, but no one had angry handprints or dirt and filth smearing their little faces.

The photo had been taken in the courtyard of the building, which had a U-shaped construction. There was laundry hanging down, sheets and some underclothes. Bridget couldn't remember a time when there wasn't wash. Between bedding, towels, pantaloons, and the smocks they wore over their clothes for everyday, there was always laundry. Sometimes in the winter it took days for it to dry. The ironing girls would just take them damp in to the irons.

So there was nothing left to it then. She'd put it off as long as she could. Bridget stepped up to the door and gave a good solid knock. Quickly, a nun opened the door. Bridget could tell by her headdress that she was a member of the Sisters of Charity. The Protestant ladies had given up on the Irish Catholic orphans. The war had given them another cause.

"Sister, may I come in, please?"

The nun opened the door to allow Bridget entry. "What may we do for you, child?"

Bridget pushed the photo at the nun. "I used to live here."

The sister took a look at the photo. "Oh, dear me. It's taken right here in the courtyard. And I bet you're one of those darling girls in the front row with all that curly hair."

"That would be me. And that's why I'm here. The little girl next to me is my sister, Maggie. I've lost touch with her and I thought perhaps she might have come by here sometime."

The nun returned the photo to Bridget. "I'm sure you realize now, if you didn't before, that the Guardian Society stopped operating the orphanage about the time the war started. Unfortunately we have none of their records. We have discussed a registry, where parents or graduates could leave their address. So many of the poor little ones from famine times were not really orphans at all. Some of their, pardon, your, parents are very much alive, they just couldn't take care of the little ones. Now they stop by wanting to find their children. We feel so helpless."

That won't be the case with the Heaney sisters, Bridget thought. No mother or father is out there looking for us.

Bridget handed the nun one of Mr. Gold's plain calling cards. She had printed her name, Maggie's name, and the Golds' address on it. "I'm Bridget Heaney. I cook at the address on here. If Maggie happens to come by here, please give her my address."

The sister nodded. "Perhaps you will be the first person in our registry, Bridget."

Bridget handed five dollars to the sister. "Thank you for your time. I know you never have enough money to go around."

"Thank you, Bridget. Would you like to see your old room?"

"No, sister, but could I see the kitchen?"

"Of course. I'll have one of the girls take you." She rang a bell and a little child about eight came bouncing to the front of the building, where the nun had a desk. She told the girl to take Bridget for a look-see at the kitchen.

The little girl, big brown eyes, sandy hair in braids, gave a little curtsy. Together they went across the courtyard to the back of the building. "I'm Marie."

"And I'm Bridget."

Marie looked at Bridget with interest. "You from here?"

"That I am. I worked in the kitchen and now I'm cooking at a big, fancy house." Bridget was embarrassed she had been bragging to a child about her great success as a servant.

Bridget didn't think it would hit her so hard, but it did.

Entering the kitchen turned her into a fiercely determined eleven-year-old again.

The room looked the same. It was big and plain, painted white long ago, grayed now with the city's dinginess. There was a monster coal-burning stove with ovens in it. Ten girls were at work, plus a couple of nuns to supervise. Her eyes fixed on a tall girl concentrating intently on frying a huge skillet full of onions and potatoes. Bridget's eyes filled with tears but she tried to act normal, nodding and smiling at the kitchen nuns so they wouldn't be alarmed. She could just hear the conversation later. "I don't know what happened, Mother Superior. She came in the kitchen, started crying, and just wanted to wash dishes. We couldn't get her to leave."

"Come to see your old haunt?" one of the nuns asked cheerfully.

"Yes, I lived here when it was the Home for the Friendless. Worked here in the kitchen." Bridget had intended to make more small talk but she was afraid her voice would crack.

The girls observed Bridget with curiosity. A few smiled at her. The girl on fried potato duty looked up briefly then continued to concentrate on her work.

Bridget saw herself, of course, in that focused potato girl. It was pathetic that she remained so softhearted. After losing her ma to the ocean, her da to despair and drink and eventually to violence, and just plain losing her sister, she was still a weepy, sentimental girl who was desperate to connect herself with others where some sense of family could be concocted. She had best leave before she made a fool of herself.

"Thank you, sisters. Marie, will you see me back to the door?" Bridget asked. She hurried out of the kitchen, the child at her side. As they walked through the courtyard, Bridget looked up. Sheets were hanging today, just like the day of the photograph, the brisk November air whipping them up in the air. Another tug to the old heartstrings.

Bridget gave Marie a dollar as they walked. "Don't give this to the sisters. This is for you. I gave the sister some money, too. Hide this, Marie. You never know when a dollar will come in handy."

Marie understood the drill. She nodded solemnly and tucked the dollar somewhere without missing a step. The nun at the door was at her desk now, writing in a big ledger. She looked up and smiled pleasantly. "God bless you and I hope you find your sister."

"I do, too. Thank you, both." Bridget indicated Marie and the nun with her eyes and hurried out the door.

It was too early to visit the brothels. She walked south. At the table the other day Kate and Karol talked about a place they went to lunch on their day off, a restaurant for women. She thought it was on Broadway around Franklin so she jumped on the omnibus.

It was called Taylor's, a ladies eatery, and to Bridget's amazement it was full of women, eating with each other in couples, big groups, or alone. There must have been a hundred tables.

"Table for one?" a young lady holding a menu asked.

Bridget nodded and followed her to a table right in the middle of the room. The restaurant was noisy with the cheerful sounds of women: talking, laughing, exclamations of all sorts, singing occasionally, and someone even whistled. Bridget ordered a chicken potpie and rice pudding. Later, she couldn't remember how anything tasted. She was just excited to be in such a place. It didn't matter about the quality of the food; the quality of the experience was worth remembering.

After dinner, Bridget walked over to Greene Street. She headed north slowly, not knowing exactly where to go next.

Soon, it became apparent she was in the right area. Men went in and out of the brownstones singly or in small groups. Bridget could hear music coming out of the open doors. It was three o'clock in the afternoon, a weekend, festive feeling on the streets.

Bridget just chose one at random. Actually, it was the draperies. They were a pretty dusky rose color that kind of matched the color of the sandstone that the building was built of.

She walked up the stairs and in the door, which was unlocked. A petite blonde was sitting at a piano, not playing, instead fanning herself with a big feather fan. "Can I help you, dear?" she asked, looking amused at Bridget's presence.

"I'm looking for my sister. Red, curly hair like mine. Younger. Her name is Maggie Heaney. She might be going by Margaret."

"Darling, I don't use Irish girls. They just don't sell. Too common, I guess."

Bridget didn't know what to say to that. She turned to leave then thought of something. "Are there any houses around here that do hire Irish girls? This means a lot to me," she asked.

The petite blonde studied her for a moment. "There are three places. O'Brien's on Wooster two blocks up. Madame Josephine's a block south, and Aunt Sally's down a block or so on Mercer."

Bridget took the dollars out of her pocket, unsure what would be a proper tip for information at a brothel. The blonde waved her fan to indicate Bridget should put her money away. "Save your dollars, dear. I bet you work long and hard in a Fifth Avenue mansion for them. Good luck finding Maggie."

Bridget was amazed that the madame, she guessed that's who it was, not only spotted her for a servant but also knew the street she worked on. Must be part of the job to figure folks out by their appearance.

Bridget dutifully went to the three houses that used Irish girls, then went to three more that looked interesting, just because she was curious. Men made comments to her all along the streets but she tried to keep her eyes down and look like a servant, which she supposed she could succeed at since she had been tagged with it earlier. She was surprised at how nice the brothels were inside and what pretty clothes the women who worked there wore. These prostitutes sure didn't look or act like the ones Bridget worked the streets alongside in her pickpocket days. She had always heard there was a big difference between street whores and the ones who worked in the fancy houses. That seemed like it was true now that Bridget had toured the better whore-houses of New York.

Bridget took the omnibus home feeling beat up. Every one of her stops had yielded little she could call positive results.

Mrs. Simon confirmed that she and more so Seth had had a moneymaking scheme on the side.

Her old orphanage had no method for keeping track of their "graduates."

The high-class brothels didn't want Irish whores.

The only really positive thing that had happened today was Taylor's. Bridget had visions of her own restaurant, she in a tall toque commanding a troop of women chefs cooking for other women.

As Bridget walked up the driveway to the back door of the Golds', she wished, just for a minute, for a boyfriend to spend her little bit of free time with. But Bridget knew what that led to, misery. She could stand to be lonely once in a while.

She tapped lightly on the door. It wasn't much after eight o'clock so the staff would still be up. She expected Justin to answer the door and he did.

"How was your day, Bridget?" he asked.

"Pretty busy," Bridget said, then she followed him back to his little office, spilling out the contents of her day in those long, convoluted sentences she used when she was wound up about something. Mrs. Simon, the orphanage, Taylor's, the brothels, all came pouring out in a tangled narrative.

"And I don't know why it hurt my feelings so much when the lady, the madame I guess she was, told me they didn't hire Irish girls because they were too common. That just took the cake, Justin. Not that I'm wanting to make a career change, mind you, but when they don't want you at the whorehouse, that's pretty bad."

Justin laughed that big hearty laugh. "Join the club. People of color are always getting turned down 'just because.' To be arbitrarily written off is a frustrating situation. You may only want to be a privy cleaner but if they say, 'No red hair or no black skin can be a privy cleaner,' it's frustrating, not to mention immoral."

Bridget nodded. She could always count on Justin for an interesting insight. "What's surprising to me is how hurt I was, as though she'd taken something away from me I really wanted."

"I would think the most difficult part of the day would have been going back to the orphanage," Justin observed correctly.

"It's not like they beat us or were cruel to us in any way. Many got a worse draw than Maggie and me." Bridget sounded miserable when she said this.

"Yes, indeed, it always could be worse," Justin commented dryly. "Last year, during those unfortunate riots, the family left for the country house. I stayed with Mr. Gold, as he was hiring guards for the store and having the windows boarded up and all sorts of unpleasant things."

"It was a hard four or five days for the city."

"Well, my point for bringing it up, Bridget, is how it could be worse. On July thirteenth, I'll never forget it. Johnny came with news that the mob was just up the street here at Forty-Third and Fifth at the Colored Orphan's Asylum. They were going to burn it down and it was their hope that it would burn with the children in it. I headed up the street, leaving Johnny with a shotgun to guard this house. Mr. Fleming was with the family out of town."

"I guess I don't need to point out that you're a Negro, Justin," Bridget said. "I would think you'd go in the opposite direction from that mess."

Justin shook his head. "Two hundred children, Bridget, were going to be burned alive. But they weren't and it was mostly thanks to them. The big kids carried the little ones. By the time I circled around and came in from the back, there was a young Irish fellow, I'll never forget it, with two children in his arms, running out the back door. I was ready to fight but he just said, 'Four more is all. I'm taking them to the precinct house.' By that time, the mob was inside the house, breaking up furniture. I grabbed the last four children, who were hiding in a cupboard, and followed Paddy to the twentieth precinct. Paddy McCaffrey was his name. I'll never forget it, or him either for going against his countrymen."

Bridget started laughing. "Oh, Justin, when a story about homeless Negro tykes being burned out of the house by a mob of murdering, thieving Irish makes you feel better, you know you've taken yourself too serious."

Justin laughed with Bridget, a couple of his big ha-haws, and turned back to his paperwork. "It always could be worse, Bridget. They didn't try to burn your orphan house down. And count yourself lucky the brothels of Mercer Street don't want you."

Bridget turned to leave, then remembered something. "Justin, what does alchemy mean?"

Justin looked up. "To turn a base metal into gold. It can also be used to reference the power of transformation."

"Thanks, Justin. You know everything," Bridget said, thinking about the spice box as she went up to her room.

CHAPTER SEVENTEEN

BRIDGET heard them talking next door in the laundry room. Rose and Sally were going to it about something, giggling and carrying on. Bridget liked it when the masters of the house came downstairs. She knew they probably didn't ever give it another thought, what they saw down here, but it must stick back there somewhere in their minds. The sheets don't get washed and ironed and all crisp-like on their own. You don't get three or four choices for breakfast without someone to fix them up. The house functions: it's warm, there are gas lamps to read by at night, you can relieve yourself indoors. The ground floor is where people are keeping all this in working order. The only one that Bridget never saw downstairs was Mrs. Gold. No surprise there.

Bridget slipped over to the laundry door. "Miss Rose, can

I ask you something when you and Sally are finished talkin'? I'm right over in the kitchen."

Rose and Sally looked up from the sink where they were working. "Hi, Bridget. I brought everything home from Spain that had a spot on it. Sally's teaching me," Rose said. "I'll come by the kitchen next."

"Thank ya," Bridget said and went back to stuffing a pork loin with a mixture of corn bread and dried apricots and pecans and bits of fried onion and celery and carrot. Chef had a name for this onion-celery-carrot mixture. It was called *mirepoix*. Lots of French cooking started with this *mirepoix* and Chef had taught Bridget to cut the dice, that's what Chef called the little pieces, small and uniform. Then she softened it up in some butter on the top of the stove in one of those copper sauté pans, not called frying pans because you sautéed, not fried, in them. She was learning a lot from Chef and also about different religions and their eating habits.

She was shocked the first time the Golds had a ham for dinner, or the meat market delivered a big rasher of bacon. She asked Mary Martha about it later, not wanting to bring it up with Chef, whom she didn't know that well yet, to show her ignorance. Mary Martha said she was right about the Jewish faith and pork products. The real religious folks that went to all the services at the Congregation kept a kosher kitchen, she said. She was proud to know something food related that Bridget didn't know. The particulars of keeping kosher, as Mr. Fleming called it, had been lost on Mary Martha but she thought you couldn't prepare meat and dairy products in the same kitchen or the same pots and pans, one or the other. Bridget still didn't know about keeping kosher. Mary Martha told her the Golds weren't religious and they liked bacon as much as the next person. No one mentioned diet restrictions in the kitchen so she never thought about it. But when Chef bought a big piece of pork like this loin, it still shocked her a bit. She worked fast so Miss Rose wouldn't have to see this much pig in the raw. Quickly she tied up the loin, tucking in the stuffing as she tied. She had it done and in a roasting pan by the time Rose came into the kitchen. Bridget covered it with a towel. It was too soon to put it in the oven. She moved the teakettle over to the hot part of the stove.

"Will you have a cup with me?" Bridget asked.

"Of course," Rose answered. "What's the question?"

Bridget was taken aback. "What?"

"You said you had a question for me. What is it? I'm dying to know what our very own cook/investigator needs from me."

"When we were at the Stock Exchange, I saw a fella down on the trading floor. He was blond, blue eyed, and had a bandaged hand. I asked your father and brother about him and they knew just who I was talking about. They said his name was Ian Strong. I wondered what you knew about him?"

"A lot. Did they mention he asked my father if he could ask me to marry him?"

"No, they sure did not, miss. What did Mr. Gold tell him?"

"That I wasn't available for matrimony at this time, that I wanted to have a career. Can you imagine? Father told Ian I was going to be a famous opera singer, and after I'd achieved my goals, then maybe I would want to get married or maybe not."

"Well, did you and this Ian court?"

"I guess you could call it that. With a man like Ian, you don't think of it in such romantic terms."

Steam started flowing out of the teakettle spout. Bridget took the kettle off the heat and poured the hot water into a china teapot she'd pulled out of the cupboard. "Do you want regular black tea or some with a bit of bergamot in with it?"

"Oh, the bergamot, please," Rose said. "Why are you interested in Ian Strong, Bridget?"

"When your father and I went down to my old neighborhood, I went to this pub that the neighbors said Katherine's da favored. The first time I was asking after Mr. O'Sullivan, I gave the barkeep a tip. He said the old man had talked of his daughter Katherine having problems. The next time we go down there, Mr. Gold and I, he tells us Katherine and her da had been there, told him they were waiting for someone, then a blond-haired, blue-eyed gent comes in to meet them. One with a bandage on his hand. The three of them leave together. The next thing you know, we're finding them shot dead, the two of them." Bridget brought over the tea and two of the plain teacups the staff drank from. She hoped Miss Rose would understand the kitchen ways.

"Oh, my goodness. Well, that's a surprising development. I never would have guessed Ian to be involved with a servant—sorry, Bridget, no offense meant."

"And none taken, miss. That's what I am and what Katherine was. Your father also made the point that just because he had a bandage on his hand when we saw him doesn't mean he had one last week."

Rose's eyes were dancing with anticipation. "I know but it's rather a coincidence, isn't it? There aren't many men who look like Ian. He's Finnish or Norwegian or something of the sort. I wish we could give the bartender a photo of him to see if it's the same man."

"Do you have a photo of him?"

"I don't know. I'll have to look through my things. How exciting. Is the implication here that Ian had something to do with their deaths?"

"Oh, miss, I surely wouldn't think so. But will you look about and see if you have a photo of him? Is this upsetting to you, ma'am? Were you sweet on him?"

"I guess so. But certainly not enough to cancel my plans for my life. I look at my brother and his wife and they seem to genuinely love each other. They met at a party when Ben was still in college. He came home and told me he'd found the girl for him. He never dated anyone else after that. With Ian you got the impression he was still always shopping, that you were the leading contender but at any minute a better prospect might come along and he'd drop you like a hot potato."

"Was there any problem with the religion, miss? Aren't those Scandinavians Protestants?"

"Actually, Ian was a quarter Jewish. I think he either talked about that or didn't, depending on the company. Being the daughter of the owner of Gold's Department Store has quite an effect on business-minded young men who come calling. It makes them forget they were taught that Jews were inferior."

Bridget and Rose had a laugh at that one. Bridget finished her tea. "I best get back to work or your supper will be late. I would appreciate you taking a look for that photo, miss. I don't suppose it's your Ian that was in The Spotted Pig but it sure would be good to know."

Rose looked pensive, as if she was thinking hard on something or remembering something unpleasant. "Yes, it certainly would be good to know."

* * *

BRIDGET had just turned down the lights in the kitchen when she heard the tap on the window.

She liked doing some project after the staff supper. Most of the time, Gilbert and Chef left the dining room and went upstairs to their rooms, to nip Cognac, Bridget supposed. They came down plenty early in the mornings; Bridget had only beaten them to the kitchen once. But she liked to have that time after dinner to do something for the next day and to be in the kitchen by herself, after Elsie and Harvey had finished up the cleaning. That was when she had the most personal talks with most of the other staff, except Mary Martha, who still came to her room three or four nights a week for reading, snacks, and gossip. One night it might be Justin who would wander in. They would have a cup of tea together sometimes. Then the next evening it might be Mr. Fleming. Sometimes he had a bit of the wine they had served at table that night. They would have a nip and he would teach her little bits about the difference between Bordeaux and Burgundy or sherry and Madeira. Even the girls went back to work some nights. Last week the ironing had got completely away from Sally. Kate, Karol, and Mary Martha all pitched in. They used every iron in the house, and spent a good amount of time around the dining room table playing dominos as the irons heated back up. It was fun to visit with them and Bridget even made them a gingerbread, and one for the family for the next day. Gilbert was so good at fancy desserts, but he didn't know about the simple ones like cobblers and gingerbread and apple brown Betty.

Tonight she had roasted some beets, and peeled them, storing them in the icebox for tomorrow. She'd talk to Chef about what to do with them. She was ready to turn in when the tapping started. She considered just walking out of the room, pretending that she hadn't heard and going on up to bed. But she was pretty sure it was Michael Murphy and she had to admit she'd be glad to see him again. She went over to the window, and there he was, bent down, waving and motioning to the back door. She nodded and went to meet him.

Bridget remembered what had happened last time so she went to Justin's office. He looked as if he was getting ready to give up and go to bed. "Sir, that reporter fella is outside. I'm going out to see what he wants."

Justin gave her a look. "Don't be too long. Let me show you something," he said and showed her the window of his office. It was unlocked, and even though it looked like there was a fancy iron grill over it outside, like the other ones on the ground floor, the grill was on a hinge. The window was open and he pushed the grill out so it was easy to slip in. "I don't leave this unlocked all the time, but I had it open tonight for air. I'll leave it unlocked so you can come in when you get done with Mr. Murphy."

Bridget was humiliated. "Justin, I think you misunderstood. I'll be right back in ten minutes. I just didn't want you to hear us outside like you did last time."

"Don't try to tell me you're not attracted to that young whippersnapper. And don't think I'm encouraging or discouraging. I'm tired, my neck hurts, and I'm going to bed. Let yourself in."

Bridget grinned. There was no sense arguing. "Thank you, Justin," she said and headed out the back door.

Michael Murphy was standing right by the door, blowing on his hands. "I left my gloves someplace today. My hands are frozen. Can I come in?"

Bridget stepped out and regretted it immediately. It was

cold and there was a wind whipping around the house. "No, you can't come in. What do you want, Murphy?"

"Are you sure we can't go inside? It looks like the troops have gone to bed. It's almost midnight."

If Bridget hadn't closed the door, she would have let him in for a cup of tea. But now she had to use the secret window to get in and she knew Justin would have a conniption fit if she let Murphy in the house, especially through an unlocked window. "Murphy, forget it. Why are you here?"

"I found your sister. Well, I didn't actually find your sister, but I found out where she was for a year and a half. Bridget, I'm sorry."

Bridget was speechless. She stuttered and finally pushed out a finished word. "Wh, wh, wh, what in the world? So, what did you do, memorize her name?"

"After the night we went up to Saint Patrick's."

"And so?"

"And so I started asking around. When I'd go to a precinct, I'd ask if anyone knew a Maggie Heaney, that kind of thing. The other day I had to go over there for a story and I asked if they had ever had Maggie Heaney as a patient and the doc I was interviewing remembered her. He was real proud of her, said she was one they had high hopes for not returning. They have a nasty return rate."

Bridget was about to erupt. "Murphy, where in the hell are you talking about. Where was Maggie?"

"On Blackwell's Island at the Lunatic Asylum," Murphy said. "I said I was sorry."

MARY Martha didn't think it was so bad. Bridget, sobbing, came to Mary Martha's bedroom and begged her to come to her room. They sat on the bed and Bridget blubbered out the story.

"You know the stories about that place. We heard them at the Friendless, you hear them on the streets, down in the old neighborhood. How many girls did you hear of going to Blackwell's Island and they just disappeared?"

"I had her dead and tossed in the river, so this is better, Brig," Mary Martha said practically.

"I have to go there, Mary Martha, to Blackwell's Island. I have to talk to the doctor. Maybe they know where she was going when she was discharged. I have to know how she got there."

"Of course you do. You know Mr. Gold will let you go tomorrow. After all you've done for him. What did you say to the reporter fella?"

"Thank you about a hundred times. I can't believe he did this. He acted like it was no big deal but I told him it was the most important thing anyone had ever done for me."

"So, are you going to see him again?"

"I told him we'd have a drink next Saturday on my day off."

"Good. I think he's sweet on you."

"He must be to find my sister, or almost find her."

"Did you ask him not to write about it?"

"What's to write about?"

"Poor Irish girl goes to the dogs, goes to the Lunatic Asylum."

"The city is full of them. I don't think anyone cares. Remember what the madame told me. We're too common for a good story."

"Well, you care about this one Irish girl. Talk to Mr. Fleming first thing in the morning."

* * *

"I can't thank you enough for this, Mr. Gold. You didn't have to come with me."

"You went to some unpleasant places with me, Bridget. We found dead bodies, for God's sake. Now it's my turn. This is very good news, in my opinion. If Maggie was released and the doctor was optimistic about her prognosis, then we may be able to find her."

They were on a ferry to Blackwell's Island, crossing part of the East River. The ferry went there from Twenty-Sixth Street twice a day. When Mr. Gold and Bridget arrived at the ferry station, they were told no visitors were allowed on the island without a permit. Only the vessels of the Department of Charities and Corrections were allowed to dock on the island and there were corrections boats patrolling the shores to make sure no one escaped or came on the island unofficially. All was not lost, however. It had been possible to send a telegraph over to the Asylum, with a small bribe from Mr. Gold to the ferry dock official, and obtain permission to visit the island.

Mr. Gold and Bridget huddled together as the wind cut through Bridget's cape and salt spray splashed up on them occasionally.

"Mr. Gold, can I tell you that I'm scared?"

"I noticed that you're trembling. We've been in some bad situations together—nothing could be worse than when we found Katherine and her father—and I can't recall you trembling before. What specifically frightens you?"

"We're getting close to finding Maggie and finding Seth's killer. I can just feel it. It's bloody terrifying. Speaking of that, what have you decided about Ian Strong?"

Mr. Gold wanted to stop Bridget. He wanted to tell her not to worry about Seth's death right now, to concentrate all her energy on her sister, but he figured she needed a distraction.

"I think we'll invite Ian to dinner, to welcome Rose home, as soon as the thirty-day mourning period is up," Mr. Gold said thoughtfully. It had been on his mind a lot these last days. He couldn't believe Ian would have anything to do with criminal acts and certainly not with hurting Seth. But it was troubling him.

"Sir, I talked to Rose about Ian. She thinks she may have a photograph of him. If she does, I think we should take it down to that bartender at The Spotted Pig."

"Yes, she told me, and I agree. She was going to start looking for it today. She remembers Ian giving her a photo before she left for Spain. He was talking drivel about how she should take this with her to remind her of what she was missing. She tossed it somewhere in the house in a fit of pique so now she has to unearth it."

"Mr. Gold, thank you for taking care of getting these permits. I would have just started bawling like a baby if that dock attendant told me I couldn't get on the ferry."

"He was a reasonable man and we were able to reach a compromise. Here we are," Mr. Gold said as the ferry docked. The next moments were consumed with showing papers and getting guards assigned to accompany them.

The little entourage set out walking to the northernmost part of the island, where the lunatic asylum was. One of the guards, probably as part of his official duties, called out the names of the other buildings on the island.

They had docked close to the prison. "The first structure erected on the island was the Penitentiary," the guard intoned. He must have been required to memorize the dates and figures. "The main building was erected in 1832, then the north wing was added a decade later. It houses about a thousand inmates," he said, gesturing to a massive building with turrets on the top, as if there were knights in shining armor patrolling on high.

He must have seen Bridget looking up at the top of the building because he added, "All the buildings here are made of granite in the fortress style."

When the guard wasn't talking, Bridget was babbling nervously about Seth's case, avoiding thinking about what they were there for.

"Have you heard any more from the Metropolitans? They made that big noise and tried to scare us about being their prime suspects. I doubt they've done a thing since then. They just don't have the manpower to conduct a good homicide investigation."

"I'm not worried about us, Bridget. If they wanted to pin the murders of Katherine and her father on us, they would have done it by now. We're at their mercy," Mr. Gold stated with a resignation Bridget had never observed before in him. He'd seemed like more of a fighter before. "If they really want to hang us for this, they will manufacture evidence against us and there is nothing we can do."

THE guard pointed to the southern point of the island. "That's the smallpox hospital down there and those small buildings on the eastern shore are for other infectious patients, such as ones with typhus or ship's fever. The large building up from the Small Pox Hospital is the Charity Hospital. It treats about seven thousand patients a year."

"This is where New York deposits all its misery," Mr. Gold said softly to Bridget, not wanting to offend the guard.

"You certainly wouldn't know it by looking at Mott Street," Bridget retorted.

"The buildings we're passing now are the almshouses," the guard explained as they passed two matching buildings. "One is for men and one for women. No children are allowed, only the aged and infirm who are destitute. In the rear there is the workhouse. It sees fifteen thousand to twenty thousand persons each year who are sent here for an average of ten days. Drunkenness is the principal crime. Most are Irish or German," he said with a quick glance at Bridget.

Bridget wondered how many of these buildings her da had seen at various times, and other gents like him, fellas who didn't mean to, but ended up in the workhouse or the penitentiary with their children or their wives across the river in the city wondering where they were. He could have been right here when they were over there cursing him, she thought, locked up in one of these fake castles.

And so had her Maggie been.

"There are lots of other buildings, like the Hospital for Incurables and the inmate workshops. At any one time, the population of the island is around seven thousand. And here we are at the Asylum. I'll wait to escort you back to the ferry," the guard said, making it clear that they were not free to roam about unescorted.

FINALLY, after their papers were examined, they were on their way to the resident physician's office, he being the reigning official over the Asylum. The physician, a nice-looking man in his sixties, greeted them with cordiality. "Thank you for your telegraph message from the city, Mr. Gold. I'm Dr. Zinitski. I have asked Margaret's attending

physician to join us and he will bring you a written statement of her treatment. In the meantime we can talk a little
about how Margaret ended up here."

Bridget was so grateful again for Mr. Gold's command of
the situation. While she was just dithering about, he had
solved the problem at hand which was getting on this
cursed island. And people respected Mr. Gold, even if they
didn't know he owned a big department store. He just deserved and received respect and that was that.

"Margaret tried to throw herself in the harbor," the
physician said. Bridget could have fainted right then and
there. "She got on a ship and climbed up on the main mast
and was going to do great harm to herself, if not commit
suicide. She seemed to think she could fly. Of course, the
sailors who were on board at the time took great amusement
in this and would have let her do so: fly, die, whatever. They
simply did not understand the seriousness of her delusions
and didn't want to endanger themselves for a drunk, I suspect. There was one young man, however, who had been left
in charge of the ship while his fellow officers went off to
enjoy an evening of pleasure and he did his duty. He was un-
happy to be chosen to stay behind but he took his responsibilities most seriously. He actually climbed up the mast
after her and I guess made a good argument for not flying at
this particular time. She was given over to the local authorities, who brought her to us. I am simplifying, of course. To
be committed here is a laborious process."

"When was this?" Bridget asked.

"Three years ago. Margaret stayed with us for about a
year and a half. She had been smoking considerable opium,
which had clouded her judgment. After the effects of the
opiates wore off, she was appalled to be here, and under

suicide watch, which involves rather less freedom than others have. After she realized her freedoms here were connected to our trusting her to not harm herself again, she became a good patient. She made rapid progress after that."

"What was the matter with her, sir?" Bridget asked, not making much sense out of the doctor's words, not because he was talking over her head but because she was addled by the image he had painted of her sister climbing a tall mast.

The director shrugged, continuing. "Two thirds of our inmates are Irish females. Most of them came to this country in a state of physical crisis, having been without proper diets for months of their childhood. Then there is the voyage itself, which I need not tell you about, as you were there by your sister's side. Then after this strenuous trip, and the death of many a loved one at sea, just like your mother, you arrive in New York City, which is a shock in itself to country folk."

"I have thought the same for a long time, Doctor," Mr. Gold said.

"Being an immigrant woman is hard enough under circumstances a great deal elevated from what you and your sister experienced. It is a testament to your own constitution that you have not suffered as your sister has, rather have made your way in this new society rather successfully from what I can see."

Bridget looked at the doctor closely to see if that was meant as an insult to Mr. Gold or her, but she saw no malice. She figured the poor doctor was just relieved Bridget was able to take care of herself and wasn't another poor Irish needing his medical expertise. "Did my sister ever speak of me?"

"All the time." This came from the back of the room

from the physician who actually took care of Maggie. He had just walked in the room, and he shook hands all around and handed the promised written statement to Mr. Gold. Bridget didn't correct him about who was the relative and who was not or even take offense that he had given the information to the man automatically. She was so glad to have these little scraps of information about Maggie that nothing else mattered now.

"Do you have any idea where Maggie was going when she left here? Did she have any plan for her future?" Mr. Gold asked, cutting to a place closer to the present in the narrative. They were still a year and a half behind Maggie. She had been released so long ago it was possible she could be lost to them again.

"She drew all the time. Sketches of hats and gowns. She said she wanted to be a dress designer. I know that doesn't help. But she did have a job. We don't like to release patients if they don't have family to help them or a job."

Bridget took that like a knife to the heart. Maggie did have family, her, although it hadn't done her much good. Bridget listened to the doctor explaining how many patients were just like Margaret. They lost touch with their family before they lost touch with reality. Months later a mother or daughter came over to the island and found their loved one incarcerated. They felt guilty, as he was sure Bridget did, but rarely was it the fault of the sane relative if they lost track of the insane one. Part of the break with reality led them to push away those that love them, the doctor said. Bridget heard all this merely as background; the words loud and clear were inside her head, the accusations, the recriminations. "What was her job? Please?" Bridget snapped, then immediately was ashamed for losing patience.

"She had a job sewing somewhere. It was a smaller place. Unfortunately, a patient set a fire in the records office about a year ago and Margaret's records were destroyed. I just found this out. But I definitely remember she was going to a small shop of some kind."

The head physician looked at the other doctor and they exchanged meaningful glances of some sort. "I think we must tell you that Margaret became pregnant when she was here. We allowed Margaret to have an abortion because she really could not have taken care of a child, although I assure you she can take care of herself."

"I think that was for the best," Bridget said softly. Would there be no end to the string of horrors poor Maggie lived through? Did some truly insane man come into her room at night? Or worse, was it one of her keepers? Perhaps one of these men right here? "Was the father another patient or one of the staff?" she asked, her voice quivering.

To his credit, the doctor did not try to get out of answering the question or protest that she would even think the staff could take advantage of sick patients in that way. His knowledge of human foibles was too extensive. "We really have no way of knowing. Even at the time, Margaret did not share that information with us.

"Would you like to see the area to which Margaret was assigned? It was Hall Three, our best hall. Sometimes it helps to set one's mind at ease."

"And I would imagine that sometimes it does not," said Mr. Gold. "If she were still on the premises, that would be necessary, but I do not believe it would help Bridget, who is still on an active quest for her sister."

Bridget got up, desperate to leave this place. She was afraid they would tell her something else unspeakable. "Oh, we found it necessary to cut off Maggie's right arm when she was here." Or "Did we tell you Maggie's eyes were put out by another patient. It's amazing she was able to sew!"

"I so thank you for all the information you've given me and most of all to know that Maggie was still alive a year and a half ago, that is the most positive fact," she managed to choke out.

"Dr. Zinitski, thank you and your colleague for your time. Thank you also for rehabilitating, if that is the appropriate word, Maggie Heaney," Mr. Gold said, shaking both of the doctor's hands.

Bridget didn't remember much about the rest of the visit. They murmured niceties, walked south to the ferry landing with the guard accompanying them all the way, boarded the boat, and landed at the Twenty-Sixth Street station. Mr. Gold hailed a cab and they rode back to Gold's, where they had met up for this trip. Bridget knew they talked, that Mr. Gold was very positive, kept discussing the possibilities. They would ask the dress buyers at the store for a list of local companies and start the search anew.

Bridget knew there were hundreds of clothing factories and sweatshops in New York, and what's more, many women did piecework in their homes and those clothing companies didn't have any record of the names of the women who made their garments. She was having trouble keeping a positive attitude. She wanted to go home and crawl in bed, though it was only one in the afternoon. When they arrived at the department store, Mr. Gold looked at her sympathetically. "I'm going to pay the driver to take you on home. I know you'll be back in the kitchen soon, which will help you calm down. Which part was the hardest for you to hear?"

"Between trying to jump off a ship's mast and being

raped by a fellow lunatic or one of the doctors? About even, I think. The hardest part was that the records had been destroyed so we can't find her. What was that they handed to you at the first?"

"A handwritten note from the doctor who supposedly treated her saying basically what they said to us, although they don't seem to do much except separate them from the real world until they calm down and the effects of drugs or alcohol wear off." He handed her the envelope. "I just skimmed it. Read it yourself and thank you for not making a scene for him giving it to me instead of you. We still have a chance. Don't give up."

Bridget shook her head impatiently "Don't worry, Mr. Gold, I'm not giving up. When we started this, whatever we call this journey, we had two goals, to find out who killed Seth and to just plain find Maggie. We won't quit until both things are done."

CHAPTER EIGHTEEN

"I found it."

Bridget turned around and saw Rose standing there, a look of triumph on her face.

"It took a week but I finally found it. The photograph of Ian Strong. Here it is." She pushed the photo at Bridget.

Bridget quickly wiped her hands on a dry towel and took the photo. There he was, handsome and cocky, with a dandy's wardrobe and a gold-topped walking stick. It was a portrait produced at a photographer's studio. Bridget thought it showed his weakness. He went out and spent money for a photo that Rose didn't even bother to take with her to Spain. That reflected his vanity and his refusal to see his relative insignificance in Rose's heart. "This should do it, miss."

"I want to go with you."

"Your father would never allow it, miss."

"Then let's not tell him. Let's go down there right now and find out if Ian was the one. Then we tell Dad."

"Your father has been so kind to me I could not stand to lie to him. Just last week he helped me get closer to my sister than I ever imagined. I can't do it, Miss Rose, I just cannot."

"Fine, then," Rose said and grabbed the photo back from Bridget.

"You don't know where to go," Bridget said with a superior air.

"I do, too. I remember you said The Spotted Pig," Rose replied as she ran down the hall to the back door.

Bridget moved as fast as she could but she was at a disadvantage. She couldn't just run out the door after Rose. She needed to talk to Mr. Fleming, explain the situation, and get permission. She ran into Justin's office. "The worst thing has just happened. Where's Mr. Fleming?"

"What's the matter, Bridget?"

"Rose found the photo of the young blond fella and she wanted us, me and her, to go down to The Spotted Pig and I told her no and she grabbed the photo back and now she's gone."

"So, in your opinion, she is headed downtown to this pub where she will interfere with your murder investigation."

"Yes, sir."

"So, you must go after her. She is not used to the neighborhood."

"That's what I thought, Justin. But Mr. Fleming and Chef . . ."

"I will tell them and explain the immediacy of the problem. Do you have things on the stove?"

"Not right now."

"Then go."

"Thank you, sir."

Bridget was steamed. She had experienced a week of relative calm. She'd even had a relatively normal day off, last Saturday, which involved meeting Michael Murphy, eating ice cream, drinking whiskey, and kissing a few times on the mouth. Michael promised to keep asking about Maggie Heaney, if he was around any clothing manufacturers. Of course, they didn't even know for sure Maggie was working in the rag trade, as Mr. Gold called it.

Now Rose was being stupid and she'd made Bridget leave work in a most unprofessional way. She realized it probably seemed to Rose that Mr. Gold and she, Bridget, had been having a high adventure. She obviously had never been in a small room with two dead bodies.

Bridget wanted to stop at Gold's and tell Mr. Gold what was happening, but Justin promised her he would send Harvey. She had to learn that she couldn't do everything herself. The cab driver pulled up in front of The Spotted Pig and Bridget hopped out, stuffing money in the driver's hand. She couldn't burst in there all fired up. She tried to calm herself and just slipped in the door. Rose was there, as Bridget had hoped, and was buying drinks for the boys at the bar. Everyone was in a good mood, because of Rose's largesse. Rose herself was leaning against the bar holding a shot glass. Maybe she didn't need Bridget, after all. The bartender acknowledged Bridget when she walked in with his usual rise of the eyebrows.

"So, I guess you've met everyone here," Bridget said to Rose anger and worry in her voice.

"Oh, Bridget, this is so fun. Ted here, he owns this place, identified our friend Ian. Isn't that fabulous?"

"Hello, Ted. Yes, Rose, that is fabulous." She pulled Rose

to her, bending her body toward her. "What should we do next, about Ian, I mean? I know what I'm doing about you. Your father will tan your hide."

"Oh, please. You would have come with me right off the bat if you didn't feel so guilty about my father. You knew it was a good idea. I saw it in your eyes."

"Rose, now we know that Ian met Katherine and her father here in this pub. That's all we know for sure."

"I understand that. But this is exciting, isn't it?"

Bridget looked around. Only to someone who had lived a privileged life did this look exciting. The bar was full of similar types, carpenters, drivers, maybe a cook or two. And those were the ones who looked employed. Two men were passed out in their barstools, their faces flat down on the bar, one of them snoring. The place was smoky and dirty. The two women could have been robbed or compromised at any time. The patrons of this slum kept looking at Rose with interest, at Bridget with less interest. She was one of them, after all, a working stiff.

"It is exciting that you got a positive identification from the barkeep. Now, how do we get Ian to tell us why he was here and if he had anything to do with the killings?"

"We'll just ask him," Rose said smugly, braver than she should be. She was a little drunk.

"I think first we should ask your brother if Ian was the one who made the sale, the trade," Bridget said, correcting herself. "Then we have to remember that even if we are sure in our minds that he's connected, we don't have much in the way of proof. The police need more than we have."

"Then let's go talk to Benjamin."

Bridget looked around. Mr. Gold would be happier if Rose was at the Stock Exchange rather than a working-class bar in the worst neighborhood in town. "I'm all for that," Bridget said, relieved.

The two women paid and tipped Ted again, for Bridget was sure Rose had spread some money around before she got there. When they hit the sidewalk, Bridget asked about Johnny. "Did you have Johnny bring you?"

"No, I thought that would take too long. I just ran down to the corner."

"And you happened to find a cab driver who knew where this place was?"

"I asked Johnny where it was the other day when he was taking me to the store to buy new shoes. I kind of tricked it out of him, I guess. If I had to come home from Spain, and I think Benjamin was right to telegraph me, I did have to come home, then I want to be a useful part of this. So, I was planning a trip down here to the old Spotted Pig on my own anyway."

They were able to find a hack on the corner. It had snowed an inch or so several days before, and now the streets were filled with black chunks of snow turned to ice. Traffic was moving more slowly than usual. Once they were safely on their way, Bridget tried to find out more about the one person in the family she knew so little about, Mrs. Gold.

"When you were young, and Estella, Mrs. Gold, was your nanny, how did you get along?"

"About the same way we get along now. We aren't close but we don't fight. She let me have my head and just tried to keep my clothes clean and my face washed. I've never had a meaningful discussion with her in my life. Seth was closer to her, I think."

"Were you surprised when she married your father?"

"Yes, but not unpleasantly so. It was better than having

some outsider come and change everything. And my father was so handsome and rich there was no way he was going to stay single. Women were after him; I noticed it even as a little girl. Plus he still wanted to have a wife."

"What was your mother like?"

"She was also Sephardim, with a Portuguese-speaking background. Her father wasn't one of the founders of the Stock Exchange but he was a stock trader. She was pretty and funny. She wasn't as dark haired and eyed as Dad and I are, and Estella, too. I was too young to know her real personality, but our life was pretty smooth. Until she died. I saw her, you know. They carried her in the house, and a doctor came to us. There isn't a Jewish hospital in New York yet."

"So, your mother didn't die when she was hit?"

"No, it was several hours later. She wasn't awake. But I crept in her room and wouldn't leave. When they realized I was there, they tried to take me away but I threw a fit and grabbed the leg of the bed and wouldn't let go. I just wanted to be near her. I thought I could heal her somehow."

Bridget certainly understood that. "My mother died on the ship, the *Jeanine Johnston,* on the way from Ireland. Lots of people did, of course. She took sick right away. I slept on one side of her and my sister on the other. I don't know where my da was—in another part of the ship, I guess, where the men were. So when she died, I didn't tell anyone for a long time. I kept hoping she would moan or turn over in her sleep. I thought I could will her alive."

Rose looked surprised. She was just realizing what Bridget had figured out a week ago. They were two young women, about the same age, who had both lost their mother at about the same age. They certainly had more in common than the average rich Jewish girl and poor Irish one.

When they got to the Stock Exchange, it was busy on the floor. It was most of an hour before Benjamin noticed them, then it took longer for him to get up to them.

"What a nice surprise," he said as he kissed his sister on both cheeks. Bridget had talked to Mary Martha about the two-kiss greeting and she said it was the European way to greet folks. She'd seen folks do that up on the first floor and had discussed it with Sally.

"And what a surprise to see you without that beard. Did you decide you didn't like it?" Rose asked.

"No, the thirty days of mourning are up. We can shave again, Dad and I."

"Oh, that's right. I lost count of the days somewhere on the Atlantic. Well, you look very handsome," she said to her brother. "I did some detecting on my own today," Rose reported proudly.

Bridget vouched for this with a nod of her head to indicate that she verified what Rose had said, and a shake of her head with a shrug to indicate she didn't approve.

"I went to The Spotted Pig and I took a photo of Ian and he was definitely the one who met with Katherine and her father. The bartender was sure of it," Rose declared with pride.

"I assume you went with her, Bridget."

"I followed her, sir. When I told her she couldn't go with me to the Pig, she grabbed the photo and said she'd do it herself. Then I followed her. I'm probably in trouble."

Benjamin looked at his sister and frowned. "Don't be foolish, little sister. We can't afford to lose any more of us."

Rose ignored him. "So, I intend to ask Mr. Ian Strong what he was doing with our cook. Also, Bridget thought we should ask you if Ian was the broker that handled the

Vermont Wool trade for Aunt Slim? Or I'll just ask him myself. When does trading close?"

Bridget and Benjamin felt as if they'd been hit with
ninety-mile-an-hour winds. Rose was barking questions
and orders right and left. She obviously was enjoying helping solve this family mystery.

Benjamin was the first one to respond. "I didn't ask who
had handled the trade and I'll find that out myself, though I
suppose Ian would have to tell us the truth. He knows I
could check up on anything he said. He's not dumb; after
all, he wanted to marry my little sister."

Rose was just not going to bite. She was totally focused.
"Should I just wait, I wonder? Bridget, you might as well go
back to the house. This will take a while."

"I think you should both go back to the house. You can
ask him tonight," Benjamin said.

"How?" Rose asked impatiently.

"He's coming to the house tonight. We are, too. Since the
thirty-day mourning is over, Estella has decided to enter-
tain. She invited Ian to dinner. I guess she's still trying to
get you two together."

BRIDGET raced back uptown, tipping the driver before the
trip just to make sure he understood how important it was
to take the fastest route. Rose had cost her precious time she
would need if they were having company for dinner. Bridget
realized that she really didn't know much about the social
dining habits of the Golds, coming in like she had when a
mourning period became necessary. It could be the kitchen
was much busier now.

When she finally got back to the house, she didn't stop,

just kept going right into the kitchen. She figured everyone would come to her for a report. Chef had his menu worked out and even posted on a little blackboard hung on the wall. They used the same blackboard to write down supplies they were out of. Chef looked up and acknowledged she was back. He had her name by the items he was depending on her to prepare, so she went right to work starting some bread dough. It wasn't long before Justin and Mr. Fleming came in the kitchen. "Did you hear we're having a dinner party tonight?" Mr. Fleming asked Bridget.

"Yes, I heard about it from Benjamin."

The two men looked surprised. "I thought Rose was headed for the pub, the one named Pig something," Justin said.

"The Spotted Pig. That was my first stop. Miss Rose had already showed the photo to the barkeep and he'd agreed it was Mr. Strong who was in there talking with Katherine and her father."

"So, how did you get to the Stock Exchange?"

"Miss Rose insisted on going down there to talk to Mr. Strong, ask him what business he had with Katherine. She was still going to talk to him when I left. Benjamin told her to wait until tonight, that Mr. Strong was coming here to dinner, that the thirty-day mourning period was over and that he guessed Mrs. Gold was trying to play matchmaker with Miss Rose and this Ian."

"But she wouldn't come home with you?"

"No, she was pretty determined."

Just then the back door bell rang and Justin went to get it. He was back in a jiffy with Rose right behind him, fussing. "I don't know how he left the floor without me seeing him. He must have snuck off. I told Benjamin to tell him I urgently needed to speak to him. He must think it has something to do with our so-called romance. I guess he's playing hard to get."

"How's that, miss?" Bridget asked.

"I marched right down to his office and he was already gone to lunch. And it wasn't more than five minutes that had passed. And he left me a note that said, 'My dear Rose, see you tonight.' Of all the nerve!" Rose said as she continued on her way upstairs.

"IAN, thank you for meeting me down here. I wanted to speak to you alone," Rose said, trying to sound very businesslike. They were in the staff dining room.

Bridget could hear them. She was still in the kitchen, as were Harvey and Elsie, but they were clear over on the other side of the room, by the sinks.

"Rose, I can't tell you what a pleasant surprise it was to look up and see you the other day. Of course you would come home from Spain to be with your father and, your stepmother. It's been rough. Seth was a friend of mine."

Rose cut right through all the niceties. "Is that why you were seen talking to his lover, Katherine?"

Bridget could tell by his voice he was surprised. Benjamin hadn't warned him, then. Good.

"I don't know what you're talking about, Rose."

"Ian, you were seen in a pub with Katherine O'Sullivan and her father. The same Katherine O'Sullivan who used to work in this house. The same one who was murdered, and her father, too."

"Who told you that?"

"I heard it with my own ears, from customers in The

Spotted Pig. I'm not accusing you of anything. I just wondered what was so important you would go into a bad neighborhood to meet with a girl that Seth was seeing who my father had ordered out of town."

"Rose, darling, it just isn't so. I don't know what you're talking about."

"Will you go with me? The bartender could have made a mistake, I guess. Will you go there in person?"

"You've been to some dive asking about me? What in the name of God is going on?"

"I guess no one understands how our family operates. My father is determined to find out what happened with Seth, and Benjamin and I are going to help him. Katherine and her father were killed on the same day, or maybe the next day, after a man who looks like you met them at The Spotted Pig. I was hoping you knew something."

Ian took Rose's hands in his hands and looked intently in her eyes. "I do, but not about The Spotted Pig or this woman, Katherine. Oh, I did know Seth was sleeping with her. Seth had also been involved in some very shady deals. He was making large amounts of money on the side that your father didn't know about."

"Tell me about them."

"I will, but not now. Have lunch with me tomorrow. It's Saturday. We can catch up. I've missed you, Rose."

"I'll go to lunch if you promise to tell me everything you know about my brother," Rose said.

"I'll pick you up around one."

Bridget was as close as she could get to the dining room without being seen. When they stopped talking, she assumed they'd gone back up stairs. She finally looked to make sure they were gone, then continued to clean her work space slowly. She didn't believe Ian Strong for a minute. He was the kind of man who would tell you that you weren't seeing what was right in front of your eyes. Surely Miss Rose didn't fall for it.

Benjamin poked his head in the kitchen door. "Good eats tonight. Did my sister and Ian come down here?"

"Yes, sir, and I just happened to hear them."

"I was hoping for that—I suggested Rose meet Ian in the staff dining room. What did they say?"

"He denied ever meeting with Katherine, period. He said Seth was doing shady business on the side. He asked her to go to lunch with him tomorrow and he'll tell her everything he knows about Seth. I guess he's going to pin everything on your dead brother."

"He may be right. I found out who handled that trade for Seth and it wasn't Ian. It was an older guy, not one of our group. He said he did about six trades a month for my brother. And Seth told him not to mention them."

"Because he knew you'd wonder why he used someone else?"

"It wasn't just me. James, that's the trader's name, said Seth was very concerned that Ian not know about the trades, more so than me. He made a special point of it, that James should not mention their business to Ian Strong. Said they were friends and Ian wouldn't understand why he was using someone else. Me, he just said I was his brother and he wanted to keep business and family separate. It smells, but there are some people who don't use their family for their trading so their father or their uncle doesn't know how much they lose or profit."

"So, what do you make of all this?"

"We'll know more from what Ian tells Rose tomorrow. I better get back upstairs."

It was a few minutes later that Bridget realized Benjamin hadn't taken a single sweet while he was downstairs. It was the first time that had happened. Either he was really full or very distracted.

It wasn't long after Benjamin left that Bridget heard something in the front part of the ground floor hall. Kate, Karol, and Mr. Fleming were still clearing the table on the main floor, and Justin was in his office. Everyone else had gone up to the third floor. She heard whispering, so she moved up the hall and slipped in the silver pantry to hear without being seen. She had never done this before and didn't know exactly what made her so curious this time. Later, she guessed it was because it was unfamiliar enough to make her suspicious. The voices were unfamiliar and no one was usually in that area of the ground floor at this time of the evening.

When she got to the silver pantry, to her surprise, she heard Mrs. Gold, the one member of the household who never came downstairs, meeting someone in the hall. That someone was Ian Strong.

"What do you want, Estella?" Ian said with irritation in his tone.

"What do you mean, what do I want? You, of course."

"Not here, and not now. You know we'll see each other tomorrow at my house. I'm taking Rose out to lunch. She's suspicious. She asked me why I was at the Pig with Katherine. I told her I didn't know what she was talking about."

"The cook who took Katherine's place has helped Isaac, and now Rose wants to play detective too. She thinks it looks like fun, I suppose. I thought I'd put a stop to it by telling the cook to stay where she belongs, but now Rose has taken right up where Bridget left off."

"They were together today at the Exchange. This is the second time."

"I'll work on Bridget if you take care of Rose. I thought getting rid of Katherine was going to help us but now we have to handle the two of them. I wasn't prepared for Rose coming home. Damn Benjamin for insisting she return. Isaac wanted her to stay in Spain, to be protected."

"Don't worry about Rose. I can handle her. Come here."

Mrs. Gold laughed one of those low, sexy laughs that women use with their lovers. Bridget heard the unmistakable sound of passionate kissing. She stood stock-still, barely breathing for fear they would hear her. Finally she heard Mrs. Gold go back up the stairs. Then Mr. Strong.

Bridget walked back to the staff dining room and sat down, holding her head in her hands. She hadn't seen this coming. Not only was Mrs. Gold involved with another man, but she was involved in the recent killings. How could she ever tell Mr. Gold this? He'd already had so much grief. She had to tell him. There was no other choice. But it could wait until morning. No reason to ruin his night's sleep.

CHAPTER NINETEEN

TODAY was Bridget's day off.

Early, before breakfast, Bridget knocked on the library door. She had no idea if Mr. Gold was in there or not, but she didn't have the patience to go ask Mr. Fleming for an audience with Mr. Gold right now, the way she should. She also knew if she spoke to Mr. Fleming first thing, she'd blurt out the awful truth of what she saw Mrs. Gold and Ian up to last night. She wasn't ready yet to tell their secret.

"Come in," said Mr. Gold's voice from the other side of the door.

"Sir, I'm sorry to interrupt you. I have to talk to you right now, before I leave for the day."

"What is it, Bridget? I hear you had an adventure yesterday trying to keep up with my daughter."

"Yes, sir. She found the photograph of Ian, and when I

said I couldn't go down to the Pig right that minute, she grabbed the photo and ran out the door."

Mr. Gold shook his head but Bridget could tell he was more proud than angry. "And you had to follow so she wouldn't be down there by herself. Mr. Fleming explained it to me."

"That's true, sir. But that's not what I came in to tell you. I heard Ian and Rose talking last night, downstairs, and he denied ever being at the Pig or knowing Katherine."

"I would expect him to do that."

Bridget had tossed and turned all night about just how much to tell Mr. Gold. No matter that she thought of him as more than a boss, as something like a friend, he still wouldn't want any little cook telling him she'd spotted his wife kissing another man. Boss or friend, no one wants to hear that kind of news and they usually lash out at the one that's done the tellin'. It's easier to get a new cook than a new wife. "Then I heard—Mr. Gold I do not want to tell you this but I think you need to know, I heard Ian Strong and Mrs. Gold."

Mr. Gold put down his newspaper for the first time. "Oh, dear."

"I just heard a little bit of it, as they walked down the hall, but I heard the name 'Katherine' more than once and I thought he said the words 'When we got rid of her . . . ' but I didn't get the last part, maybe something about Rose."

There was silence for a minute or two while Mr. Gold digested this information. "I suppose Mrs. Gold could have been saying something unkind about Rose, like 'I thought when we got rid of her, Isaac and I would spend more time at the country house' or some such. After all, Ian had pursued Rose. And it would be natural for them to be talking about her. But where did Katherine come into the picture?"

"Yes, Mr. Ian still seems sweet on Rose," which was the truth even in light of what Bridget had seen and heard between him and Mrs. Gold last night. It was another example of how men and woman were different about their loving. "He's taking her to lunch," Bridget added.

"I'm not sure that's an entirely safe thing for Rose to do," Mr. Gold said gravely.

"This is my day off but I will do anything you want me to," Bridget offered. "I can follow them and keep an eye on Miss Rose if you like."

"I have to think about it. I really don't know what I want. What do you think really happened, Bridget? You know almost as much as I do about these awful events," Mr. Gold asked.

"I worried about it all through the night. I think it started with the stock. Seth wanted to make some extra money. Katherine fell in love. And I still don't know what Ian Strong or Mrs. Gold might have to do with it."

Mr. Gold went over to the fireplace. "Human behavior is so hard to predict. Someone stops for a newspaper, or turns right instead of left, and their life changes, they get run over by an omnibus or a barrel falls off a wagon and crushes them. A happy woman steps out in front of a carriage and it sets a series of events in motion that cause death and destruction ten years later. I failed Seth. In my grief after his mother died, he did not receive the love and nuturing that Benjamin had received. I didn't teach Seth the basic moral principles that he needed to become a man."

"But it could be Seth and Benjamin just weren't the same," Bridget said gently. "Maybe even if his ma, his mother, hadn't been taken and all that, maybe Seth just didn't have it in him. You can't worry on the ifs. Mr. Gold, I could go through the same kind of recitation. If my mother hadn't died on the way to America, if my father had decided to take care of us girls instead of becoming one of the local Irish drunks, on and on. I haven't told you how my father really died."

"You said in the Civil War."

"I lied, or told a half truth to you. He died during the time of the Civil War but I let you believe he was in the Civil War. Actually, he was shot by a Union soldier during the Draft Riots last year. He was a terrible man."

"But he was your father. I don't blame you for keeping it to yourself."

"I tell you now because I think you are being too hard on yourself, Mr. Gold. Fate is fate. If the damn potatoes hadn't failed, we wouldn't have been on the boat. If you start with ifs, it's hard to stop. The good things in life are few and far between. If you found some solace with Estella, and maybe spent less time with Rose and Seth, it doesn't mean everything that has happened since then is your fault. And Rose turned out beautiful, inside and out, it seems." Bridget knew that was not going to make Mr. Gold feel better right now. His son was a scoundrel and had been shot for it.

"Good try, Bridget. Next time we go looking for your sister, I'll remind you of that. Fate is fate so there's no reason to go out searching New York City for her. Right. You wouldn't pay attention to me because you feel responsibility to your family, just as I do to mine. You and I won't figure this out. Jewish scholars have been arguing these kinds of issues for five thousand years."

And Bridget's problem remained. She was happy she hadn't told Mr. Gold about Mrs. Gold and Ian kissing. But she knew what a skunk Ian really was and still didn't like the idea of Rose being alone with him. "Do you want me to keep tabs on Miss Rose today, real quiet-like?"

Mr. Gold shook his head, his mind still full of questions about his failings as a father. "Go on about your day off. I have to ruminate about all this and determine just how involved in these tragedies Ian Strong really is."

Bridget left the house soon thereafter, thinking of how our lives never go the way we want them to. She had no intention of leaving Mr. Gold without her help today. She knew in her heart that if she'd told him the truth about Mrs. Gold and Ian Strong, he wouldn't want his daughter with a man like that. That would have hardened his heart.

She walked over to the gardener, the one she'd seen in the German pub long ago, and gave him a dollar. "I'm going to wait to follow the fellow who is coming to pick up Miss Rose, to make sure she stays safe. When he comes, I want you to go over to his carriage. I bet anything he'll have a driver. Talk up the driver and try to find out where the gent lives. I have another dollar for you if you find out. I'm going to go across the street and perch on that stone wall over there but I don't want anyone but you to know I'm there. I won't make a sound. Don't look over my way." The gardener grinned, nodded, and pocketed the dollar.

Bridget spent at least an hour across the street behind, on, or in front of the stone ledge, her body turned away from the Golds' house as much as she could. She was antsy, but she didn't know what else to do. She could have told Miss Rose what she heard last night, and begged her not to go with Ian Strong, but somehow letting her know that her boyfriend and her stepmother were lovers was worse than telling Mr. Gold himself.

Even if Ian Strong didn't have a thing to do with Seth,

his trading scheme, and his death, he was sure a no-good for courting Miss Rose and bedding Mrs. Gold. Even Bridget was convinced Ian was at the core of all these troubles, though she didn't for a minute think she could convince the Metropolitans about any of it. She'd seen many a time in the early days when an eyewitness to something terrible had run to the police with it and they'd just laughed it off. And Bridget hadn't been an eyewitness to any of the killings that had beset this family, so she knew she wouldn't stand a chance of getting the coppers to believe her.

Bridget swung her legs back and forth like a kid as she sat on the little wall. Maybe she should kill Ian herself. Good riddance to bad rubbish, she thought. And it would save the city of New York the expense and bother and Mr. Gold the embarrassment of it all.

As she sat there contemplating Ian's death, he pulled up across the street. The gardener did a good job, going right over to the carriage driver and slipping a flask out of his back pocket, offering him a drink. By the time Rose and Ian came out of the house, surely he had the address.

As soon as the carriage pulled out, Bridget ran across the street. The address the gardener gave her was on Bleeker Street, so she hurried to the omnibus down Fifth Avenue. It was a quicker method of transportation than a private hack most of the time.

Bridget didn't have much of a plan. She was going to Ian's house on the hunch that he would take Rose there instead of to a restaurant, or would take her there after they ate. She figured she could peep in at the window, and if she got to feeling uneasy, she could always just pound on the door and say Mr. Gold had sent her for Miss Rose, bold-like. That was it, as far as what she had planned out. Not much at all. She fretted all the way downtown, then walked the block from the bus stop to Ian's address.

Bridget found a perfect hiding place at Ian's house with a bush just in front of the window. It looked into the dining room. It was on the street side of the house, but the bush was so tall that she could stand between the house and the bush and be hidden from the street traffic, which was moderate on a Saturday afternoon.

Rose and Ian were already there. They seemed to be having a festive lunch because they were drinking champagne. Bridget couldn't hear what was being said as they sat at the dining room table, but they weren't having a fight; in fact, they looked compatible and friendly. Ian had a butler who served them and Bridget assumed he had a cook because the food didn't look store bought. After dessert, which was pumpkin pie, Ian and Rose started having a serious conversation. They didn't even get up from the table and go to the drawing room.

Soon an older woman, the cook it must be, and the butler gent came out of the back door and walked around to the street where Bridget was. Bridget ducked down behind the shrubs. She could hear them talking about the shopping, one going to the shoe repair, the other to the bakery, as they divided up the errands. When they disappeared down the block, she stood up and tried to stretch a little to get the kinks out of her back and neck from her hiding. Then she stood on her tiptoes and peeked in the window again.

Bridget could tell by the postures of Ian and Rose and their friendly expressions that there wasn't an argument but she stayed where she was. About three in the afternoon, Ian sent Rose off by herself. The carriage and driver were nowhere around and Rose walked off to the east. Bridget

thought that strange and rude of Mr. Ian. Young women of
Miss Rose's status didn't go about New York by themselves
too often. But Rose was an independent one and she seemed
to be perfectly fine when she left, kissing Mr. Ian on both
cheeks quickly before she went out the door. Bridget walked
a few steps to the corner and sneaked a look around the
house as Miss Rose headed toward Washington Park. She
was almost ready to follow her, to make sure she got in a carriage all safe and sound, when it became evident why Ian
hadn't escorted Rose home.

Estella pulled up in a hack. She went in Ian's front door
without knocking; he must have left the door ajar for her.
Bridget saw them embrace in the hall through the open
door of the dining room that led to the entry hall. Then Ian
disappeared out of Bridget's narrow sight lines and Estella
pulled off her bonnet and coat.

Bridget was torn. She crouched down to relax her feet
and think about it. Should she stay and watch more proof
that these two were romantically entangled, proof that she
had no intention of telling Mr. Gold in on? Or should she
do what she had intended, follow Rose until she was safely
in a cab? Bridget knew that she wanted to stay partly because the romance between Mrs. Gold and Ian Strong was so
terrible and forbidden that it fascinated her. She'd been
truly shocked and surprised last night. She didn't like Mrs.
Gold but Bridget hadn't pictured her cheating on Mr. Gold,
not even in her most vivid imagination, which had gotten a
workout lately. Yes, she wanted to stay and see them together again. But she was going to do what was useful and
best, and follow Miss Rose. After she took one more peek.
She stood on her tiptoes once more to look in the window.
That was the last thing Bridget remembered.

* * *

WHEN she came painfully back to consciousness, she was inside the house. She had a terrible gash on the back of her head, where Ian—she guessed it was Ian—had whacked her good. Blood was seeping from the wound, and from the looks of her clothes, her head had bled quite a bit while she'd been unconscious. She tried to move and felt a stabbing pain travel down from her head to her neck and back. She realized she had been tied to a chair.

"Bridget, what a silly girl you are, thinking you could spy on me in such an obvious way," Ian Strong said.

Bridget was in an unfamiliar room, one she hadn't seen from the street window. She was tied with enough rope to tie a piano on a bicycle. She wasn't gagged, though, so she didn't waste time. "Why did you kill Seth?" she asked.

Estella was drinking brandy. She looked shaken; her hand around the glass was trembling. She glared at Bridget.

Ian answered that one. "I really am sorry about poor Seth. He stopped by here uninvited one Saturday. Estella hadn't closed the door properly," he began, looking over at Estella as if to remind her it was all her fault. Bridget bet they had spent plenty of time tossing the blame around. "The servants were out of the house doing their errands as they are now. And when Seth saw Estella and I being, ah, close, he really had a fit. I had no idea he would care so much, not that I would have told him. Estella wasn't his mother, after all. He whipped out this silly pistol, knocked me to the floor. I do think he would have shot me. He was defending Estella's honor, and his father's, of course. We struggled and I shot him in the thick of it, quite by accident."

"Then why didn't you send for the doctor, send for his

father, get him help instead of stuffing his dead body in a chest in his own home?" Bridget asked, still spunky, wriggling her fingers against the ropes at the same time.

Ian looked over at Estella. Bridget couldn't read the look and she wasn't sure whether she should believe Ian or not. It sounded logical. Seth probably saw Estella as his mother, more of a mother than he would admit to his friends. She had been there to pick up the pieces of the Gold household when they lost their mother and wife. It was a real breach of trust, a breach of all that he held dear, to see Estella in the arms of his friend Ian. Seth had reacted like a loyal son, not as the self-centered brat he'd become. "It was Estella's idea to take the body home. She was supposed to be up at her country house but she was here with me. She left immediately for the country with a hired driver and gave me her key so I could let myself in the front door. It was a bold move." Ian was walking grandly around the room, lecturing Bridget, exhibiting pride in his cunning, the touch of regret he'd shown over Seth's death gone for now. "I went by the Golds' and talked to Mr. Fleming, said I needed to see Seth, learned that no one knew where he was. I returned that night. I didn't know Justin wasn't at his usual guard post so I brought Seth in through the front door. Estella suggested leaving him in the front hall, as if he'd just made it home, wounded. I thought that was rather crass and took him downstairs. It seemed better for the help to find him, rather than his father."

There it was. Even in the midst of murder, rich folks depend on their servants, Bridget thought.

Ian continued his narrative. Estella's eyes followed him around the room, her look cold and angry. Bridget didn't know if she was angry they had been discovered again or if she was just generally angry about the bumbling of Seth's death and those that came after his.

"Then someone tried to get in the back door. I now know it was Katherine. That's when I jumped into that storage room, dragging the body by this time. It was bloody heavy. I saw the chest, and with a little manipulation Seth was a perfect fit. I was just trying to be thoughtful and not lay him out in the middle of the kitchen, Bridget," Ian said, as if Bridget would think this a good joke, not remembering or perhaps not knowing that she had been the one who found Seth.

"And what about Katherine?" Bridget asked, still clawing away ineffectively at the ropes around her wrists.

Ian shrugged and Estella looked at Bridget. It was her turn to talk. "Katherine had the bad timing to show back up at the house the evening Ian was moving Seth," she said. "She was insolent and disobedient and ran away from Isaac's cousin. Then I guess from what your snooping found out, she came back to New York and made up with Seth down at the factory. She must have slipped back in the house through Justin's window like everybody does. My guess is she planned to wait in the kitchen for morning, when she was going to throw herself on Mr. Gold's mercy and beg for her job back. Ian heard her but he didn't see her. She saw him, unfortunately. She always was good at sneaking about the house," Estella continued, still drinking brandy and talking in an offhand manner. "So when she saw what she saw, her plans changed. Her rich boyfriend wasn't alive anymore. She must have snuck back out, and talked it over with her father."

Ian resumed his telling of the tale. "She sent a message to the Stock Exchange and asked me to meet her at The Spotted Pig. She and her father figured I'd pay a good sum not to have her tell on me. I was all for letting them yap. Who are the police going to believe? A member of the New York Stock Exchange, or some Irish cook who just got thrown out on her can for sleeping with a member of the family?"

Bridget was getting frantic. When the story was over, she knew it would be her turn to die. "But you didn't let him take that chance, eh, Mrs. Gold?"

Estella looked at Bridget to see if she spotted insolence in the manner Bridget had said "Mrs. Gold." Estella wasn't ready to admit defeat in any realm. "Ian was wrong about that. We had to get rid of Katherine and her father. Ian met them at the pub, and I followed them back to O'Sullivan's room and walked in firing. It was easy. I enjoyed it." Mrs. Gold got up and fetched her hat and coat, started putting them on, obviously ready to leave before Bridget was disposed of. "We thought it was all over. Then you kept stirring up Isaac by actually carrying on some sort of investigation. No one meant for Seth to die. I'm sure I could have talked to him, reasoned with him, and made Seth keep quiet on his father's behalf. We always got along so well, Seth and I. It was a stupid accident."

Bridget suddenly got an idea. "Like that carriage hitting Mrs. Gold?"

A sly look crossed Estella's face. "When you want something, you sometimes have to make it happen."

Bridget's heart sank. Estella had been masterminding the lives of those around her for a long time. She wasn't going to let another Irish cook, a small obstacle really, stand in her way. If Bridget couldn't get her arms free, she'd be dead very soon. Even if she did get free, she didn't know how she'd fight them both and win. Ian had a gun—maybe that's what he had hit Bridget over the head with. Bridget looked around frantically. Mrs. Gold was leaving so Ian could take care of Bridget privately. What could she do to save her own life?

The next few minutes were filled with events that never seemed real to Bridget, no matter how many times she looked back at them. In real life, no one comes in with guns blazing to rescue the damsel in distress.

But that is just what happened.

THEY were dressed in the uniform of the Union Army. Their hats were pulled down on their heads so the shadow of the brims hid their faces but they also had handkerchiefs over their nose and mouth, bandit style. They were brandishing Colt revolvers.

The two men strong-armed their way into the house, shattering a pane of glass in the front door, then unlocking the door through the empty pane. Ian and Estella didn't have a chance. The men walked into the room where Bridget was held. Ian tried to reach his gun, which must have been on the desk, Mrs. Gold looking around disapprovingly as though she expected it to be a servant interrupting them. Without a word the two uniformed men just simply shot them. It didn't take a minute.

Ian died with a surprised look on his face, arm outstretched. Estella crumpled like a hankie in a heap on the floor. Then they untied Bridget, and the three of them left by the shattered front door.

They walked quickly, one on each side of Bridget, practically lifting her off her feet to keep up with their stride. When they reached the corner, a double brougham pulled around the corner. Justin was driving. "I thought you might need a ride home," he said. He hopped down and pulled the reins around the footrest. "Why don't you ride up here with me?" he said and offered a hand, as gallantly as Bridget had come to expect from him.

For a split second, Bridget didn't know whether to trust this man or not. She thought about running down the street or screaming at the top of her lungs. Hesitantly she took his hand and climbed up.

As he did this, the two men got inside the cab and quickly changed clothes. Justin handed them each a knapsack and they pulled out striped shirts with no collars and simple cotton pants, stuffing the uniforms in where the other clothes had been. They handed Justin the knapsacks and he, in turn, handed them each a small sack that Bridget assumed contained money. They still had not uttered a word. Silently, the two split up, running in different directions. Justin got up on the coach seat and put the two knapsacks between them.

Bridget was surprised at her reaction. Now that her fear and panic were subsiding, the distrust melted away and she was only relieved. It was as if Justin had read her mind as she sat on that ledge this morning and taken the action she'd thought about. Or was it Mr. Gold who sent Justin to obtain justice?

Justin was silent and solemn for a few minutes as they drove down closer to the harbor, where the usual barely organized chaos was going on. And that was just fine with Bridget. She wasn't ready to coax the truth out of Justin about whose idea it was to follow her or Rose or Estella, or who had led the assassins to Ian's house.

When they got close to the waterfront, she didn't even need to be told what to do. She jumped down with the knapsacks, grabbed four good rocks from the side of the road, put two in each knapsack, and slipped them in the water quietly. Justin watched all this and gave an approving nod, then turned the team uptown.

"Well, there you have it," Bridget Heaney said.

All that was left was to get home safely. "Murders happen in New York City every day," Justin commented, as if they were talking about the weather. "The police always say, 'If you don't find someone standing there with a smoking gun, you probably aren't going to find the killer.'"

Bridget could hardly wait to get home to take a hot bath. "Thank you, Justin," she said and touched his arm as he maneuvered the horses through the crowded streets.

He gave her a little smile. "We'll talk about it later."

CHAPTER TWENTY

A week had passed since Mrs. Isaac Gold had been found murdered in Ian Strong's house, along with Strong himself. Someone had seen two Union soldiers entering the house. And Miss Rose had been there earlier in the day. It would have been even more terrible if those rogue soldiers had come to murder and pillage while she was there. Apparently it was fate that kept her safe. Or the Good Lord, as Mary Martha always said at this time in the tellin' of the story.

Of course everyone was sorry about Mrs. Gold. Mr. Gold said that she had wanted to talk to Mr. Strong about his intentions toward Miss Rose. No one in the house really believed it, but Justin and Mr. Fleming were strict about no one speaking against Mrs. Gold. Everyone was just fine with that, and covered the mirrors up with the black cloth as they were told.

The house was in the middle of another Shiva. Bridget was going to take a half day off, instead of a whole one. She'd volunteered to stay on duty but Mr. Fleming said everyone needed a break and that they should all take half days. She stayed around until noon and helped Chef and Gilbert get ready for the visitors.

Now she was going to do an important errand. She didn't know why she hadn't thought of it before. It had come to her a couple of days ago and she had hardly thought of anything else since. The horror of last week was just a blur. She would let herself think about it more when some time had passed. Now she pushed it out of her mind when she started to feel that panic of being tied up, or to think about the amazed look on Mrs. Gold's face just before she got shot.

Mr. Gold walked in the kitchen and right over to Bridget. "Where are you going to look for Maggie this week?" He had been down on the first floor often these last days, talking in the office with Justin and Mr. Fleming or going over details with Chef. Obviously he enjoyed the company.

"Mr. Gold, if it weren't for you teachin' me to think about this logical-like, I don't think I would have remembered this. After tellin' you how Maggie and I were little thieves that never got caught, the other day I thought of how our stash place had been so important to us, so why hadn't I thought to look there? It makes sense that she might leave me a message there. I'm going to take a look."

Mr. Gold smiled. He looked years younger. Rose and Master Benjamin were very considerate of their father, telling everyone how devastating it was for him to lose another wife, not that losing wives was so strange in this day and age, what with women dying in childbirth all the time. But Bridget could see Rose and her brother relaxing together in a way that didn't look like they were devastated themselves, not that Bridget for a minute thought they knew anything about what had happened, or what Mrs. Gold and Ian had been up to.

Justin had been very closemouthed this week, busy making arrangements, and of course Bridget couldn't mention anything to Mr. Gold or ask him about it, but he hadn't made a big to-do about finding the identity of his wife's killer like he had with Seth. If Mr. Gold hadn't actually sent Justin out to find those men to do the killing, Bridget bet he'd uncovered the truth by now. Or maybe not. Maybe Justin knew his employer so well that he just did what was best for him. "You're not going to tell me where this famous stash is, are you?" Mr. Gold asked.

"No, but I might show you sometime." She grinned at him as she pulled her cape on. "I'll be back this evenin'."

Broadway and Wall Street hadn't had any significance to a young girl from Ireland, but now as she took the omnibus downtown, she was amazed how her life in New York had come back around to Wall Street. She and Maggie had chosen this particular place to hide their loot, and then years later she would work for a man whose family was so linked to the activities of the same street.

She got off the bus and walked over to Trinity Church. There, some of the most important men in America's history were buried. Bridget remembered the signs. But that didn't mean a thing to two young pickpockets. She remembered why she and Maggie chose it. The graveyard wasn't closed, so they could get in and out. And it wasn't a Catholic church. That had been very important to Maggie, who back then was more religious than Bridget. Maggie didn't want to involve the Catholics in their criminal activities.

Bridget went to the part of the cemetery closest to the church building and picked out the small child's tombstone right away. Divinity Smith. Bridget remembered how they laughed about that name and wondered what her mother called her for short. They settled on Di. Bridget still knew how to kneel down so she looked like she was praying and lift the small tombstone up. And son of a gun if there wasn't still a tin box under the stone, right where she and Maggie had placed it.

Now she leaned back and took a deep breath. She had really talked herself into believing she was going to find something here. If there wasn't word from Maggie, she knew she was going to be terribly disappointed. But in a twisted way, she'd even been disappointed when Maggie's death certificate wasn't filed neatly under the H's in that dusty office or when Maggie wasn't still residing at the lunatic asylum in the middle of the East River. She wanted some word of her sister and even bad news would be a help. But in truth, another dead end was what she expected.

No message from Maggie here at Trinity Graveyard could just mean she was out there in the world, getting on with her life, maybe married with children and living in Albany by now. This was Bridget's last idea of how to find her sister, and she prepared herself for another disappointment.

Bridget opened the tin and it had only one thing in it. There was a business card lying there. It was on good paper; Mr. Gold had taught her the difference. It was engraved and looked very expensive, just like Mr. Gold's calling cards did. It was a beautiful color, not ivory and not altogether pink but a combination of the two. Bridget picked it up. It smelled good, like the fancy perfume they sold at Gold's.

The card said: *Madame Lambert, 23 Christopher Street, New York City, Couture Françoise Erotic.*

Bridget wanted to get up and run to Christopher Street. But this grave had been a good stash for almost ten years. She wasn't going to compromise it now, just in case she needed it again someday. She quickly put the business card in her purse and replaced it with one she had hand printed out before she left the house, one with Mr. Gold's address. Maggie would know to ask for her, and if anyone else found it, they would not know what it meant. She put the tin back in the hole and was careful not to force it in the ground too hard. If you did that, you could scrape up against Divinity's coffin and she had never liked seeing or feeling that.

"Rest in peace, Di," she said as she always did as she set the stone carefully back in the ground and then pushed the dirt with her hands to make sure it was secure.

She got up, wiped her hands on her skirt, that same navy blue shirt she wore every day off, and headed north, walking as fast as she could.

THE shop on Christopher Street was elegant. The store's front windows were curtained with thick burgundy velvet drapes. There were also rows of silk flowers, the same ambiguous color as the business card, hanging from silk ribbons in front of the drapes. The ribbons were other shades of ivory and rose and peach and pink, all so delicate you had to stop and think about what color you were seeing. The window reeked of good taste and money. Without there being any real underthings showing in the window, it also told of forbidden sensual pleasures. All those flesh tones.

Bridget hadn't forgotten the word "erotic" on the business card. Maggie must have been sewing for some fancy French lady, making fancy silk underwear. The only sign in the window was in the same script as on the card, in gold gilt. *Madame Lambert, Couture Françoise Erotic.*

She opened the door and there was a beautiful young woman playing an elegant instrument like a small piano. Bridget couldn't name the instrument but the tinkling sound was lovely. It made her feel calm.

The racks in the shop were very spare, not crammed full like at Gold's. Bridget saw beautiful nightclothes, and also things to wear out of the house, like ball gowns, then things a little more personal. On one shelf there were underpants with no crotch at all. Next to them were some that exposed your bottom completely. She picked up something off another shelf and it turned out to be a bejeweled piece of black silk that would fit completely over the head like a hood, with a red satin slit for the mouth and a red satin lining.

There were six women who seemed to be customers, and a seventh woman with red hair piled high. She wore a fitted dress that was the color of the business card and the silk flowers, ivory blushing with hints of pink. The color itself was erotic. This woman was helping a lady at the back of the shop, bent over retrieving a red satin camisole out of a drawer. When she turned around, it was Maggie.

Maggie looking like a lady—no, much more elegant than any lady Bridget had seen. Maggie, only it couldn't be. This person was so beautiful, so complete, so womanly. But it was Maggie, who gave her a wink and a little bow. "Ah, Mademoiselle Bridget, your things are ready. Come with me to try them, just to make sure," she cooed, slick as a whistle, and took Bridget by the hand like she was a paying customer.

She led Bridget into a changing room and they hugged.

"Did you finally check in that damn grave?" Maggie whispered. "I thought you'd never think of it. But I wasn't goin' to stop lookin' for you. I've been to a hundred and fifty-seven German boardinghouses. That's where the lady who cashiers at Delmonico's said you'd gone to but they didn't know which one."

"Now I'm at a big, fancy mansion on Fifth Avenue, cooking with a French chef," Bridget said proudly, then immediately blushed at her bragging. "I've been looking for you, too, all over to hell and gone," she said, thinking of Blackwell's Island.

"Stay right in here. This woman is driving me crazy trying to decide what color she wants her dressing gown made up in. I want to make the sale, so I'll finish with her, then I'll turn the shop over to Nadine. She can work out the day."

Bridget hugged her sister again. "No, you go back to work. We can meet up after you close. I don't want you to get in trouble with Madame Lambert."

Maggie smiled at her mischievously. "Don't you worry about that, sister. I am Madame Lambert. I'll be right back."

She left Bridget speechless in the dressing room.

THE cab was almost at the house. Bridget and Maggie were on their way to the Golds'. It was about the time the servants had supper after dinner upstairs. The women from the congregation, the mourners, would be changing shifts right about now, too.

When they left Maggie's store, they'd gone to a ladies' oyster house Maggie knew about. Then they went in a pub and had a shot of Irish whiskey to celebrate.

Bridget had told Maggie about going to the death certificate office and Blackwell's Island. She didn't mention what the doctor had told them about Maggie trying to jump from the top of a ship's mast, or anything else for that matter. She told it like an adventure, she off with her boss to Blackwell's Island, and never let on that it sent her for a spin. She could tell that Maggie had shut the door of her heart concerning period that time, and Bridget could respect that. Maggie had always been one to look ahead, not behind.

Bridget also told Maggie about all the goings-on at the Golds' since she came on staff, finding the body and going with Mr. Gold all around the city, and getting a new cape and ice cream, and learning from Chef and being needed by the house. As she spilled it all out, she felt a good bit of pride about it all. She told everything except the most important.

She hadn't told about what happened last week, not even Mary Martha. She didn't want Mary Martha to have to live in the house and pretend to all the rest about Mrs. Gold. It would be so much easier for her if she truly thought Mrs. Gold was on a good and righteous mission to that "awful man's" house.

Bridget told everyone that she spent her half day with Michael Murphy down at Mr. Barnum's museum, a lie that reflected what Bridget would like to have happen sometime. She had expected Murphy to come around when Mrs. Gold died. All the newspapers had written stories about the "Gold curse." But his wasn't the byline on the Gold story in the *Recorder* and he hadn't been hanging around the back door either, to Bridget's disappointment.

No, Bridget hadn't told anyone what had really happened last week. She pretended to be as upset as everyone else when the coppers came to report the robbery gone bad, or whatever it was. Justin acted just as surprised as Bridget.

The police seemed to think maybe soldiers had done all the killings, stalking rich people. Or maybe it was a disgruntled department store employee, as some of the newspapers speculated, getting even with Mr. Gold for some slight by killing off his family and staff. Such silliness, but everyone on the staff seemed to believe one of these theories, or said they did. Bridget wondered why no one was afraid if they were all supposed to be potential victims. Instead, Mrs. Gold's death, however shocking, had left the household with an almost cheerful disposition.

Benjamin and his wife were going to move into the house with Mr. Gold. He said it would be theirs someday and the country house was for Rose, so they might as well have their family here. Mrs. Simon had also agreed to come back and live with the family. Mr. Gold told her she didn't have to do a thing, that she had worked long enough, that she could just spoil the babies everyone hoped Benjamin would father soon. It looked like things were working out.

Bridget was lost in these thoughts as the carriage rolled along when she realized Maggie was still jabbering away. "So, when I was on the island, I decided I would start my own business. I've never been good at working for the other fellow, you know that, Brig. I can't take orders worth a hoot."

"That's a fact," Bridget said. "But where did Madame Lambert come from?"

"Haven't you ever seen those ads in the back of the newspapers? 'Dressmaking by French seamstress' or 'French Couture for You.' I tracked down dozens of those ads and only three were real Frenchwomen sewing things up. Most were Irish who had learned how to do handwork at a sweatshop downtown or working in a big department store like your boss owns." Maggie had been very impressed when she learned Bridget worked for the man who owned Gold's Department Store. "Then they dye their hair and take on some airs, maybe an accent or a special embroidery stitch. I love a good scam, Brig, so I wrote a whole story for myself, gave Madame Lambert a proper history. She's the widow of a lingerie manufacturer in Paris. She goes over to see her in-laws every year and brings back all kinds of pretty things for her customers. They eat it up."

"Do you?"

"What?"

"Do you go to Paris, or is that part of the scam?"

"Oh, I go, or I did once, last year. I've only been in business a year and a half, you know. I am taking French lessons from a lady in Brooklyn who used to live in Paris. And I'm also taking hand-sewing lessons from the women I hired to make up the things I design. Two of them are French. I want to be able to do it all, not that I have time for the sewing but it never hurts to know. All the French women helped me with letters to their relatives who lived in Paris. I rented a room from one of them, a cousin of my French teacher, and I had enough money just to walk the streets of Paris and sketch what the ladies are wearing and go around to all the dressmaking houses where they make everything to order all fancy. And of course I went to every lingerie store. It was wonderful. I want you to go with me."

Bridget didn't understand. "Where?"

"I want you to go to Paris with me. It came to me right away when you said you work for a real French chef. Let's go see what the ladies are wearing and eating. You will love it, Brig; it's nothing like Ireland, or New York, that's for sure."

"When?" Bridget asked, her head swimming with the very idea of such madness.

"I'm planning to go in January, close the store up for six weeks or so. Last time I made up the money I lost by closing three times over. I charged more for the fancies I brought back from Paris and made up for the trip easy. This time I have plenty of money for us both to go."

"Oh dear Lord, Maggie, you can't spend your hard-earned money on me."

"Oh, it's not mine, really. It's Madame Lambert's. You might as well help me spend it."

Bridget smiled. She couldn't even imagine Paris. "Why did you, why did Madame Lambert settle on lingerie?"

"There's a lot to be said for selling people what they dream about. You can charge more for that. Not everyone can afford a ball gown but most everyone wants something pretty. And it's for the men, you know. They'll pay a pretty penny for the naughty panties and such. Women who live in these big mansions come to me and say, 'Oh, Madame, I don't know what to do. My husband wants me to dress up in a maid's uniform when we go to bed at night.' "

Bridget blushed. "What do you say?"

"I say, 'Then we will make you the sexiest maid's uniform in New York City. Your husband will never be interested in the real maids after our version. Of course, this will cost quite a bit of his money.' So it satisfies the rich wife two ways. She can keep her husband interested and she spends lots of his money doing it, which is like punishing him at the same time she gives him pleasure. It's perfect, really. They never complain about the price. The wives, and the husbands when they come in, they *want* it to cost a lot."

Bridget couldn't believe her rebellious little sister had grown into this woman, so confident and good looking and smart. It was amazing. She was ashamed she thought Maggie would go to the dogs without her. She couldn't tell Maggie the kinds of places she went searching for her.

"Of course, most of the time the husbands come to my shop, it isn't to buy things for their wives," Maggie continued. "They let the wives buy their own lingerie. They come in to buy presents for their mistresses. I get in the gents' pocketbook twice," she said, laughing.

The carriage pulled in the driveway. Bridget paid the driver and rang the bell, anxious and nervous and excited all at the same time.

Justin opened the door and looked at the two women, his eyes narrowed. Then he tipped back his head and laughed, that big voice ringing out in the cold air. "Come in, come in. You must be, let's see, Maggie, is it?"

He took Maggie's coat and her fur muff, looking at Bridget with a smile. "You found her. Good for you."

Mary Martha stuck her head out of their dining room, then started rushing toward them, eyes wide with surprise. "Lord Jesus, it's Maggie," she shouted and wrapped her arms around Maggie in a bear hug. "I can't believe it. Your sister has been so worried about you."

Bridget slipped her arm through Maggie's arm on one side and Mary Martha on the other. "Believe me, Maggie is doing just fine. Have you eaten?"

"Just started," Mary Martha said.

Bridget started the three of them down the hall. "Then let's go. I promise you, Maggie, it will be better than the last time the three of us ate together."

Justin followed the three women back to the dining room, smiling the whole way.

THE Gold household was a sleepless one that night.

Mr. Gold hadn't been sleeping much since Estella's death. He spent a good part of the nights wondering if he had done the morally correct thing or if his actions—instructions to Justin that produced other people's actions, to be more accurate—were base and had been rooted in jealousy and revenge. He was willing to live with these questions. He had saved his daughter from a relationship with her brother's murderer, and saved Bridget's life. Part of his heart was broken by Estella's treachery. Part of his heart had known about it long ago but wouldn't admit it. Thank God Justin had come to him and told him what he'd seen, Ian and Estella together, not just the evening that Ian came to dinner but for months. Justin was willing to do the difficult jobs, such as tell the truth or keep quiet, whichever was necessary.

JUSTIN was thinking about tomorrow, which was the last day of Shiva. Tomorrow they would have a large crowd of friends who had waited until the last day to pay their respects. Justin had a remarkably clear conscience for someone who had engineered a double murder. It was his job to help Mr. Gold and that's what he had done. It seemed fairly cut and dried. Bridget had made it easy. He had seen Bridget peering in the window, then the next time he and the "soldiers" went around the block, she was gone. Not only was he righting a wrong in Mr. Gold's life but he was keeping

Bridget safe. That reminded him, he wanted Bridget to make potato rolls for tomorrow.

BRIDGET tossed and turned. The last week had been unusual, to say the least. She'd been hit over the head, hog-tied and almost killed, witnessed two murders, and found her long-lost sister. And then there was the part where her sister asked her to go to Paris with her. It was a lot to think about. The idea of leaving this house was difficult. The idea of letting Maggie go across the ocean without her was impossible to comprehend. It had been hard enough letting her leave tonight, knowing she was just going down to Greenwich Village. Maggie was her anchor. Bridget would have to talk it over with Mr. Fleming and Chef and, of course, Justin.

CHAPTER TWENTY-ONE

BRIDGET knocked lightly on the door.

"Come in," Rose said. She had three big steamer trunks open and in various stages of being packed. "I don't know how I'm ever going to get all this organized," she said cheerfully.

"Can I help?" Bridget asked.

"No, well, do you mind rolling up these stockings? I'm not very neat until it comes to packing. Daddy gave me so many new clothes he had to give me two new trunks at the store."

It must be nice to have a whole department store to choose from, Bridget thought. "Are you anxious to get back to Spain?"

"I'm anxious to get back to my voice lessons. I didn't practice much while I was here."

Bridget had heard her a few times, going up and down

the scale in her clear soprano. Rose's voice shimmered. "I have big news," Bridget said, hesitating.

"You're going to Paris!" Rose said and her eyes lit up with delight. She leaned over and patted Bridget's back with a big pat. "I told you you'd be a fool to turn it down."

"I know what you told me, but for us working folks, it's hard to quit a good job like this when you know there's a chance you won't get one so good the next time. Your father is wonderful to work for, even during these hard times."

Rose pulled two suits out of her wardrobe and hung them on hangers in one of the trunks. "I'm sure he is but that's nonsense. Do you want to be cooking for us when you're old and gray? Go see the world. I know it will change your outlook on life."

Bridget nodded solemnly. "I talked to Mr. Fleming and Justin and then to your father, after Mr. Fleming told him. The truth is I don't want my sister out of my sight, let alone across the ocean without me. We were a team growing up, just the two of us, and I don't want to lose that again. She has the funds to take me and I have to go."

Rose walked over to a closet and started pulling out another big steamer trunk. Bridget hurried over to help her. "Bridget, this is beat up but it will take another trip back and forth across the ocean. I don't need this anymore, now that father has insisted on giving me new ones. I want you to have it for your trip."

Bridget was flabbergasted. "Oh my goodness. I guess I will need something, although I could just take my carpet-bag for all I have to pack. But this will be good because Maggie buys all kinds of lingerie there in France and we can use the space to bring it all home."

"And another thing," Rose said as she started wrapping

her shoes in tissue, one by one. "I would love it if you would come to visit me in Spain. It's not far, you know, just the next country over."

"I thank you, miss, for this trunk and for the invite. I best be going now so you can pack without having to talk to me at the same time."

"Don't worry about getting a job when you get back. My father doesn't like to lose good people. He'll find a place for you. You showed true grit."

Bridget was surprised Miss Rose knew anything about true grit. Rich people mostly didn't need it. But she was proud of the compliment. "Thank you, miss. If it's all right with you, I'll leave the trunk today and Mary Martha can help me haul it up tomorrow, after you leave."

Rose nodded in agreement and sat down on the bed, her hands full of shoes. "Before you go, what do you think my stepmother was doing down at Ian's house? I hardly think my father would send her on a diplomatic mission of any kind, she not being much of a diplomat. If he really wanted to caution Ian about me, he would have sent Benjamin, I think."

Bridget had been avoiding this conversation for weeks. Now that she was trapped into it, she would just have to lie.

"Well, even if your father didn't directly send her like he says, maybe she took it on herself to go warn Mr. Ian off. She and your father could have talked about the worry of him maybe having something to do with Katherine and her da getting shot. And Mrs. Gold could have been trying to help, no matter how wrong it turned out to be for her. That's what I like to think."

"Yes, well, that's better than she probably deserves," Rose said tartly. "Come see me in Spain, Bridget," she added with a wave and then dove headfirst into her hat closet.

"Have a good trip, Miss Rose," Bridget said and slipped out. It was her last day off and she had to go downtown.

WORKERS were taking down the Christmas decorations around City Hall when Bridget took the bus to Printer's Row across the street.

It had been a quiet holiday season at the Golds'. Them not being Christian and being in mourning had meant no decorations or big Christmas dinner. Mary Martha said they had more of a celebration the year before. On New Year's Eve, the family had come round and the kitchen made a fancy dinner.

Bridget made a puree of spinach soup and Gilbert had built these puff pastry shells he called *vol au vent,* which meant something light enough to fly away. Chef filled them with lobster in a champagne sauce. Even though lobster was thought common, Miss Rose liked it so they were serving it. The staff got a lobster each for their dinner so they were happy. Then there was a fillet of beef with Madeira sauce, a pair of roasted capon, lots of vegetables, and dessert was crepes fried in butter and with some orange liquor and apples served with whipped cream. Everyone had more champagne than they needed and everyone giggled too much, upstairs and downstairs both needing a little release. That was three days ago.

Bridget pulled her wool scarf close around her neck as she hurried into the *Recorder* office. The scarf was Mary Martha's Christmas gift to her. The same woman was sitting at her desk, in charge of all the hustle and bustle as usual. She greeted Bridget with a tiny smile. Bridget figured the woman wasn't sure if she recognized Bridget or not so she wasn't smiling the way you do when someone is a good customer or a friend.

"Is Michael Murphy in, please?" Bridget asked as if she were working and had been sent to fetch Murphy.

The woman looked for the little boy. He came out of one of the mysterious doors and ran up to the desk. "Murphy," the woman said and he took off, heading into another door.

Bridget sat down, fidgeting. She was impatient to get to her sister's shop. She was going to run errands for the both of them through the afternoon, then they were going to supper together.

In a few minutes Murphy came to the lobby, looking suspicious. When he saw Bridget, he grinned. He nodded at the receptionist.

"Bridget Heaney. Happy New Year." Bridget stood up and stuck out her hand.

Murphy shook it with some reservation. "What are you doing here?"

"I came to thank you. I found my sister and it was because of you. At least you certainly helped."

Murphy ducked his head. "This is strange. People usually come down here to yell at me, not thank me. Was your sister still on Blackwell's Island?"

"No, she wasn't. She came out of it and now she owns her own business. And we're going to Paris together," Bridget said brightly.

Murphy searched Bridget's face. Then he smiled and shook her hand again. "A happy ending. You don't get that much here in New York."

"I thought you'd be down banging on the kitchen window again when Mrs. Gold was killed," Bridget said.

"Yeah, wasn't that a weird coincidence. Another Gold bites the dust."

"Why weren't you?"

"What?"

Bridget stomped her foot once, involuntarily. "You know what I mean, Murphy. Why weren't you still poking around when Mrs. Gold and Ian Strong were killed?"

Murphy shrugged. "Remember when I told you the editorial and publishing arms of the paper were separate but equal? Well, I was wrong. The publisher told me that I was definitely off the story. I guess your boss didn't like me hanging around the back door."

Bridget smiled at him. "You were too good at your job, Murphy, and I thank you for that. Maggie thanks you, too. When we get back from Paris, Maggie and I want to take you to dinner."

Murphy grinned, his old confident self back now that he knew he wasn't in trouble. "I don't know if I can handle two Heaney sisters. But I'm willing to give it a try."

Bridget gave him a little hit on the arm as she turned away. "We'll be in touch."

"Have a good trip. When you come back, I have some questions to ask you about Mrs. Gold's death," Murphy called to Bridget as she walked out.

MARY Martha and Bridget were both still writing, sitting on the bed with books under their papers since there was no desk. The trunk Rose had given to Bridget was standing at the end of the bed. They'd started this project after they ended their duties downstairs. Now it was near eleven. Mary Martha rubbed her neck and Bridget pulled on her fingers. There were several crumpled papers on the floor. Bridget insisted that they have no mistakes, no crossed-out words on the finished product.

It had started the night before. Bridget had the spice box out on the bed when Mary Martha came down to her room. When she saw the box, she wrinkled her nose in distaste.

"Stop that," Bridget scolded. "I decided that I'm going to add a recipe to the box. I wished I'd taken some of these others around to have them translated. Benjamin recognized French and Italian and Ladino."

"What's Ladino?"

"It's Hebrew and Spanish mixed together. It's what Mr. Gold's relatives spoke. Benjamin could recognize it but he can't speak it or write it."

Mary Martha looked slightly irritated for once at this bit of insider information Bridget had. "Why did you show Benjamin this box?"

Bridget ignored the question. "I showed it to him and it's a good thing, too. We found a piece of paper in there that had the name of a stock Seth was buying up. It helped us figure out that Mr. Ian was up to no good."

"This box helped you?"

Mary Martha still didn't know about Bridget's experience at Ian Strong's house. The murders were not entirely solved in her eyes. "Yes, or Katherine did for hiding the piece of paper in it, so I'll thank you to stop talking ill about this box," Bridget said, then rapidly changed the subject. She pointed to the carving of the woman stirring the big pot. "I want to have a bit of me in here. Maybe some other cook will find this box and take the time to decipher all these recipes and here will be my potato roll recipe along with all the rest."

Mary Martha looked suspiciously at the box again. "You're not taking it to France, with you?"

"Oh, Lordy, no. I can't be wasting space in my trunk on pretties such as this. My sister has made me the most beautiful clothes, or her sewing ladies have. And she said I should save room for buying some more in Paris. Besides, once I put my recipe in there, I'm a part of the box, just like the other cooks who put their recipes in the drawer. But there is still a puzzle about it."

"What?"

"Why didn't Katherine add a recipe?"

Mary Martha nodded her head up and down knowingly. "Oh, I think I know. She didn't write. She could read enough to get by, but she didn't write much in English. She wrote a bit in Gaelic."

"Oh, Mary Martha, you know Gaelic, don't you? You were eleven when you came over, you must have learned it in school back there. I've forgotten the bit I learned."

Mary Martha hesitated, glancing at the box sideways. "Yes, I can read and write it a little. Why?"

"Would you write down a recipe for Katherine that we could add to the box? I don't want her to go unremembered. It was her box after all."

"That's right sweet of you, Bridget. You never even met her."

Bridget thought of the young woman cowering in death in the corner of a dank room. "It's a box for us women cooks. She belongs. How about those delicious pickled beets?"

"They were always tasty," Mary Martha conceded.

"I'll ask Chef if he watched her make them enough times to know what she put in them. Then you can write it down in Gaelic. And I'll ask Mr. Fleming for some paper."

And so tonight they were doing just that. Bridget was writing out her potato roll recipe and Mary Martha was copying what Bridget had jotted down on a piece of butcher paper about the pickled beets from what Chef and Gilbert remembered.

Finally they had two sets Bridget was satisfied with.

"So one of each goes in here. And may the next cook add her own recipe," Bridget proclaimed solemnly, placing them on the top of the pile of recipes in the bottom drawer of the box, then closing it.

"What about the other two?" Mary Martha asked, glad they were done with the box. She believed it was all falderal, but if it made Bridget happy, she was willing to do it.

"I'll give them to Chef. Gilbert can make the potato rolls when you miss me."

Mary Martha's eyes filled up with tears. "That'll be all the time. We talked about it this morning after you'd gone to the kitchen. I wish Mr. Fleming didn't have to replace you. Even though he said over and over he'd try to work you back in, I don't like you not havin' a job when you get back."

"Well, he has to. What with Mrs. Simon and Benjamin and the missus moving back in the house, I think you'll be busy. And the mourning periods stole the holidays away. Mary Martha, the truth about this trip is I just can't let my sister go so far without me. I lost her and I found her and it's a miracle I did. If it means I don't have a place to work in six weeks, well, so be it." Bridget got to her feet and placed the box in Mary Martha's hands. "Now I want you to keep this down in your room. See if the new cook deserves it or not before you give it to her."

"I'll do it. Even though I still think this box could be wicked," Mary Martha said stubbornly as she got up.

Bridget gave her a big hug. "It's just a box. It's how people use what's inside that's bad or good, just like most things. Night, my friend."

Mary Martha started crying and Bridget pushed her out the door before she burst into tears herself. She couldn't start blubbering yet. She had more goodbyes to say.

JUSTIN and Mr. Fleming were in Justin's little office, their heads bent over the accounts.

"You two should go to bed, you can't cipher so late at night," Bridget said as she stood in the doorway.

Both men looked up. "We just have a few more pages, then we'll be done with December," Mr. Fleming wearily explained. Just then, the bell rang on the first floor. It must be Mr. Gold wanting something, Bridget figured.

Mr. Fleming got up. "I'll see you off in the morning, Bridget. And don't forget, you're to come right here when you get back in town. There's an empty bedroom on the third floor. If we haven't scared off the new cook by then, I'll find you another position," he said, then gave Bridget a kiss on one cheek and passed by her on his way to the first floor.

"Thank you, sir, for all the time you let me take to help Mr. Gold," Bridget said as he passed her. "I'll see you in the morning, then." Her eyes followed him down the hall then she turned to Justin. "Does he know?"

Justin smiled. "On that fateful day in December, Mr. Fleming saw you leave, me leave, Mrs. Gold leave, then saw you and me come back. It was he who received the police with their sad news about Mrs. Gold. I imagine that is rather more than he wants to know. I haven't burdened him with the details."

Have you burdened Mr. Gold with the details, Bridget wanted to ask, but she didn't. "You are a good friend to Mr. Gold, Justin, and to me. Thank you for saving my life."

Justin brushed away the compliment. "Oh, it was nothing. I just happened to be in the neighborhood. Now, remember what I told you. When you cheat death, you have to enjoy life like never before. That's why you must go to Paris."

"I'll be back by spring, unless I run away with a French chef," Bridget teased, wanting to break the tension between them that was bordering on sentimentality. She certainly couldn't start crying in front of Justin.

Justin stood up and bowed low to Bridget, then did something unexpected. He took her right hand and kissed it. "The men will be lining up in Paris to do this, only they won't be the chefs, they'll be the counts. *Au revoir,* Bridget."

Bridget was speechless for a minute. Then she recovered and made as graceful a curtsy as she knew how to. "Au revoir, Justin," she said, mimicking him. "I'll see you in the morning," she said and marched back down the hall, her chin stuck out.

"COME," Mr. Gold said.

Bridget entered the library. Mr. Gold was in the last few days of the mourning period. His beard had grown and his hair was long, brushing his shirt collar. Bridget still thought him the most handsome man she'd ever laid eyes on. "Sir, I leave in the morning and I just wanted to thank you again for understanding why I had to go with my sister."

Mr. Gold had a stack of paperwork on his desk. He'd been bringing work home from the office each night. Bridget suspected he missed Estella and wanted to keep busy in that lonely time after dinner. Neither Mrs. Simon nor Benjamin had moved in yet.

"Of course, I understand. I have something for you, Bridget," Mr. Gold said. He got up and opened a drawer in his desk then handed her an envelope.

Bridget looked inside the envelope. It was full of money. "Oh, no, sir. My sister really has enough money for both of us."

"No, that is not my money. And you can help me by using it to experience Europe and to learn more about cooking, not that you aren't a good cook already."

"Then whose money is it, sir?"

"Seth's. I went down to the factory yesterday. There it was in the safe. Thank goodness I remembered the combination because no one else had it. The factory doesn't take in money; those accounts go through Gold's. They just have a small amount of cash for incidental expenses. Erasmus sent me a note telling me Seth had been using the safe and I should come open it to see what he'd put in there. I found neat stacks of cash."

"Then the money's yours, sir."

"Seth was not a good man and I have taken the responsibility for that. I could never use that money as my own and I don't need it at any rate. I plan to use his ill-gotten gains to help people. You are the first recipient. Mrs. Simon will be the second. I don't want her to ever feel that she is trapped without her own funds again. Then I'm going to challenge the Congregation Shearith Israel to meet my contribution to start a Jewish hospital here in New York. I think that would be a fitting thing to do with Seth's money."

"Mrs. Simon, yes, the hospital, yes, but I'm not in that category."

"You are a better tonic than any a doctor ever prescribed, Bridget, and your cooking makes everyone feel happy and well fed."

"Thank you, sir," Bridget said, feeling the weight of the envelope in her hand.

"Now remember, take your time. You have the letter to Chef's sister. That will help you in Paris. Rene's father was also a chef and the family knows people in the cooking trades. You may want to work somewhere for a bit, just to learn. You don't have to come home when your sister does. And Rose really meant it when she asked you to come to Spain and visit her. She considers you a special person. I do, too. I know what you've done for this family." He looked directly in her eyes.

Bridget felt faint. Her temples were pounding suddenly. Was Mr. Gold finally going to talk about Ian and Mrs. Gold? Should she start telling him about that day? Could she ever share her suspicions about the first Mrs. Gold, and what the second one hinted about the carriage accident?

But Mr. Gold continued on another subject. The moment was gone. "You know, I've been thinking of expanding the ice cream parlor into a lunchroom for the ladies. When you come back, we'll talk about you creating a menu for it, possibly being the chef. If you're still interested in our little project after you've seen the grand cafés they have in Paris."

Bridget couldn't believe her ears. A lunchroom in Gold's Department Store. She realized there was a relationship between the two subjects, subtle and unspoken though it was. There probably was a relationship with the cash in her hand as well. To ensure her silence about Ian and Mrs. Gold, Mr. Gold was willing to offer Bridget a wonderful advancement in her career and cash to travel for a while. Not that she was anywhere near Ian Strong's house the day of the murders. From now on, that was what she had to tell herself. And not that she wasn't the perfect person for the lunchroom job. "You know I'll be interested, Mr. Gold. I can't think of anything I'd like to do better."

"I'll say goodbye then," Mr. Gold said and without a bit of warning he moved around to Bridget's side of the desk and embraced her, both his arms around her, drawing her close. She ducked her head, then closed her eyes for a minute and leaned against him just a little. She felt Mr. Gold's heart beating through his woolly vest. In a moment, he released her, holding her at arm's length formally.

"Thank you again, sir. I'll see you in the spring," Bridget said with a little bow to him. She didn't look back as she walked out the door, envelope in hand. A deal had been made and now she had to finish packing. There was no more to say.

Maggie was calling for her early.

MUSTARD FRUIT COMPOTE

1 tablespoon mustard seeds
1 teaspoon turmeric
1 teaspoon dried powdered mustard
½ cup brown sugar
¼ cup honey mustard
2 cups apple juice
15–20 pitted prunes, chopped
15–20 dried apricots, chopped
1 cup raisins
1 cup dried cranberries or cherries
6–8 dried figs, chopped
3 fresh pears, or apples, chopped

1. In a small sauté pan over medium heat, heat the mustard seeds and turmeric until the seeds began to pop, about 2 minutes. Be careful not to inhale directly over the pan, as the mustard gas is strong. Remove from heat.

2. Combine all ingredients in a large, heavy saucepan. Bring to a simmer and cook until the pears are soft, about 25 minutes. Serve with ham, turkey or a prime rib of beef or pork.

PICKLED BEETS WITH GINGER

2–3 lbs. beets
¼ cup strips of peeled ginger
1 tablespoon orange zest
½ cup orange juice
¾ cup red wine vinegar
¾ cup red wine
¾ cup brown sugar
1 teaspoon allspice berries
2 teaspoons cloves
1 cinnamon stick
2 teaspoons kosher salt
1 teaspoon freshly ground black pepper

1. Cook the beets in boiling water until tender, about 30–40 minutes.

2. When they are done rinse with cool water. When they are cool enough to handle, slip the skins off under running water. Slice into ¼ inch slices.

3. Transfer to a storage container.

4. In a nonreactive saucepan, bring the remaining ingredients to a boil over high heat. Reduce heat and simmer for 7 minutes, stirring occasionally.

5. Pour the liquid over the beets and cool to room temperature.

6. Cover and refrigerate. They will keep 3–4 weeks.

OXTAILS WITH TURNIPS AND RED WINE

You could make this dish all in one day, but please don't. Cook the oxtails a couple of hours the day before you need them and finish them off the day of serving. It makes such a difference in flavor.

4–5 pounds oxtails

2 tablespoons butter

2 tablespoons canola oil

2 tablespoons olive oil (Bridget would have used all butter—but we have our health to worry about these days!)

2 teaspoons kosher salt

1 teaspoon black pepper

1 large onion or 2 medium, peeled and sliced

2 carrots, peeled and sliced, plus 1 lb. carrots, peeled and sliced (the 2 are for the *mirepoix,* the 1 lb. for the stew)

4 celery stalks, sliced

4–6 cloves garlic, peeled and sliced

4 leeks, sliced just up into the green about ½ inch, soaked and rinsed

1 lb. turnips, washed and cut in chunks

1 lb. "B" size red potatoes or other new potatoes, washed and quartered

1 bottle Rhône wine, a Côtes-du-Rhône will work fine

4 cups stock, veal, or chicken

1. In a heavy Dutch oven, season with salt and pepper and brown the oxtails in the oil and olive oil. Remove them and set aside.

2. Melt the butter in this same pan and add your roughly chopped *mirepoix* (sliced not diced) and the garlic. Sauté slowly until the onions wilt.

3. Add the oxtails to the *mirepoix* with the bottle of wine and 2 cups stock. Simmer covered for two hours, stirring every once in a while. This is the place to stop, store, and start again tomorrow.

4. If you did stop and store, put the sauce back in the Dutch oven, and heat slowly. If you are cooking this all in one day, just continue. Now is the time to add the leeks, turnips, and potatoes, then reintroduce the oxtails and the vegetables to the pot. Cover and simmer another two hours on low heat, stirring occasionally. In a fancy restaurant you would remove the meat from the bones but we don't have to do that. The fun is in finding those wonderful morsels of meat that have been basted in their own juices. Just turn this out on a big platter and serve it with some mashed potatoes or rice.

Wine Tips: A Côtes-du-Rhône will be just fine for this gutsy dish.

POTATO ROLLS

1 cup cooked and riced potatoes
½ cup butter
2 cups buttermilk
1 tablespoon active dry yeast
2 tablespoons sugar
2 eggs
dash salt
7–8 cups all purpose flour, sifted before measuring

For the egg wash:
1 egg
2 tablespoons cream or milk

1. Peel and cook enough potatoes to make 1 cup, which will be approximately 2 medium potatoes. Cover with water, bring to a boil and cook until tender, about 10–20 minutes, depending on the size of the potatoes. I prefer red potatoes but many folks like Idaho bakers for this recipe. I have recently used the larger Yukon Gold variety and I liked the flavor and texture. Experiment. We have more potato choices than were available in New York City in 1864.

2. If you have a ricer, push the potato through that. If you don't, you can rig a ricer by pushing the cooked potato flesh through a colander a couple of times or forcing the flesh through a large mesh strainer. The idea is to "grate" the cooked potato, not mash it, which releases more starch.

3. While the potato is still hot, mix with the butter.

4. Heat the buttermilk to warm over low heat so you don't scald it. Heat to 110 degrees.

5. Remove 1/2 cup of the warm buttermilk to a large bowl. Add the yeast and the sugar. Let set 5 minutes or until the yeast starts bubbling on the top of the milk.

6. Add the remaining buttermilk and the potatoes. Add the eggs and salt and beat until its combined and fluffy.

7. Add the flour, a cup at a time, working it into the dough before adding another cup. When the dough will not absorb any more flour, knead it for 5 minutes. This whole process can be done with an automatic mixer or by hand.

8. Put the dough in a greased bowl, cover and let rise to double.

9. Punch down the dough and roll out to about 1/4-inch thickness.

10. Cut out circles with a biscuit cutter.

11. Fold the circles of dough in half to form semicircles.

12. Wash the top of the rolls with French egg wash: a combination of an egg yolk and the cream or milk.

13. Let them settle into their new shape by setting for 20 minutes.

14. Bake in a preheated 400 degree oven for 18–20minutes.

Turn the page for a special preview of
Lou Jane Temple's next novel

DEATH DU JOUR

Available from Berkley Prime Crime

Fanny returned home from her daily trip to the boulangerie, her hands full of bread and packages, but as soon as she opened the outer door Henri grabbed the bread from her. "I can't believe you left without me. We normally go together," he scolded.

Fanny had her usual reaction to being around Henri: extreme discomfort, acute self-awareness, dizziness and tingling in various parts of her body, her cheeks one of them. Henri was tall and lanky, with chestnut brown hair worn long, green eyes, and the most beautiful hands Fanny had ever seen. Fanny always told him he should be playing the piano with those hands instead of using the rolling pin and cleaver. "I thought you might still be exhausted from your weekend and I didn't want to wake you. When did you get home?"

Henri's facial expression changed. His eyes left Fanny for

the first time and he turned and started walking toward the house. Fanny could feel a lie coming. "Oh, I don't know. I didn't look at a clock. It was almost dark. I fell asleep as soon as my head hit the pillow. Why?"

"Oh, I just wondered. I saw these two men when I was coming home and they were arguing out in the middle of the square and I could swear one of them came in here."

The moment when Henri should have replied came and went as they entered the house. He seemed to be searching for words. Fanny sensed his awkwardness and stopped what she was doing to regard him. But the arrival of the maid who attended the master and his wife broke the uneasy silence.

"Oh, there you are. The master is already up and wants his coffee, Fanny," Josee-Marie said with a little stamp of her feet. Josee-Marie was responsible for giving both the master and the mistress their morning trays.

Henri looked relieved to end the conversation. "I'll see you later. Don't forget we have a lesson this afternoon," he said as he put down the baguettes and sacks on the work table and hurried out the door.

Fanny brewed the coffee. Paris was coffee mad. The first coffee house had opened more than a hundred years before and now they were scattered across the city. Coffee houses were where Parisian husbands went to see their friends, conduct business, read the newspapers. At first wives complained about this new fad but after several years, it was clear no one would give up their coffee and by that time women were enjoying it as well, and began to serve it at home.

Fanny ground the roasted coffee beans in a crank-operated grinder. She poured boiling water from the kettle that was always hanging on a hearth hook over the grounds, which she'd placed in a porcelain teapot. Then she cut several slices off one of the loaves of bread and placed them in a napkin-lined silver basket. She fetched a small ramekin of butter out of one of the cool storage rooms, then put all of this on a large silver tray, along with a pot of honey, a small pitcher that she filled with milk warmed over the fire, and a bowl of the precious white sugar that the master favored.

Josee-Marie took the tray and paused at the doorway. "You might as well make another tray. I heard the mistress stirring," she said as she prepared to climb up to the master's suite.

And so went the morning. Fanny hurried from task to task, concentrating on the job in front of her with her whole being but still trying to watch the rest of the kitchen, as Henri had taught her. She had a capon she was stewing over the hot part of the fire, her cast iron pot with the bird next to the teakettle on the second hook. She also mixed up a no-yeast barley bread that had a cake-like texture. She poured this thick batter in a greased Dutch oven and covered it, placing it in the back of the fireplace where the embers were low. And there were some green beans and zucchini squash that she had bought a couple of days before when the green grocer cart came around. She'd throw them in with the chicken in a while. They should be used up today.

Now she needed to make a cold dish for Henri, for dinner. She soaked and cleaned some leeks, and blanched them until the whites were tender. Then she made mustard dressing for them, whisking together some mustard from Burgundy with grape verjus and walnut oil. She dressed the leeks and let them set to absorb the flavors.

They had delicious tarts at the baker's and Fanny had

purchased one with cheese and chard. That was for the master's table, that and the leeks. The capon and vegetables were for the staff. And the barley bread was for the staff, too. It was much too coarse for the master and mistress but Henri said it was one of the best things Fanny baked. He said her crumb was beautiful. Fanny wasn't really interested in baking, but it was nice to be complimented any time.

Henri cooked most of the dinner for the master and mistress and their table, with Fanny's help. Fanny cooked most of the dinner for the staff, which numbered eight adults and two boys about ten, who ate more than anyone. Fanny and Henri met every evening about five, after dinner was served, and discussed the next day's menus, what the mistress and master had ordered, what was available at the markets, then Henri gave Fanny assignments. It was the best time of the day. Although they were rarely completely alone, the whole household staff wandered in and out of both kitchens all day, no one was really paying attention to them. Spending that time together, talking about food, looking at cookbooks and recipes Henri had collected, that was where Fanny had fallen in love, with food and Henri.

After the meeting for the next day, they went through the leftovers and discussed what would have to be made for supper. Usually they could make do with what was on hand, making soup for the staff out of odds and ends, and rearranging dishes for the masters' table. The master and mistress ate simply at night unless they invited someone to supper after the opera, which they did often. The master loved the opera.

If there were guests Fanny and Henri would come up with something fresh to put out for them. Except for special occasions, the staff did not serve supper; rather the dishes were laid out in the salon or dining room in covered silver containers, along with bottles of wine, plates, and glasses.

The staff ate before and after the real meals, at noon or one, then they ate leftovers after dinner had been served for the master and mistress, around six or seven in the evening.

Fanny was almost ready for this first staff meal. She was just sugaring some peaches that she had bought last week that had been hard as a rock. She'd ripened them and had used the best ones for a peach melba for the master's table. The ones with brown spots she had peeled and cut up for the staff. M. Desjardins stuck his nose in the kitchen and she nodded. She knew he would ring the bell up on the ground floor, then step out in the courtyard and ring it again, so Henri and the driver could hear. Today they were eating outdoors, on a trestle table set up by the footmen and M. Desjardins just by the entry door. They could still let any deliveries in and eat lunch at the same time. They had a couple of worn out linen tablecloths they spread over the wooden boards for this purpose, ones with holes and stains that wouldn't do for the master's table anymore. They didn't send them to the laundry every time, using them until they were too soiled. It was just fine for the staff.

Fanny had pulled apart the capon, discarding most of the bones. She put the meat on a platter and surrounded it with the vegetables. She had some marinated cucumbers and onions, had prepared the barley bread, and had also made a kind of a pudding with stale bread, cheese, and eggs. They had peaches for dessert. Vera, the second maid, had set the table with the old pewter plates and the scratched wine glasses. M. Desjardins had already put out all the bottles of wine that had been opened but not finished in the last couple of days by the master and his family. That was what the staff normally drank unless there were no leftovers, and then they drank Beaujolais from a barrel the maitre d'hotel kept under lock and key in the wine cellar.

Fanny filled a pitcher with water and went out the delivery door to the courtyard. She put the water by the wine bottles so everyone could combine water and wine to their own liking, then took her place next to Henri at the table.

The household staff was seated according to their station. M. Desjardins, as maitre d'hotel, was at the head of the table. Henri, as the chef, sat at the other end. To Henri's right, Fanny was seated, and to her right was the scullery maid, Henriette. Henriette had the lowest job in the house. She cleaned and scrubbed and lifted and moved from daylight to dusk. She was responsible for washing all the dishes as well, although Fanny tried to clean up as she went. Next to her was one of the two young boys that ran errands and did all the odd jobs around the house. His name was Simon. Next to Simon sat the driver, Charles. He was responsible for the horses, carriages, and equipment, as well as driving the family about. Charles was stretched thin with all his responsibilities and the two boys helped him more often than anyone else. On his right was Jules, the footman, who served at table and also rode on the carriage when the occasion warranted having a footman. Jules was very handy at fixing things, both out in the carriage house and inside. Next to Jules was Nicholas, the other boy. Nicholas and Simon had previously been seated next to each other as their lowly station warranted but they bickered and pinched each other and teased so much that M. Desjardins had separated them. Vera, the second maid, sat on Nicholas's right. Vera took care of the young master Monnard, the son, and his family, who occupied the third floor of the house. Josee-

Marie, the first maid, attended the master and mistress of the household, thus her place of status next to Henri on his left. That was the ten of them, all with as many duties as they could possibly successfully accomplish in a day. Fanny thought them to be an average amount of servants for a house on Place Royale. She knew the nobility had more, and some of the judges, who weren't paid terribly well, had less. Fanny couldn't imagine how you could get by with even one person less.

The dinner table topic today had started with the Fete de Federation which had invariably led to politics. Fanny's mind wandered as other people talked and ate, using their hands for emphasis. She looked around the table. They were a handsome group, well dressed and well fed. It wasn't such a disaster as her parents had thought, her wanting to be a cook.

A guest chef at the Culinary Institute of America and the James Beard Foundation, **Lou Jane Temple** is a caterer in Kansas City, Missouri. She has also been a restaurateur and a food and wine critic. She is the author of the culinary mystery series featuring caterer Heaven Lee. She lives in Kansas City.

The *Tea Shop* mystery series by

LAURA CHILDS

DEATH BY DARJEELING
0-425-17945-1

Meet Theodosia Browning, owner of Charleston's beloved
Indigo Tea Shop. Theo enjoys the full–bodied flavor of a town
steeped in history—and mystery.

GUNPOWDER GREEN
0-425-18405-6

Shop owner Theodosia Browning knows that something's
brewing in the high society of Charleston—murder.

SHADES OF EARL GREY
0-425-18821-3

Theo is finally invited to a social event that she
doesn't have to cater—but trouble is brewing at the
engagement soiree of the season.

THE ENGLISH BREAKFAST MURDER
0-425-19129-X

Just as she's about to celebrate her work to help protect
the sea turtles of Charleston, Theo spots a dead body
bobbing in the waves.

THE JASMINE MOON MURDER
0-425-19986-X

Theo is catering a Charleston benefit, a "Ghost Crawl"
through Jasmine Cemetery, when the organizer drops dead—
and it looks like foul play.

NANCY FAIRBANKS

The Culinary Mystery series with recipes

Crime Brûlée   0-425-17918-4
Carolyn accompanies her husband to an academic conference
in New Orleans. But just as she gets a taste of Creole, she gets a
bite of crime when her friend Julienne disappears at a dinner
party.

Truffled Feathers   0-425-18272-X
The CEO of a large pharmaceutical company has invited
Carolyn and her husband to the Big Apple for some serious
wining and dining. But before she gets a chance to get a true
taste of New York, the CEO is dead. Was it high cholesterol or
high crime?

Death à l'Orange   0-425-18524-9
It's a culinary tour de France for Carolyn Blue and her family
as they travel through Normandy and the Loire valley with a
group of academics. But when murder shows up on the menu,
Carolyn is once again investigating crime as well as cuisine.

Chocolate Quake   0-425-18946-5
Carolyn's trip to San Francisco includes a visit to her mother-in-
law, a few earthquake tremors, and a stint in prison as a murder
suspect. A column about prison food might be a change of pace.

The Perils of Paella   0-425-19390-X
Carolyn is excited to be in Barcelona visiting her friend Roberta,
who is the resident scholar at the modern art museum. When an
actor is killed during a performance art exhibit, Carolyn must
get to the bottom of the unsavory crime.